Look for light in the shadows.

Todd A. Gipstein.

Aboard Ledge Light

IN THE SHADOW
of the LIGHT

by
Todd A. Gipstein

First published by Dog Ear Publishing
4011 Vincennes Rd
Indianapolis, IN 46268
www.dogearpublishing.net

ISBN: 978-1-4575-3863-6

This book is printed on acid-free paper.

This book is a work of fiction. Places, events, and situations in this book
are purely fictional and any resemblance to actual persons, living
or dead, is coincidental.

Printed in the United States of America

Cover photograph by
Todd A. Gipstein

Dedicated to Marcia, the light of my life,
and my partner in the madness of preserving
Ledge Lighthouse.

and to

The memory of the lights in my life
who have gone dark,
but whose spirits are still beacons in the darkness.

PROLOGUE

There are more things in heaven and earth, Horatio,
Than are dreamt of in your philosophy.

— William Shakespeare, Hamlet

1

AVERY POINT
GROTON, CONNECTICUT
2009

Like a lost shadow, the single black cloud drifted over Long Island Sound. It crackled with lightning, its thunder a distant rumble. It was the only cloud in an otherwise clear blue sky. Everett Line Fine was walking along Groton's Avery Point, on the memorial brick path that ran along the shore. Next to the path, a series of modern sculptures dotted the landscape. The path ended at the Avery Point lighthouse, a short tower of stone.

Fine took little notice of the distant aberrant cloud. He was heading toward a black steel obelisk that sat perched on a granite rock. It was a stark sculpture, like a finger pointing to the heavens. A small sign gave its title: "Mythic Mystery." Its four sides were covered with 6-inch metal letters bolted to the 12-foot pylon. Except for letters forming the sculpture's title, running vertically down the north side, the jumble of letters, though grouped, spelled no obvious words. Many had pondered the meaning of the cryptic characters. Were they a code? Or random and meaningless? The sculpture was tantalizingly evocative and frustratingly obscure. It lived up to its name. Its monolithic silhouette was indeed mythic, and the iron letters it wore were certainly a mystery.

The black cloud continued north, nearing Ledge Lighthouse, a mile offshore from Avery Point. A loud crack of thunder made Fine stop and look out to sea. Fine watched as the cloud seemed to settle in above Ledge Light. Like the fingers of a blind man, bolts of lightning arced downward to touch the lighthouse.

For a few minutes, Fine stood on the path and watched the cloud unleash its fury on the lighthouse. It was a one-sided argument. The building took the wrath of that angry cloud again and again, absorbing the lightning bolts it sent down.

The cloud began to move again, toward the land. Toward the steel obelisk. Toward Fine. Seeing the cloud would be over-head in just a few minutes, Fine decided to head for cover. He veered away from the obelisk and headed to the sprawling stone mansion a hundred yards away. As he stepped up his pace, a leading edge of wind swept across the point. A minute later, Fine found himself in shadow.

Somehow, time compressed. Or perhaps Everett just lost track of it. More quickly than he would have imagined, the cloud was overhead, black, sizzling with sparks of light. Sud-denly panicky, Fine started to run. Lightning began to hit behind him. Rain started to fall in torrents. The broad grass lawn he ran across turned to mud. His feet sank in. The light-ning continued. He was desperate to get to safety, but each step was difficult and slow as the mud sucked at his feet. He felt like it was all happening in slow motion now, like being in a dream.

A sizzling lightning bolt, 50 million volts of white-hot elec-tricity, hit the steel obelisk. Something popped off the metal sculpture and bounced to the ground, smoking. The strike knocked Fine off his feet, and he tumbled onto his side. There was a low deep hum in the air that was an eerie counterpart to the howling of the wind and the hiss of the rain.

Fine scrambled to his feet and continued his terrified run to the mansion's portico. He was thirty feet away when another bolt slammed into the ground to his left. He felt the concussion and smelled the ionized air it left in its wake. The cloud was above Fine and its lightning bolts surrounded him.

His clothes were wet and heavy, and the lawn was a muddy mess. He slipped as he ran and picked himself up and ran for-ward. Twenty feet to go.

Another bolt hit one of the lightning rods that stuck out of the top of each gable and pediment of the stone mansion. The carved falcon below the rod seemed to twist and tilt as if pierced by an arrow.

Ten feet to the portico. Ten agonizingly distant feet in this rain across this mud in this freak storm. Fine took a few final strides and tumbled inside the stone columns just as a bolt hit the ground where he had been just seconds earlier. It was so close it knocked him off his feet and against the wall.

Panting, exhausted, terrified, Fine huddled in the shadows of the portico as bolt after bolt raked across the lawn. The lightning reminded him of a tiger prowling back and forth in a cage, eyeing its prey but unable to reach it.

The storm was after him.

For five long minutes the lightning continued, a curtain of violent light just yards away. And then with a final grumble of thunder, the cloud began to drift west toward New London, carrying the rain and wind with it. As the cloud drifted away, the sky cleared. The sun shone brightly, sparkling on the raindrops that clung to trees and grass and railings and sculptures. The cloud left behind it an eerie, suspended calm, a profound silence. The change in the scene was so abrupt it seemed as if someone had switched off the sound in a movie.

Fine slowly emerged from the shadows of the portico into the daylight. He blinked in stunned wariness. He stood and watched the distant dark cloud dissipate and fade away. Recovering his senses, Fine walked over to the path and moved along it. Leaves and twigs were scattered across the bricks.

Had it really happened? The wet ground said it had. But it was so strange. He had never seen a single black cloud like the one that had come in over Ledge Light. It had seemed to willfully come after him. What a strange thought — a cloud with intention. A cloud possessed.

Fine walked toward the metal obelisk, up ahead and to his right. Ledge Light was to his left. Both were dark shapes against the sky. Both had tasted the storm's fury. And, Fine felt, they were somehow connected. He reached Mythic Mystery and climbed up the granite rock that was its base. The rock broke through the grass in a misshapen oval of striated grey granite.

The sculpture, by Penny Kaplan, had been installed in 2004. It looked like a miniature Washington Monument that had been dipped in black ink. Over time, that steel surface had weathered into a mottling of red rust. Some of the letters were missing, only their shapes left in the rust like ghosts.

Fine saw on the ground the letter that had been blown off by the lightning. It was a "K." He picked up the metal letter, still warm from the lightning's hot caress. He turned it over and saw the melted stubs of the rivets that had held it in place. He turned to the metal sculpture and studied it. He could see where the K had been on the pylon. The letter below, an "A," was also missing. But its shape was still discernible in the rust.

Fine thought about those two letters. K. And A. "Ka."

What the other letters might mean Fine didn't know. But he knew what Ka meant. Ka was in some ways at the heart of what Fine did. He was a paranormal investigator. To Fine, the odd black cloud, the way it seemed to stalk him, the dramatic blowing off of the K, all seemed to have significance and meaning. He felt he was being drawn to something. He just didn't know what.

And there was more.

Standing at the obelisk, Fine looked across the sea to Ledge Lighthouse, a square red structure out in the ocean a mile from the mouth of the Thames River. Past Ledge Light, Race Rock Lighthouse was a silhouette against the horizon. To his left a few hundred yards, the Avery Point light was a small tower. And to his right, across the river, New London Harbor Light, a regal white tower, cast a bright reflection upon the waters. All these lighthouses seemed to define a geometry — of places, of history, of architecture, and of legend. Each had a unique story.

To Fine, the geometry was compelling. He was working on a theory he called proximal affinity. He believed that places near one another had connections — paranormal connections. It was a geography of a different nature. Its components were not mountains and rivers and seas. They were spirits and phantoms and hauntings. Fine was convinced that Ledge Lighthouse and Mythic Mystery were somehow entwined. According to local legend, Ledge Light was haunted. And Mythic Mystery — tall, black, and clothed in a skin of letters — seemed an apparition from another realm. The storm had hit them both. It could not be without meaning.

Today, he would study the obelisk. Soon, he would go out and spend the night alone on the lighthouse. He'd investigate. Collect data. Feel for himself the aura of the building. He'd see if there was any evidence of the ghost that haunted the lighthouse. He would explore his proximal affinity theory, and test his Phanoptiscope, a device he had created to see spirits.

Everett Line Fine turned his attention back to the Mythic Mystery sculpture. He took some photographs of it and made some notes in his slightly damp field notebook.

He looked at the K again. Blown off before his eyes. Perhaps *for* his eyes? The K also might have another meaning: it was the first letter of "keeper." The ghost at Ledge Light was that of a keeper. Was it a sign of a proximal affinity? "K." "Ka." "Keeper." It all connected.

Fine put the metal letter in his pocket. He stood by the obelisk and stared out at Ledge Lighthouse. What mysteries lay within its walls? What would a night alone out there reveal to him? Did its shadows hold answers or just more mysteries?

He turned and walked down the memorial path. Though the day was clear and the sun was out, the foghorn on Ledge Light came on. Its low distant cry drifted across the water.

Fine wondered if it was calling out to him to come.

Or perhaps warning him to stay away.

2

FIVE YEARS LATER
2014

S cott Edwards walked into the New London Antique Store with no particular intention other than to see if anything in the place might suggest a story. As a writer, he found antique stores an endless source of inspiration. Creativity is essentially the art of combining unconnected things into new relationships. And that's exactly what antique stores did. To Edwards, the jumble of an antique store, its kaleidoscopic mix of forms and functions, eras and ideas, was wonderfully evocative. And since he was new to the area, he could learn a lot about its history and culture by the knickknacks, books, old photographs and clothes he found.

Scott browsed the narrow aisles formed by tables and cabinets and cases. It was always strange to see so many parts of lives taken out of context and jumbled together. It was as if boxes of memories had been emptied and mixed together. Were there any connections, any affinities between the objects casually resting against one another on the shelves? Did the wide-eyed doll see the tiny tin Civil War soldier across the way? Did the ventriloquist's dummy have anything to say to the bust of Lincoln? Was it just coincidence that a volume of H.P. Lovecraft's stories rested atop "Davidson's Compendium of Phobias, Revised Edition"? Was there any meaning to the Purple Heart medal peeking out from beneath a dented peace symbol button? From tarnished silver dollar to dog-eared family album, every object had a story. A story that was usually impossible to know. But for a writer, the perfect starting point for invention.

Scott especially liked boxes, as his father had. Similar to doors, boxes beckoned us to open them. The myth of Pandora taught the folly of this, but few heed the warning. A closed box is just too seductive.

Scott was on the second floor of the sprawling antique store when he spotted a light in the gloom. Drawing closer, he saw it was the hinge on a box. Curious, he dug through the old record albums, books, magazines, and board games that surrounded and all but covered it. When he finally unearthed it, he saw the box was beat up, grimy, and had no doubt been buried in the pile for some time. He brought it to a nearby counter.

The box was about the size of a briefcase, with a handle and brass combination lock. It was covered with dark, worn leather. Two faux straps crossed over the top and over the ends. A bunch of travel labels, faded and worn, still clung to the top and sides. When Scott tipped it he heard and felt something shift.

Scott wondered what was inside. Was it full of letters and postcards, or money, or old photographs? Were they the treasures of somebody's life or random junk? He took the case downstairs and asked the man behind the counter what he wanted for it, as he could not find a price tag. The man held the box, gave it a gentle shake.

"There's stuff inside," the man said.

"It's locked," said Scott.

"Could be valuable, whatever's in it," said the man.

"Or worthless crap," said Scott. "And I may never get it open," he added.

"True," said the man. "There are 1,000 permutations of three digits."

"You know that?"

"Yes, I do. I get a lot of things locked with 3-digit locks, so I looked it up. Discouraged me from ever trying them all to unlock something to see what's inside, curious as I may be."

"So how do you price a locked box?"

"Not easy. What's inside this box could be stale bubble gum."

"Or a million dollars."

"You wanna give me a million for it?"

"No. More likely it's stale gum."

"Eighty-one dollars," said the man abruptly.

"How did you arrive at that?"

"No idea. Just popped into my head."

"Seems pricey."

"Maybe. But if it's a million dollars, you got a helluva deal."

"If its stale gum, I got ripped off," Scott countered.

"So we settle for something between a few bucks and a million," the man said. He leaned on the counter with his hands resting on either side of the box.

Scott thought it over. It seemed a lot for a box, but maybe there was something inside, and maybe it was worth something. It was a gamble.

"How about fifty bucks?" he asked.

The storeowner thought it over. "No, I think eighty-one is good. It's a nice box. Worth at least forty or fifty empty. So you're only gambling thirty-one bucks on what's inside."

"But I'll have to cut the hasp, which will ruin the box."

"Not if you cut it carefully, just the hasp. You can replace that if you want. Easy. I sell 'em."

Scott started to protest and wanted to bargain. The owner held up his hand.

"Listen, I don't like haggling. Eighty-one bucks popped into my head and I trust my gut. You can buy it or not. I don't care, really. I half hate to part with a lot of this stuff. I like being surrounded by all these bits and pieces of lives. I tend to grow fond, to feel an affinity for 'em."

In his years buying stuff at flea markets and antique shops, Scott had found that a lot of the dealers felt this way. They didn't want to part with things they had no real connection to. They became possessive of anonymous stuff. Scott had come to suspect that it was not about the stuff, really. It was about parting with things. Losing them. Life was full of loss. Holding on to things was a sometimes desperate way to try to balance that.

But the box intrigued him, and his gut, too, told him it was worth buying.

So Scott Edwards walked out of the New London Antique Store with a locked box. There was something inside. What, he had no idea.

It was a mystery.

3

The box sat on the dining room table for a few days. Scott was busy with other projects and didn't feel like dealing with it quite yet. Though every time he walked by, he stopped for a moment and wondered what lay within. Maybe, subconsciously, Scott was toying with himself. Building the anticipation and curiosity. Letting his imagination run a little wild.

Ding! Ding!

It was a text from his wife, Anne. She was away for two weeks at a conference. Since she often worked at home, they spent almost all their time together. This might have driven some couples crazy. But for Scott and Anne, it was the opposite. They were as one, sharing space and adventures and a deep love. They were also best friends. He really missed her.

Anne: What's up, Sweetie?
Scott: Not much. Missing you. I bought a box.
Anne: A box?
Scott: Yes, at the antique store in New London.
Anne: That's thrilling.
Scott: It's locked. I need to cut it open, see what's inside.
Anne: Maybe priceless gems.
Scott: Or stale gum.
Anne: Yuck! Be careful when you open it.
Scott: I will. I promise. How are you doing?
Anne: Okay. Busy. This conference is nuts. But it's a good distraction Keeps me from obsessing about the test.

Scott: Good. Don't worry. Everything will be fine.
Anne: We hope. I wish we'd hear.
Scott: We will soon.
Anne: I hope so. Well, gotta go. Lecture starting.
Scott: Maybe something good?
Anne: I wish. Probably another horrible PowerPoint. Miss you.
Love you!
Scott: Me too. Talk later. XXOOOXXX

It was Saturday, and he had a lonely dinner of leftover spaghetti Bolognese, arugula salad, bread, and wine. He hated eating alone when his wife was away. He had had more than enough solitary meals in his single days. But her work took her to conferences a few times a year, and he was left alone. As he ate, he eyed the box through the doorway to the dining room. It sat in the shadows on the big wooden table, a thing of mystery. After dinner, he could wait no longer.

Scott had a small shop in his basement. It was well equipped with tools he used to keep the house in shape. He set the box on his worktable and found a thin jigsaw. He turned on the radio, and being Saturday, tuned it to PRI to listen to "Hot Jazz Saturday Night," coming out of WAMU in Washington, D.C. He and his wife had listened to it for years. The host, Rob Bamberger, played jazz of the 1920s, 30s, and 40s. They just don't make music like that anymore, and Scott and Anne had fallen in love with the old classics of Ella Fitzgerald, Glenn Miller, the Mills Brothers, Fats Waller and all the rest who had created such wonderful music. The tunes took them back, at least in their minds, to the Roaring Twenties, the Great Depression, and World War II. The music evoked speakeasies and smoky nightclubs, men in uniform, and young couples sitting out in the summer night, falling in love, facing their futures. He could imagine people gathered around a radio listening to these songs. It was hard not to wax sentimental over the love ballads and the feelings they conjured up. Scott and Anne knew those times were fraught with difficulties and problems. They knew history. But somehow, the heart triumphed and cast a golden light on the music. The couple spent countless Saturday nights on the couch, in the shadows, looking out the picture window at the lighthouse flashing, as clarinets and crooners swept them into romantic dreams.

As Cab Calloway sang about Minnie the Moocher, Scott began to saw at the tarnished brass hasp that kept his box of mysteries locked.

What was inside? Tipping the box he could hear things, but what? It could be almost anything.

The brass was hard to cut. It took him nearly half an hour to saw through it. Once the hasp was severed, he sat back. For some reason, Scott wanted to draw this moment out. Maybe it was the writer in him. Maybe it was the music, now Glenn Miller's "Moonlight Serenade." But he felt that the moment of opening the box was meaningful. It might send his life in a new direction. He laughed at himself. Always so dramatic!

He went upstairs and poured himself a shot of Licor 43, then returned to his shop. He sat down and positioned the box in the middle of the table under his work light. The wind rattled a basement window. He took a sip of the sweet drink, as golden as the music. Glenn Miller had given way to Ella singing "Bewitched, Bothered and Bewildered." Perfect.

"Okay," he said to the box. "Let's see what my eighty-one dollars bought me."

Then he undid the two clasps and slowly raised the lid. Inside was a very strange assortment of items, and Scott knew immediately he had made a wise purchase — at least for him. He just stared at the contents for a moment, a bit awed, a bit excited that the objects that presented themselves were fascinating, strange, evocative. An antique shop in miniature. Or maybe a glimpse into a single life.

It was a box full of mysteries. Scott was determined to figure them out, one at a time, and see if they solved a puzzle or just created new ones.

Eight or nine items were in the box. He picked up the first and took it out. It was an old 35mm Voigtlander camera with big silver dials and knobs. In an age of iPhones and sleek digital cameras, it seemed a strange, cumbersome thing. But there was also a beauty to it. A classic 35mm camera is a precise and functional sculpture of metal and leather and glass. He put the camera to his eye and focused on the box, spun a few dials. Scott put the camera aside.

Next, he took out a black metal letter "K." It was about 6 inches high, made of steel, he thought, and rusting. A few holes in it suggested it had once been bolted to something, probably a sign. Curious. Why would someone keep a metal K? He put it on the table next to the camera.

Something called an EMF meter, made by the ACME Company, was next. In small print he saw that EMF meant Electro-Magnetic Field. It was about the size of a TV remote, with a few buttons and a meter. A camera. A metal letter. A meter. Scott saw no connection yet. Maybe the case held random junk?

Another gadget was next. It was a metallic box, about the size of a hardcover book. Its surface was a cluttered complexity of brass and silver gears, wires, levers, switches, and lights. It reminded him of an anatomical model where the skin had been stripped off revealing the underlying muscles, nerves, and blood vessels. Except these were all mechanical parts, their function unimaginable. A wire led from one side of the box to a bumpy glass cone on top that seemed to be some sort of lens or projection lamp. Scott raised the lid and saw more mechanisms and lights inside, a glass disk in the center. It was a device of some sort, but that was about all Scott could guess. He had never seen anything like it. He had no idea whatsoever what it was for. In its bronze and silver complexity, it was beautiful, whatever it was. He put it next to the camera, meter, and letter K.

A small wood figure lay nestled against a side of the box, and Scott took it out. It was about 5 inches high. It was a crudely carved wood figurine of a sailor. It had a sailor's cap, coat, and buttoned vest, a scarf, and wide pants. Scott stood him on the table next to the box. Scott pondered the little figure a while as he sipped his drink.

"Okay, my little friend," Scott said to the wooden sailor, "let's see what other mysterious cargo you're sailing through time with."

The next item to emerge from the box was mysterious indeed. It was a set of goggles, made of brass. One lens had several small lenses on a post that could be swiveled down in front of it. The other lens had what looked like a magnifying eyepiece attached to it, and next to that a small light. It looked like something from a Jules Verne story — Victorian in design and appearance. Did it somehow work in tandem with the strange projection device he had already taken out?

What was this stuff?

Scott took out a simple Radio Shack microcassette recorder. He popped open the lid and was disappointed to see there was no cassette inside. The final item was a notebook. Scott opened it and thumbed through the pages. They were filled with field notes and diagrams of various buildings and rooms. Scanning the entries, he realized it was the journal of a ghost hunter, a paranormal investigator. This was confirmed when he thumbed to the first page, which was blank save the following identification text:

Field Notes 2008-09
Everett Line Fine
Groton Paranormal Group

A paranormal investigator! So these gadgets had something to do with sensing and maybe recording ghosts. Scott wondered if all the items in the box belonged to Everett Line Fine or if some had been added in. Or were things missing? And what a strange name! "Everett Line Fine." The rhyme in it gave the name a magical quality, Scott thought. He wondered who he was and how this box of his stuff, assuming it was all his, had ended up in the antique store.

The box had proven to be full of intriguing things. Scott had gone in search of inspiration for a story. He had certainly found one.

The radio was playing "Caravan" by the Mills Brothers, who had the uncanny ability to simulate, with their voices, trumpets and trombones. Their music was not what it seemed to be. Scott sipped his drink and looked at the items on his worktable.

An odd mechanical box.
A strange pair of goggles.
A small carved figure.
An EMF meter.
A metal letter K.
A camera.
A tape recorder.
The notebook of Everett Line Fine, ghost hunter.

It wasn't a million dollars. But it wasn't stale gum, either!

Scott wondered what to do next. He wondered if this was the end of the story. A box of fascinating things, to be sure, but maybe no more than that. They may lead him nowhere. Then again, he had learned that coming up with a story, or uncovering a real one, was a lot like archaeology. He had to dig. He had to chase ideas. Some led nowhere. Others led him to unexpected places. Places that were sometimes as vivid and wonderful as dreams. Or as dark and terrifying as nightmares.

He wondered where this box of mysteries might lead him.

Scott sipped his drink, gazing at the objects in the pool of light cast by his work light. The wind rattled the basement window, and on the radio, Nat King Cole sang "Forever." Scott heard neither. He was lost in thought, his imagination beginning to work on the story of Everett Line Fine, paranormal investigator.

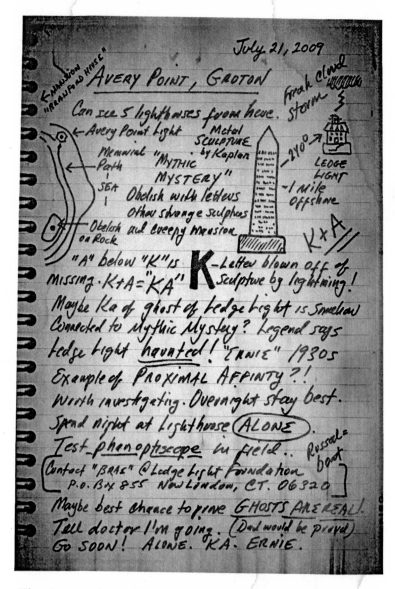

July 21, 2009

AVERY POINT, GROTON

"Marrison House" "Branford House"

freak cloud storm

Can see 5 lighthouses from here.

← Avery Point Light

Memorial Path

SEA

Metal SCULPTURE by Kaplan "MYTHIC MYSTERY"

Obelish with letters

Other strange sculptures

← Obelish and creepy mansion on Rock

LEDGE LIGHT

-240°↗

~1 Mile offshore

K×A //

"A" below "K" is missing. K+A = "KA"

K — Letter blown off of sculpture by lightning!

Maybe Ka of ghost of ledge light is somehow connected to Mythic Mystery? Legend says ledge light <u>haunted</u>! "ERNIE" 1930s Example of PROXIMAL AFFINITY ?! Worth investigating. Overnight stay best. Spend night at lighthouse (ALONE). Test phenoptiscope in field.. Russell's boat

Contact "BRAS" @ Ledge Light Foundation P.O. Box 855 New London, CT. 06320

Maybe best chance to prove GHOSTS ARE REAL! Tell doctor I'm going. (Dad would be proud) Go SOON! ALONE. KA. ERNIE.

Final page from Everett Line Fine's field notebook for the Groton Paranormal Group. July, 2009

4

S cott had a name, Everett Line Fine, and a group, the Groton Paranormal Group. Maybe he could find out more about him and them. It was a start.

He looked through the notebook and was especially intrigued by the last page. It was cluttered with notes and ideas and a few small drawings. It seemed to document a trip by Fine to Avery Point in Groton, and indicated that he was planning to investigate New London Ledge Lighthouse. Reputedly, it was haunted. The few notes gave some clues to the path Fine might have followed next, and Scott decided to see if he could retrace it and piece together some pieces of the puzzle. Scott loved this part of writing a book. The sleuthing, the researching, the reverse-engineering of tantalizing tidbits to tease out their origins and meaning. And he loved the unpredictability of it all, how his path to a story took unexpected twists and turns.

An Internet search for Everett Line Fine turned up nothing. But searching for the Groton Paranormal Group showed their address as 450 Thames Street. Not far away.

He texted his wife:

Scott: Hi, Sweetie, hope conference going well. The box had interesting stuff inside. Belonged to local paranormal investigator. Will try to track him down. Maybe a good story.

It took a while before Anne wrote back.

Anne: Good to hear from you. Busy here. A ghost hunter? Sounds interesting. Don't get into trouble.
Scott: I'll be fine. Miss you.

Anne: No call about the test?
Scott: No. Nothing. Don't fret.
Anne: Easy for you to say.
Scott: Not really.
Anne: Sorry. I know it's hard on you, too.

He decided to move on to something else.
Scott: Any old friends there?
Anne: Yeah, a few. They all say hi.
Scott: Hi to them. Have fun. Go crazy.
Anne: Easy with that gang! I'll pass that on. Off to another lecture. Miss you. Love you.
Scott: Miss you too. XOXOXXXOOO

Scott stared at the phone. He shook his head. Communicating with his wife this way, *she* was something of a ghost. There with him, but not there with him. He put the phone away and gathered the items from his worktable and put them back in the case. With the hasp sawed through it didn't stay closed, so he tied it with a rope.

* * *

Monday morning, Scott put the case in his car and set out for 450 Thames Street in Groton. As he drove, he thought about how much history the area had. Pfizer, the pharmaceutical giant. Electric Boat, where submarines were built. The sub base, where they were docked. The Coast Guard Academy. Connecticut College. The Avery Point campus of UConn, where they taught marine biology. It went on and on. The past was very much alive in the area, and vestiges of earlier times and history were everywhere. Groton was indeed a palimpsest of history.

He drove down Thames Street slowly, looking for addresses. He spotted 450 and parked across the street in front of Electric Boat. A sign on the fence warned it was a sensitive military area. No photography. It would be considered espionage! He wondered if taking a picture of the sign would be considered an act of espionage. He didn't intend to test it.

He made his way over to 450, part of a small storefront group. Peering in the window, he saw a few desks and chairs, some shelves with papers, and a torn "X Files" poster with its signature line: "The Truth Is Out There," though the ripped poster only showed "The Truth Is..."

The Groton Paranormal Group was no longer at this address, and all that remained were a few remnants of their time here. A dead end.

Scott noticed an old-fashioned barber's pole a few doors down from the vacant headquarters of the Groton Paranormal Group. He walked to it, passing a tattoo parlor on the way. The front window of the barber had big letters painted on it:

Danielle's Barber Shop
Barber on the Thames
Military and Walk-Ins Welcome

Most likely if anybody knew what had happened to the Groton Paranormal Group, it would be Danielle. Barbershops, like diners, were community places. Places where locals mixed, where news and stories were told and overheard, and where gossip was spread.

He walked into Danielle's. It was pretty quiet. A woman with tattoos up and down her arms was giving a customer dressed in fatigues the requisite military buzz cut. Danielle catered to the military guys who were stationed at the nearby sub base. They and her non-military regulars kept her busy. In a corner sat an elderly man wearing a white smock. He was just staring ahead, lost in thought, as if in a trance. A TV perched on a shelf above the wall of mirrors was tuned to a daytime talk show. In an irritating drawl, Dr. Phil was asking a couple why they thought breeding llamas would help their marriage.

The place was cluttered with photos of submarines and military badges, postcards taped to the mirrors, a bulletin board, and piles of magazines. Scott smiled to see some of them were vaguely raunchy girlie magazines — as much a staple of barbershops as brass and leather chairs, white porcelain sinks, and jars of combs and scissors. Below the mirrors, a counter that ran the length of the wall held clippers, shaving cream dispensers, tins of Pinaud Gentlemen's Powder, small whisk brooms, and other tools of the trade. The black-and-white checked floor completed the classic look.

Scott loved the place immediately.

"Hi," said a pretty blonde who was sitting in a chair by the window. "I'm Danielle."

"Hi, Danielle, I'm Scott. Scott Edwards."

"Have a seat."

Scott looked at the man in the smock sitting in the corner and wondered why he wasn't next. He turned his head back to Danielle, who just smiled at him. Scott shrugged and sat down. He hadn't planned on a haircut, but it seemed a better way to ease into a conversation than just starting cold.

"I'm not military, so not too short. Neaten me up and leave it a little longer in front." He liked to have it a bit fuller in front. His wife liked it shorter. He'd see if Danielle could find a happy compromise. If not, he and Anne might have to breed llamas.

"New to the area?" she asked as she draped him with a cloth and wrapped his neck in that tissue paper collar that only barbers use.

"Fairly. About eight months."

"Like it?"

"I do. I've lived in New York and Boston and D.C. This area is a nice change of pace from the big cities."

"Lots of history here," said Danielle as she began to snip his hair.

"So I am discovering," said Scott.

"What do you do here?" Danielle asked. He could hear her close to his ear — feel her breath, actually — a disembodied voice. He could only see her when he faced the mirror. It was a strange way to talk to someone.

"I'm a writer," he said.

"Really? What sort of stuff do you write?"

"Oh, different things. Some articles for magazines. Short scripts for documentary films. A few novels. I've just started researching a new book."

"Cool! What's the book about?"

"Well, until a few days ago, I wasn't sure. But now I think it will be about ghost hunting. And paranormal investigators."

"Fiction or nonfiction?" Danielle asked.

Scott hadn't really thought about that. He really wasn't sure.

"That remains to be seen," he said. It was true.

Her hands darted around his head. The scissors gleamed when they caught the light. Curls of his graying hair drifted down like feathers.

"We used to have a neighbor here, just down the street. The Groton Paranormal Group. They did that kind of stuff," the voice said.

"Oh yeah? I should talk to them."

"They moved out a few years ago. Something happened to one of their guys, I think. They stopped for a while, then moved and started up again. Got a fresh start."

"Interesting. Where did they go?"

"Not far. They moved to an office over in New London. In the Dewart Building on State Street, I think. I get a card from them at Christmas. Even though they're in New London, they still call themselves the Groton Paranormal Group."

That was easy.

"Thanks, Danielle. I'll look them up."

"You should. Might be helpful to your book. I'm not sure how many of them are still doing it. The main guy was Chuck. Chuck Freedman. Nice guy. Funny, too. He did a great Jerry Lewis imitation. And one of the Three Stooges, too."

"I'll see if I can find him."

"Say hi, if you do. He'll remember me. Always got his hair cut here. Had some amazing stories to tell about ghosts." She laughed, but it was half a shudder.

She continued: "Creepy line of work to be in, if you ask me. Lots of time in dark basements and attics. Sometimes they'd spend the night in some old deserted building. Not for me. I'm scared of my own shadow."

Danielle had finished trimming his hair. She would finish him off by shaving his neck. She spread hot lather on the back of his neck and around front to his throat. It felt wonderful. She opened a six-inch straight razor and began stroking it along a piece of leather that hung from the counter. It glinted in the light of the shop. Scott eyed it. There is always something menacing about a straightedge razor.

"Do you believe in ghosts?" he asked.

Danielle was about to shave his neck. The razor was right in front of him.

"I don't know. I've had some things happen that make me think that maybe there's something to all that paranormal stuff."

She began shaving him as she answered. He let her talk. He never liked to move much when someone had a razor at his throat. Always the worrier.

"Yeah?" Scott said, like a ventriloquist, barely moving his lips.

"Yeah. We think this barbershop is haunted."

"Really?"

"Yep. Strange things happen sometimes. I think it might be the ghost of Andy Chapelli who used to own it. He was a barber, too."

"Hmmm. Have you ever seen him?"

"No. But I may have seen a ghost once."

"Where?"

"Well, about fifteen years ago, I was in this empty building they were trying to get going again with businesses. It was before I moved here, and I was looking for a space for the shop. The real estate agent was showing me around, and I saw this guy sitting in one of the rooms, half in the shadows. Just sitting at a desk. Not doing anything. Just sitting there. He looked like a mannequin, but he was real. His eyes moved and I saw him breathing. And he had on this outfit that looked, I don't know, old. Like something you'd see maybe a hundred years ago. A double breasted suit. Pocket watch. Wide short tie. Old fashioned hat, too. I went in the next room where the agent was fiddling with the lights, and I asked her who the guy was. She gave me a blank look and asked: 'What guy? There's nobody here but us. I have the only key.' Sure enough, when I looked back in the room, he was gone. But I swear I saw him. I didn't imagine it. Chuck told me that sometimes only certain people can see a ghost."

Danielle stopped shaving his neck, the straightedge razor poised in mid stroke. He felt it pressing against his skin. She stared at him a moment, then continued.

"Yeah, maybe there are ghosts. I think he was one. He was someone who had worked in that building a long long time ago. I'm pretty sure of it." She shaved him with long smooth strokes and asked: "What about you?"

"Hmmm," said Scott, playing for time, not wanting to talk until she was done with that damned razor. She finished finally, and he answered.

"I'm not sure, Danielle. I've never had anything like that happen to me. Not exactly. But I did have one experience that was kind of spooky." Scott said it without really thinking, and he surprised himself with the sudden memory.

"Tell me!"

"Well, a few years ago, my grandmother died over the winter. I couldn't make the funeral. I got snowed in in D.C. Never made it out of the airport. I regretted it. We were close, me and my grandma. She was a great lady. She traveled with us. We played Scrabble with her. Went fishing. She made us her special brownies.

"Anyway, a month or so later, I visited my folks. I stayed with them. Their house used to be her house. I was asleep. In the middle of the night. I had this overwhelming sensation that my grandmother was standing next to the bed, looking at me. I started to wake up. The feeling got stronger. I could even smell her perfume — a lilac scent. I didn't open my eyes. I don't know if I was scared or thought that if I opened them it would break the spell and she would vanish. I'm not sure. I was fully awake, my heart was pounding, I kept my eyes closed, and I felt her there looking at me. I could feel ... I don't know ... her loving gaze. It lasted a few minutes and then I think I fell back asleep. I know — you'll say I was asleep the whole time. It was a dream.

But I know it wasn't. She was there, visiting me. From the here-after."

"No, I believe you. I really do. Weird, isn't it?" Danielle put a hand on Scott's shoulder. "I think we only know the half of it," she said.

Scott looked at her in the mirror. Danielle finished shaving him, wiped off his neck, dusted away the hair, and powdered him with talc. Then she whisked away the sheet like a magician revealing the climax of a trick.

"All set," she said.

Scott liked Danielle and her cozy barbershop. In an age of modern salons her shop seemed a throwback to an earlier time. A simpler time.

"Fifteen dollars," she said.

Yes. Definitely a throwback. He gave her a twenty and told her to keep the change. As Scott turned to leave, he was surprised to see the man in the white smock in the corner was still there. Scott frowned. He thought a moment then asked:

"How long has this building been here, Danielle?"

"A long time. Close to 90, 95 years. I think it was a lot of different things over the years, including a cobbler's shop, a watchmaker, and a bait shop. Then it became a barbershop around 1950 or so, and it's been one ever since."

Scott just nodded his head, looking at the man that Danielle seemed to be ignoring.

"Good luck with the ghost guys. Hope you can find Chuck," Danielle said.

"Thanks, Danielle. You've been a big help."

"Let me know what you find out sometime."

"Will do. Thanks."

Scott knew he'd found a friendly place to get his haircuts. He'd return. Outside, he peered back through the window. The man was still sitting in the corner. Danielle made no move to acknowledge him. Odd.

He walked back to his car, stopping to look in the window of the Groton Paranormal Group's former headquarters. He wondered what had happened to them. He hoped he'd find Chuck. Maybe Chuck could tell him about Everett Fine, whose case of strange objects sat beside him in the car, their mysteries intact.

5

Scott drove along Thames Street in Groton, over the Gold Star Bridge, and up State Street in New London. He parked in front of the Garde Theater. "Merloc The Magician & The Mysterium" the marquee read. Scott liked magic. Maybe he'd take Anne to the show. A night of illusions might be fun.

He crossed the street to the Dewart Building, one of the city's fine old structures. Scott had Fine's case with him. He scanned the directory in the entryway and sure enough, found the Groton Paranormal Group. He pushed the button and a few seconds later a voice came over the intercom.

"Yeah?"

"Hi. My name is Scott Edwards. I'm doing some research about paranormal investigations and I'd like to talk with you."

There was nothing for ten or fifteen seconds, then a buzzer sounded. Scott opened the door and took the creaky old elevator to the second floor. He exited. A few doors down the dim hallway was a wood door with a frosted glass pane, on which was stenciled:

Groton Paranormal Group.
Shedding Light on the Dark Side.

Under the lettering was a stylized U-shaped graphic that looked a bit like the horns of a steer, with tiny hands on the tips. The hallway and the door reminded him of something from a 1940s film noir. Scott thought everything should be in black and white. All he needed was a sultry blonde in high heels waltzing down the hallway to complete the scene.

But the hallway was empty.

Scott walked to the door and opened it. He entered a small office. The walls were covered with a cluttered assortment of maps, photographs, and beat up bulletin boards with file cards pinned to them. There was another "X Files" poster just like in the abandoned office in Groton. A foot-tall inflatable version of Munch's famous painting *The Scream* sat perched on top of some file cabinets, sagging over from lack of air. There were some movie posters, too. One of *Nosferatu*. One of *The Thing from Another World*. Beneath a poster for *Horror of Party Beach*, which showed a bug-eyed, vaguely reptilian monster terrorizing nubile girls in bikinis, a man who looked to be in his mid 60s sat at a computer terminal. The man looked up at Scott.

"Yes? May I help you?"

"Are you Chuck? Chuck Freedman?"

"Yes, I am."

"Hi! Pleased to meet you. My name is Scott Edwards. As I said on the intercom, I'm a writer doing some research about paranormal investigators. Actually about one in particular who is part of the Groton Paranormal Group."

"Yeah? Who?"

"Everett Line Fine."

The man did a bit of a double take. He leaned back in his chair. It squeaked.

"Everett Fine *was* a part of Groton Paranormal. But he hasn't been for years. He was only with us a short time. Less than a year."

"Oh," said Scott. He didn't quite know how to proceed. He decided to make small talk. He pointed to the *Horror of Party Beach* poster.

"Looks terrifying," he said with a smile.

Chuck chuckled. "Oh yes, it was terrifying. It was terrifyingly bad."

"Really?"

"I guarantee it. Get it from Netflix if you don't believe me. But I should know."

"You've seen it?"

"More than that. Not only have I seen it, I was in it."

"You were in *Horror of Party Beach*?" Scott was amazed.

"Yeah! That's me. I'm the monster. My mom worked on the production. I was in high school. They needed someone to crawl into the rubber monster suit and chase girls. What high school boy wouldn't want to do that?"

"Was it fun?"

"Not really. The suit was hot. The hours were long. And I had to kill all the girls when I caught them. I had hoped for maybe a kiss. But as you can see, the monster has what looks like hot dogs — a whole bunch of them — coming out of his mouth."

"What were they?"

"No idea. I didn't design the costume. It had something to do with nuclear radiation. All the monster films of the 60s did. I guess it was some sort of hot-dog mutation." Chuck laughed and shook his head.

"A terrifyingly bad film!" he repeated, laughing a bit. "It had no clue as to what really scares people."

"Which is?"

"Lots of things. But not guys in silly rubber suits with bulging ping-pong eyeballs. People are scared of the unknown. Of stuff they are familiar with that gets twisted, off kilter. Lots of stuff." Chuck pointed over his shoulder to the poster. "But not that."

Scott remembered he was holding the case. He'd broken the ice with Chuck.

"I have some of Everett's stuff here, Chuck. Maybe you could explain it to me?" He put the case on the table and untied the rope holding it shut. He opened the lid and turned it sideways so they could both see inside. Chuck looked a bit stricken. He just stared at the stuff — ten, twenty seconds. Finally he spoke.

"That's Everett's gear all right. How did you get it?"

"I spotted this case at the antique store over on Bank Street. It was buried under a bunch of stuff. It was locked. You can see — I had to cut the hasp to open it. I was surprised by what was inside. A strange mix of things. His name and the name Groton

Paranormal Group are in that notebook. I Googled the Groton Paranormal Group, found the address, and went over to Groton. You weren't there, but Danielle at the barber shop told me where to find you."

Chuck nodded and regained his composure. Mention of Danielle seemed to have brought him back from wherever the sight of Fine's case had taken him.

"Danielle! I miss her place. It's classic. How is she?"

"Fine. She says hi."

"Have a seat," Chuck said, then asked: "Mind if I look through this?"

"Go ahead."

"I haven't seen it since he left for the lighthouse."

Chuck moved things around seeing what was there. After a moment he looked up at Scott. He seemed to be considering something. Maybe weighing whether he should talk or not. Then he looked Scott in the eye and said: "Okay, let's see if I can shed any light on Fine's box of stuff."

"So where is Everett now?" Scott asked.

"To be honest, I don't really know. After the incident, he went away, and we lost track of him. Our little group kind of got spooked and disbanded. It was a rough time. We were small to begin with, and a few drifted away. A few of us got together a year ago and got going again. Ghosts get in your blood. Hard to give up." Chuck was thumbing through Fine's notebook, occasionally stopping to study a page.

"The incident?" asked Scott.

"Yeah. Out at Ledge Lighthouse."

"What happened?"

Suddenly wary, Chuck asked: "What are you writing about? For whom?"

"Don't worry. I'm not an investigative reporter trying to expose anyone. And I have no agenda regarding paranormal stuff. I'm a novelist. I had no interest in paranormal investigations or investigators until I happened upon this box of stuff a few days ago. I was looking for inspiration for a new story. I often find it in antique stores. So I was roaming around, found this case, got it opened, and have been, to say the least, intrigued by what's inside. There may be a story, there may not be. I don't know. But it's weird enough to at least explore."

Chuck nodded. "Yeah, I can see why what's in here would pique someone's interest. Especially someone with a good imagination. What did you pay for this?"

"Eighty-one bucks."

"Well, maybe it will be worth your while." Chuck picked up the strange box with its gears and wires and projection lens.

"What can you tell me about Everett Fine?" Scott asked as Chuck fiddled with the contraption.

"Everett Line Fine. Hmmm. Where to start? He was a young guy. Maybe about 30 or so. He just showed up at our office one day. I don't know a lot about his background. He seemed smart. A little geeky, as those of us in this line of work tend to be. I interviewed him a while. We try to weed out people who are really into role-playing games and are already convinced they live surrounded by ghosts and goblins and demons. You know, young men who live in their folks' basement, dress in black capes, and obsess on Facebook about doing battle with the Wroth of Gar and saving the Wee Sperlibogs or whatever the hell it is they do in their folks' basements. They aren't objective. They want to believe a little too much. And though people may not always take what we do seriously, WE are serious about it. We try to apply scientific methods and reasoning to paranormal investigation. We are skeptics, looking for proof. We try to gather evidence and analyze it. Basic forensics, really. But, you know, about things that may or may not exist.

"Everett seemed sincere and pretty reasonable. He was kind of quiet and introverted. One of those guys who mumbles and doesn't look you in the eye. I thought he was maybe a little troubled. I think he had lost his dad fairly recently so that may have been why.

"Anyway, his awkwardness aside, I liked him and how he answered my questions. And he said he was working on some gadgets that might provide some breakthroughs in paranormal investigating. That piqued *my* interest. So we invited him to be on our team."

"How big is your group?"

"It varies. People come and go, and occasionally we add someone for a while for their expertise with a particular subject. Like if someone thinks they have the ghost of a Revolutionary War soldier sitting in their kitchen, we might hire a guy who knows a lot about the Revolutionary War. But our core group is only four."

"Did Everett do many investigations?"

"Well, like I said, he wasn't with us too long before the incident. He did a half dozen or so, if I remember right. He was the lead investigator over at the train station, and at some residentials we did. He helped me look into the "Bloody Murder" legend over at a house on Parkway North. And, if memory serves me, he debunked the "Ghost of the Guthrie Mansion" myth.

Chuck turned his attention back to Fine's case. "Let's look at this stuff piece by piece. Maybe it will tell us more about what happened at Ledge Light. I'd like to know myself." He saw Scott tilt his head again as if to ask what happened.

"I'll get to it," Chuck said.

Chuck removed the old camera.

"This is a camera. He'd use it to take pictures."

Scott smiled. Gee, no kidding.

"Nothing special about it." Chuck put the camera aside. He took out the small microcassette recorder.

"This is a small audio recorder. He'd record field notes, observations, impressions. Things he'd want to get down without taking the time to write. Recordings are good. Very immediate. Unfiltered by analysis or contemplation. You get a real feel for things unfolding in real time, especially if the investigator just leaves it on so it records everything — what he's saying, how he's saying it, and what he's hearing. With luck you might record a spirit speaking."

Chuck pushed a button and the lid to the recorder popped open. There was no cassette inside.

"Tape's missing. Too bad. Might have shed some light on that night."

Scott was about to ask again about the incident, but Chuck put up his hands as if to say "wait." He rummaged in the box and pulled out the notebook and thumbed through it again.

"We keep field journals like this. I've got drawers full of them. They have research notes, directions, to do lists, theories, measurements, phone numbers, and so on. Let's see…here, on the last page of entries: Fine was at Avery Point, along the memorial path, studying a sculpture called Mythic Mystery as well Ledge Lighthouse. Here's a diagram of the area. He describes a little bit of what is going on. Looks like a violent thunderstorm rolled in quickly. A strange black cloud. Looks like the page got a little wet. There are some streaks on it. You can see he has some contact notes, compass headings, some things to check out and remember. He wanted to go out to the lighthouse. Alone. That came back to haunt him. Oh, yeah, here he mentions 'proximal affinity.' I remember that. It was a new theory he was working on. Fine was pretty imaginative. He writes about a ghost named Ernie, too. He mentions some other stuff, as you can see. And down here, a note that for some reason he needs to tell a doctor he is going to Ledge Light.

"But beyond that day, nothing. The pages are blank. This was his last entry. He didn't make any notes when he went out to the lighthouse. At least not on paper."

Chuck put the notebook down. He took out the letter "K."

"He referred to this on that page of notes. It was part of the Mythic Mystery sculpture. It's a black steel obelisk out at Avery Point. Near the sea. In line with Ledge Light. This steel letter got blown off by a bolt of lightning. Wow! That must have been something! He saw significance in it. Thought it might connect to Ka."

"Ka?" asked Scott.

"I don't know a lot about it, really. Fine was pretty into it. You'd have to ask an expert. But basically it's an Egyptian belief that the life spirit goes on after someone dies and looks for a body or something to inhabit. You want to know more, I can tell you who to talk to. Oh! — Ka is represented by two upraised hands, like a football ref signaling a touchdown. Our logo, in fact. Ties into what we do. It was Fine's idea. It's a hell of lot better than a ghost that looked like a sheet with two holes cut in it."

Chuck turned back to the case and took out an EMF meter.

"What's that?" asked Scott.

"This is an EMF meter, which stands for Electro-Magnetic Force. Ghosts and the like tend to have electromagnetic fields that can be detected. In fact, they often act like electricity."

Scott frowned. "Can they shock you?"

Chuck laughed. "They can shock you as in scare you, but they can't shock you like a bad electrical plug might, if that's what you mean. But we think they are in large part electrical fields, or more precisely, electrical clouds. They have their negative and positive aspects — no pun intended — just as electricity does. And they behave like electricity does, being attracted or repelled by other charges, sometimes creating light, and so on."

"Could you use electricity to kill a ghost?" Scott asked.

"You can't kill something that is already dead, Scott. But in theory you could use electricity to attract and capture a spirit's energy field, so long as you had a place to store it."

Chuck turned on the EMF meter and pointed it at Scott. The needle didn't move. Chuck shut it off.

"You're not a ghost," he said.

Chuck put the EMF meter down. He picked up the strange box full of gears and levers, knobs and small lights. The box was so festooned with things it looked almost organic, as if it was growing a skin of mechanical parts. Along with the box, he took out the brass goggles bristling with strange little lenses and eyepiece extensions. A cable dangled from them. It was clear that they plugged into the strange box and worked with it somehow.

Chuck shook his head and smiled. "God, I remember these. I only saw them once, just a few days before Fine went out to Ledge Light. He came in the office and was all excited. He said he had created a new tool for seeing paranormal apparitions. He couldn't wait to try them out at the lighthouse."

"They look like night-vision goggles," said Scott.

"No," said Chuck. "They were something new, I think. Ghost-vision goggles."

Chuck was turning the box over in his hand, flicking a few of its switches. He was hoping the strange glass cone thing on top might start to shine. But nothing happened. Scott tried on the goggles. The room was dark through them, almost pitch black. Apparently, they needed some sort of special light from the box to work.

"Doesn't seem to work," Chuck said. "Fine had some name for this device. Let me see…I think he called it the Phantometer. No, wait…the Phanopticon? No…the Phanoptiscope. Yeah, that was it! A viewer to 'see phantoms.' Phanoptiscope. I think the box projected a web of light that could then be focused outside the wavelengths of the visible spectrum. If there was a ghost in the beams, the goggles would pick it up, and then process and enhance the image. Something like that."

"Did it work?"

Chuck looked up.

"Given what happened to Fine out there, I would say it probably did."

Scott took off the goggles and Chuck put the Phanoptiscope down.

"Can you see ghosts without something like that?" asked Scott.

"Let me tell you a little bit about the world of the paranormal, Scott. At least as I understand it."

Just then, an attractive woman appeared from the back office. She was short, perky, with dark hair and a big smile. She had a messenger bag over her shoulder with "Groton Paranormal Group" stenciled on the side, and under it: "Shedding Light on the Dark Side."

"Mary Angela!" said Chuck. "Scott, this is Mary Angela Lenska, one of my associates here at GPG. Angie, this is Scott Edwards. He's researching a book. He found Everett Fine's field case. We were just going through it."

"Call me Angie," she said as she shook Scott's hand then looked at the stuff on the table. "Cool! Wow, never thought we'd see any of this stuff again. Shed any light on what happened out there?"

"I'm afraid not," said Chuck.

"Too bad. That seems to be one mystery we may never solve," she replied.

"Where are you off to?" asked Chuck.

"Seaside, over in Waterford. There have been reports of some strange lights and sounds recently. Probably just kids partying, but you never know. Could be a paranormal party. Thought I'd go over, poke around, take some readings, see what I can find. Maybe I'll leave a remote data collection unit there for a few days."

"Remember, Angie: no solo overnights."

"Yeah, I know. But I have no plans for an overnight just yet."

She eyed the Phanoptiscope. "I'd use that if any of us knew how it worked." She smiled an incandescent smile.

"How's the research going?" asked Chuck.

"Good. It's harder than I thought, and I suck on the computer, but I'm getting there."

"Mary Angela is getting her PhD. She's doing her doctoral thesis on the paranormal."

"Really?" said Scott. She didn't look like a typical student. She was a little older and more worldly. She wasn't geeky. She had an outgoing personality and a sparkle in her eyes.

"Yes," Angie said. "I'm exploring how the paranormal, horror, fear, and madness are represented in popular culture — books, films, TV. How we tell stories about these says a lot about our current beliefs, fears, and so on. For example, back in the 50s and 60s, everyone was afraid of communism and nuclear radiation. So a lot of films dealt with people being taken over and becoming mindless and heartless. Commies, basically. A classic like *Invasion of the Body Snatchers* was really a thinly veiled warning about the perils of being taken over by communists. They wouldn't snatch our bodies. They'd snatch our souls. Even worse! And then there was the fear of nuclear radiation. Lots of movies dealt with people or critters who were exposed to radiation and become horrific mutations. Like Chuck's monster that terrorized all those girls in their bikinis."

"They loved it!" Chuck piped in.

Angie rolled her eyes. "In your dreams, Chuck!"

She continued: "The truly scary movies showed us the dangers of screwing around with nuclear bombs. Take *Godzilla*, the

Amazing Colossal Man, or *Them!* They threw giant irradiated lizards and men and ants at us. After seeing one of those movies, you'd be thinking that good, old-fashioned gunpowder bombs were a much better idea. With gunpowder, you blow stuff up. With nuclear bombs, you blow stuff up and also get ants the size of buses."

"Or monsters with hot dogs growing out of their mouths," mumbled Chuck.

Angie was on a roll, happy to talk about her area of expertise, and Scott was happy to hear it.

"Then there is the whole genre of the paranormal and madness. *The Mummy, The Sixth Sense, The Shining, Poltergeist, Dead of Night* — all great movies. And don't forget the fiction. Tons of great writers like H.P. Lovecraft, Richard Matheson, Stephen King, Dean Koontz, Peter Straub — the list goes on and on. And most of these stories are rooted in their times and the changes taking place in the world: the industrial age, the depression, the nuclear age, environmental disasters, computers and cyborgs, new weapons — you name it. They all become the backstories for horror and the supernatural."

"I can't say that I've ever looked at it that way," said Scott, "but I certainly see what you mean. Our fears change with the times."

"And as we age," said Chuck. "Stephen King said in an interview that our fears change from the monster in the shadows under our bed to the mole on our arm or a lump we feel somewhere. You know, medical stuff."

"Right," said Mary Angela. "Fear is largely in our imaginations. We wear it like jewelry."

Scott knew all about the fear of medical stuff. His wife's illness had started with the tiniest shadow on a routine scan. It had turned out to be the start of a long dark journey for them both. A journey not yet over.

Angie paused to look at the stuff in Everett's box a moment. Then continued:

"Actually, I think I'm going to have to limit my topic. It's too big. I went on Amazon the other day and searched for books of 'paranormal fiction' and came up with 155,874 titles! I did the math. If I read a book a day it would take me 427 years to read them all. Hell, I'd be dead and well ensconced in the hereafter in 427 years! I suppose by that time I'd be writing from a position of authority. But I'm not sure how I'd get my manuscript to a publisher. My topic as of now is just too broad. No, I'm going to have to focus my work somehow. Maybe I'll just look at contemporary films or how the paranormal has been featured in novels since 9/11 or something like that. Anyway, I can give you a list of books and films if you're interested."

"Sure," said Scott. "Just not hundreds of thousands. I'm a slow reader."

He glanced up at the poster above Chuck. "How about scary movies?" he asked Angie. "Maybe you could focus on them."

"Yeah, maybe," said Angie, following his gaze to the poster. "I know my horror films. You gotta pick carefully. Like *Horror of Party Beach*. Not a good one. It's funny, not scary."

She gestured to the two other posters on the wall.

"On the other hand, those two movies, *Nosferatu* and *The Thing*, were scary. *Nosferatu* was the first vampire movie. A silent classic from 1922. A German expressionistic masterpiece. Look at that creepy guy: thin as a rail, long fingers with claw-like nails, big pointy ears, bald head, fangs — something out of a nightmare! *The Thing* was different. Howard Hawks made that in '51. In that movie you barely saw the monster. He was an alien from another world a bunch of Air Force guys found frozen in the arctic ice. He was a shadowy, silhouetted figure most of the time. It engages your imagination: you have to fill in the scary details. The monster had a habit of stalking guys down the long hallways of the Arctic research station or popping up unexpectedly behind a door. They finally get him with electricity. The best movies are quite entertaining and have some content, too. They make you think. But leave the lights on. Some of them are pretty scary."

"The more serious ones are good for us," said Chuck. "They show people we aren't mad."

Angie rolled her eyes. "Come on Chuck...we ARE mad. Who else but a madman would spend a night alone in a deserted dark building searching for ghosts or ectoplasm or phantoms?"

Chuck laughed. Scott wasn't sure if she meant it or was just needling him.

"Mary Angela, you just think we're mad because you're mad and you want company, because if you have company, then being mad becomes the norm and then you aren't mad anymore."

Mary Angela Lenska was about to say something but stopped, her mouth agape. She was trying to disentangle Chuck's convoluted statement, and Scott could tell it wasn't easy. He was replaying it, too, trying to follow its logic. Which, he finally decided, was sound. She gave up, frowned and said, simply: "That's crazy."

Then she turned to Scott.

"Nice to meet you, Scott. If Chuck doesn't answer all your questions, get in touch with me." She opened her purse and took out a business card. "I may be mad, but I know a lot about all this. More than he does." She took out some lipstick, touched up her lips, puckered them and blew Chuck a kiss. "I'm mad about you!" she said in a German accent like Marlene Dietrich. Then she breezed out the door, like a squall moving on.

Chuck smiled. "She's a little bundle of energy. I'm surprised she doesn't throw off sparks. But she's a great investigator. Really smart. And she's right: she knows a lot about all this stuff. She has done a ton of research. Published a few papers, too, and she'll no doubt expand her thesis into a book. The only problem is, she gets so immersed in her horror fiction, films, and TV shows she sometimes loses sight of their being fiction. I think she thinks that TV show 'Walking Dead' is a reality show."

Scott laughed. "So she blurs the line between the real and the imaginary?"

Chuck smiled.

"Hell, Scott. The whole damned paranormal world blurs the line between the real and the imaginary! We try to tease out that border that separates them, except you soon realize that that border isn't very well defined. In a dark attic in the dead of night, how does an investigator separate his own imagination — his own fears — from what may or may not be in the shadows? We're humans trying to investigate the inhuman."

"You were going to explain some of the types of paranormal apparitions to me," Scott reminded him, taking out his own little notebook to write in.

"Right. Before the apparition of mad Miss Lenska appeared. Well, she touched on a few. Here's a quick lesson. Paranormal 101.

"Now, there are ghosts. Ghosts are the apparition of a dead person that becomes visible or in some way manifest to living people. Some ghosts are what we term 'earthbound.' They are spirits that for some reason were unable to cross over to the other side at the time of death. They are trapped on earth.

"We speak of ghosts haunting places. And that's accurate. A haunting is when a ghost returns to a place where no one is physically present; though sometimes, someone stumbles upon a ghost haunting a place. Apparently, ghosts don't always read the rules.

"A 'residual haunting' is when a ghost repeats something over and over, like a video being replayed.

"A 'reciprocal apparition' is a more rare type of spirit phenomena. Both the spirit and the person encountering it are able to see and interact with one another. Maybe that's what's going on at the lighthouse.

"Then there are poltergeists. I'm sure you've heard of them or seen the movie. A poltergeist is a non-human spirit entity. They are usually more malicious and destructive than the ghosts of dead human beings. You want to stay clear of them.

"'Materialization' is like a magic trick. It is the feat of creating something solid from the air. You make a spirit materialize and you'll outdo Houdini. Who, by the way, spent a lot of time trying to conjure up the spirit of his mother after she passed away.

"A 'simulacrum' is when we see a face in something. The bark of a tree. A reflection in a window. The shadows on a sandy beach. It may just be our imaginations, and a tendency we all have to see faces in things. Or, they may be faces that are really there."

"How do you know which it is?" asked Scott.

"You seldom really do," said Chuck. "So much of all this is a matter of perspective and predisposition and your mental state at any given moment. Some of it may be quite real. It's not easy to untangle the two, to separate dreams and reality."

"This gets complicated," said Scott. "I had no idea."

"Few people outside the field do. And we're just getting started," said Chuck, who continued: "This gets us into the realm where the imagination plays a role. For example, there are 'subjective apparitions.' These are hallucinations of apparitions or other spirit forms that are created by our own minds. They are similar to what we term a 'thought form,' an apparition created entirely by the power of the human imagination.

"You can't confuse those with a 'crisis apparition,' which is an apparition that is seen by someone seriously injured or ill or about to die. It's the mind projecting something at a time of extreme stress, as you can imagine.

"A strange phenomena is a 'false awakening.' This is when a person believes they are awake but are actually dreaming. People in the psychology field sometimes call this a 'waking dream.' What the person experiences seems completely real to them, but it's a dream, even when they think they wake up."

"Don't we always believe in the reality of our dreams?" Scott asked.

"We do. But when we wake up, we realize we were only dreaming. Sometimes that's a relief, like if you were having a nightmare. Sometimes it's a disappointment, like if the Swedish bikini team had just showed up to party. But imagine if you woke up from a dream and thought you were awake, only to wake up again and realize your waking up was just part of the dream?"

"You'd never know if you were really awake would you? Kind of scary."

"Very. Something like that happened to my cousin Rick. He was on a swing in preschool. Just sitting there. He nodded off.

He never remembers waking up. He wonders to this day — like 60 years later — if he might wake up someday and his whole life would be a dream. Scary part is, since I am his cousin, maybe *my* whole life is just part of *his* dream. He wakes up and — well, who knows what happens? I might just disappear."

"Me, too," said Scott frowning. "Since I'm part of your world."

"Well, if we both vanish, we'll know cousin Rick woke up. Anyway, what else can I tell you? Let me think."

"There are more?" asked Scott, his mind spinning with visions of ghosts and apparitions and dreaming tykes.

"Lots. But those are some of the main ones."

"Seems like plenty," said Scott.

Chuck smiled. "'There are more things in heaven and earth, Horatio, than are dreamt of in your philosophy.' Shake-speare. Hamlet. People have been wondering about this since people began wondering."

"Seems so."

"There are lots of categories of things that go bump in the night, Scott. We are still learning about them. There may be more yet to be discovered. And some phenomena we deal with in the paranormal realm may combine facets of these. They may overlap. The field is always evolving. Our assumptions are always being challenged. It's not like dissecting frogs. Half the time we can't even see what it is we are trying to describe."

"These spirits and apparitions and ghosts — all the things you mentioned, Chuck. Do you think they bear us malice? Are they enemies?"

"There are no enemies in science, only phenomena to be studied."

"Well put," said Scott.

"Not mine. It's a line from Dr. Carrington in that movie on the poster up there: *The Thing from Another World.* But I believe it, actually."

Chuck turned his attention back to Everett's case and took out the last item, the carved wooden figure of a sailor.

"Morgan!" he said, turning it over in his hands and smiling fondly.

"Morgan?"

"Yeah, Morgan," said Chuck. "This little guy was Everett's good luck talisman. His paranormal rabbit's foot. Don't ask me why he was named Morgan. I have no idea. Fine took it on all his field trips, and when he came back to the office, Morgan was always on his desk, like a tiny boss watching him work."

Chuck handed the little figure to Scott. "Take care of him. Maybe he will bring you luck. Protect you in a pinch."

"When I'm done with my research, maybe I'll give some of this stuff back to you guys."

"Sure," said Chuck. "With luck we can figure out how to use the Phanoptiscope. Angie probably could given enough time. She's pretty good at figuring out strange devices. She's the only person I know who actually knows what all the buttons on a TV remote do."

"I'd like to see her in those goggles poking around some deserted building," said Scott.

"That would be frightening! Might even scare away the ghosts."

There was a pause.

"The incident?" asked Scott. "You were going to tell me what happened to Everett out at Ledge Lighthouse."

Chuck nodded. He looked reluctant to talk. He sighed, sat back in his squeaky chair and turned it a bit so he could look out the window, losing himself in memory.

"Well, you can see from the notebook Everett was keen on going out to Ledge Light. He had heard it was haunted. It's an old local legend. I don't remember the whole story very well. You can talk to Jim Streeter at the Groton Historical Society. He's a lighthouse guy. Head of the Avery Point Lighthouse Society, and he knows all about Ernie."

"Ernie?"

"The name of Ledge Light's resident ghost. Ask Streeter. Anyway, Fine wanted to go out there and see if the place really was haunted. He finally got permission to do an overnight. Alone. As you heard me tell Mary Angela, we don't do solo overnights anymore, and it's because of what happened to Fine."

Scott cocked his head as if to say "which was?"

Chuck continued. "Everett was working on a theory he called proximal affinity. He thought that a haunted place might have an area around it where certain things kind of shared some of the haunting energy. Hence his term: proximal affinity. He went to that obelisk at Avery Point to take some readings and, if you can believe what he wrote, a storm rolled in, the obelisk was hit by lightning, and that letter K was blown off."

Chuck picked up the notebook and opened it to the last page of notes. "See: he writes about that and then says the K was above a missing A, which spells KA, and wonders if maybe the obelisk and Ledge Light have some connection. Don't forget: the ghost of Ledge Light was a keeper, and keeper begins with a K. So — a proximal affinity? Maybe it was the ghost of Ernie moving from place to place, looking for a Ka or something. It was one of the things Everett wanted to check out.

Chuck picked up the metal K from the Mythic Mystery sculpture. "You know, this might have some relevance. There is something called 'psychometry,' which is detecting the presence of a spirit by touching something. Maybe when Everett found this K he held it and felt the presence of Ernie. That would tie into his proximal affinity theory.

"So he went to Ledge Light to spend the night. Looking back on it, we kind of screwed up. We should have had better communication with him — had him check in every hour or something. But we didn't. We just let him go out and spend the night on this deserted, run down, creepy old lighthouse out in the middle of the ocean. A place everybody says is haunted."

Chuck stopped. Scott could feel his emotion, and thought that maybe his eyes teared up. He waited. Chuck shook his head.

"I went out on the small boat to pick him up the next morning. We tied up to the light. I'd expected Fine to greet us, but there was no sign of him. There was just me and the boat driver, Russell. We went inside calling his name. No answer. I started to get a bad feeling. We looked in all the rooms on the first floor and then the second floor and then the third floor. No Everett Line Fine. Some of his stuff — this stuff — was scattered here and there, but no Everett. We climbed the ladder to the lantern room, which is in two sections separated by a hatch. Nothing. We went out on the catwalk around the light and scanned the roof. Nothing. Then Russell and I looked at each other. 'The basement,' Russell said. 'We haven't checked the basement.'

"So down we went to the first floor, where there is a doorway in a back room that leads to some steep stairs to the basement. The big metal door was closed. Locked. Russell had the key. Seems like one key unlocks everything at the lighthouse. We unlocked the door and when we opened it, we were in for a surprise."

Scott had tried to imagine the scenes of what Chuck was telling him. But having never been on Ledge Light, he couldn't see the place in his mind's eye. He pictured a big metal door opening to a stairway.

"What did you find?" he asked.

"Everett, curled up on the top stair. Somehow, he'd gotten himself locked in the basement. He was mumbling his name, over and over. 'Everett Line Fine. Everett Line Fine. Everett Line Fine.' He was saying it with a kind of desperate urgency. It was scary. His eyes were shut and he was all tensed up and rigid, just mumbling his name. Over and over. 'Everett Line Fine. Everett Line Fine.'

"'Everett? I remember saying. Everett?'

"It took about ten minutes of coaxing to get him to unwind and open his eyes. He blinked. Looked around. He was dazed and confused and then started to look around wildly."

I told him to calm down.

"'Get me out of here,' he said quietly. 'Take me away from the shadows.' And then he said: 'I am Everett Line Fine. Everett Line Fine. Everett Line Fine,' which is all he would say. We gathered his stuff. And all the while, he was just saying his name over and over. We got him up and out of the building and down the stairs and into the boat and back to shore.

"I was really scared. It was obvious something had happened to Everett out there that night and it had pushed him over the edge. He'd had some sort of mental breakdown. It was pretty disturbing to see him in that condition. Who's ever seen a raving madman?

"I was wondering what the hell had happened to scare him out of his mind. We got him to shore and into my car. All he would say was his name. Over and over and over. It was creepy. I took him to the ER at the Lawrence & Memorial Hospital here in New London. They admitted him for psychiatric evaluation."

"Did he tell them what had happened?" Scott asked.

"No. When I went over a day or two later to check on him, they told me he'd been transferred to the Miskatonic Mental Hospital in Arkham, Massachusetts."

Chuck paused, and Scott saw that a teardrop was slowly making its way down Chuck's cheek. After about twenty seconds, he whispered: "I never saw him again."

"What happened to him?" Scott asked.

Chuck was silent a moment. He wiped away the tear and shook his head.

"Better you talk to them, I think. To the hospital," Chuck said quietly. The memory of Everett Fine and his disastrous night alone on Ledge Light clearly haunted the man.

Sensing enough was enough, Scott slowly put the items back in Fine's case.

"Sorry to bring up bad memories," Scott said as he tied the case shut with the rope.

"Yeah, well, it's an occupational hazard, I guess. You delve into the paranormal and you put your sanity on the line sometimes. Angie may be right. Maybe we are all mad. It's tough to spend so much time in the darkness, at the edge of fear. Sometimes, you lose your way. Everett Fine went into the darkness and never came out."

"I appreciate your time," said Scott.

Chuck Freedman, once a monster in a movie, now head of the Groton Paranormal Group, looked at Scott with eyes full of sadness. To Scott, the world of paranormal investigation took on a seriousness it had not had when he walked into this office. The stakes were higher than he had imagined.

"Talk to Streeter," said Chuck. "He can tell you all about Ledge Lighthouse. About Ernie. As for Ka, I'd go to the Lyman Allyn Museum. They have a curator up there — she's called Fuzzy — who knows a lot about Egyptian beliefs and symbols. Knows a lot about everything, actually."

"Thanks, Chuck. I'll talk to both of them. I hope to see you again."

"Take care," said Chuck. "Be careful. Things aren't always what they seem."

Scott Edwards left the office of the Groton Paranormal Group. He knew a lot more about what was in Fine's case and about Fine himself. What he didn't know — maybe nobody knew — was what happened to Fine that night at Ledge Lighthouse that had driven him mad.

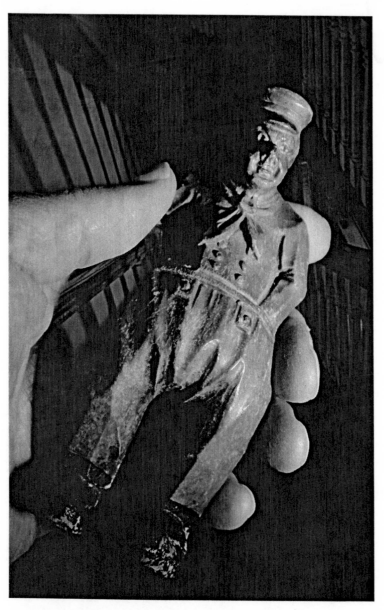

Everett Fine's good luck sailor carving "Morgan"

Everett Line Fine's Phanoptiscope and Goggles

6

Par 4 restaurant sits at the edge of the Shennecossett golf course, owned by the town of Groton. It's not far from Avery Point, and sitting in the restaurant you can see several lighthouses blinking away at night. It's a friendly, bustling place that features a sports bar area and lots of dining tables. The bar is home to a bunch of regulars. The menu is American and the helpings are huge. It's a welcoming neighborhood gathering place. Like Danielle's Barber Shop, a place where neighbors run into one another, where stories and gossip are shared.

Jim Streeter was a regular, there with his wife, Irma. They had been high school sweethearts. She was a pretty redhead. They were in their 60s and both looked great. They'd agreed to meet Scott for dinner. Streeter had been many things in his colorful life, including a cop and a security guy. He was also a leading forensics expert in handwriting, boot, and tire imprints. He had been the mayor of Groton. He was also president of the Avery Point Lighthouse Society, a group of volunteers who had restored the small lighthouse on Avery Point. The lighthouse was at the turn of the path that curled through the sculpture garden and ran by the Mythic Mystery obelisk.

Along with a busy private practice doing forensics, Streeter was the Groton Town Historian. He had thousands of photographs and knew as much as anyone about the history and lore of the area.

Martha, one of the four managers of Par 4, bustled over and greeted them. Scott ordered a Shenny Burger, a side salad, and Bass Ale. Jim went for the ribs special, and Irma opted for scallops. They both got red wine with ice on the side.

"You want oil and basmatic vinegar for the salad?" Martha asked.

Frowning, Scott said: "Sure"

"How you doing, Jim?" Martha asked Streeter.

"Great, Martha. We were up in Vermont, and I did some hunting. Did pretty well. How is it with you?"

"Same old. Busy. Crazy, really." She bustled off.

"So what do you want to know about this area?" Streeter asked Scott.

"I'm interested in Ledge Lighthouse. And Ernie the ghost," Scott replied.

Streeter nodded. "I could tell those stories in my sleep," he said.

"You have," said Irma with a smile.

Streeter chuckled. "Really? I don't remember."

Irma rolled her eyes.

"So you're interested in ghosts?" asked Streeter.

"Yes, and history. I'm working on a book."

"This area has a lot of history. And a lot of ghosts," said Streeter. "I've written some small books about local history. Picture books, mostly."

Ding! Ding!

It was Anne

"Excuse me a sec," said Scott, and they began a quick text exchange.

Anne: How goes it my love?
Scott: Great. Having dinner with the Streeters. He's Groton town historian and can help with background of Ledge Lighthouse.
Anne: Lighthouse? When did that enter the picture?
Scott: One thing has led to another. You know how it goes. How's the conference going?
Anne: Really well. Some old friends I went through training with here.
Scott: Glad to hear. Any word on your test results?
Anne: No. I wish they'd call. The waiting is driving me crazy.

Scott: Hang in there. Be brave. I'll check the home machine for messages after dinner.

Anne: Okay. Thanks. We'll get through this.

Scott: We will. I don't want to be one of those people who texts while he's with other people so I'll say bye.

Anne: Ok. Bye. Love you.

Scott: Love you too!

Scott put away his phone. "Sorry. That was my wife. She's away at a conference. Just a quick catching up."

"I understand," said Streeter. "Irma and I keep in touch when I'm away testifying on a case."

The food arrived, and as they ate, Streeter began to talk.

"Okay. First, Ledge Lighthouse. An interesting story. To begin with, it shouldn't be called New London Ledge Lighthouse. It's in Groton waters. It should be Groton Ledge Lighthouse. But then again, the Navy submarine base is in Groton and they call it the New London Sub Base. I don't know why. We don't get the credit or respect we deserve in Groton. What bugs me is that...."

"Jim," Irma interrupted, "don't get started on that. Stay on Ledge Light."

Jim sighed. "Right. Back around 1900 or so, shipping and trade out of this area took off. Though there were already two lighthouses — Race Rock and New London Harbor — the Lighthouse Board decided they needed another one at the mouth of the Thames River out where it meets Long Island Sound. The harbor light was hard to see if you were coming up the coast from the southwest. So they decided to build a new light.

"Building the lighthouse was authorized by the United States Senate in 1906, and in 1908 the contract to build it was awarded to the T.A. Scott Company of New London. The total cost allocated for the project was something like $115,000. Nowadays, we need almost that much just to replace the windows! But in the early 1900s, it got you the whole thing. Scott and his engineer, Francis Hopkinton Smith, had already made the base to Race Rock, and Smith had done engineering work on the base to the Statue of Liberty.

"The first stage of construction was to build a large crib for the foundation of the lighthouse. The crib was made of wood and big: 52 feet square and about 35 feet high. They made it here in Groton."

As Jim got deeper into the barbecued ribs, he asked Irma to tell the next part of the story.

"She knows it, too," he said.

"Yeah, I've heard it in my sleep," Irma said with a chuckle. "Many times." Between bites of scallops, she continued the narrative.

"In August 1908, the crib was towed from its location in Groton to its final position on top of the southwest ledge, about a mile from the mouth of the river. The three-mile journey down river wasn't easy. The crib drew almost 30 feet of water, and at one point it got hung up on the rocks off Eastern Point. Just offshore from here. So they got a fourth tugboat, freed the crib, and after about eight hours, got the thing out to the ledge."

Irma paused to take a sip of wine, and Jim, done with a few ribs, jumped in.

"The crib was filled with rock boulders and about 3,500 barrels of cement. Then they sunk it in 28 feet of water. Underwater divers piled more boulders around it to keep it in place. Hard to imagine guys in those big brass helmets and lead boots moving giant boulders around underwater, but they did. They were tough men, no doubt about it. Next, a concrete pier, about 50 feet square and 18 feet high, was built on top of the crib as a foundation for the lighthouse building."

"Heavy construction," Scott commented.

"Very," said Jim. "Hell, the basement walls of the foundation are 9 feet thick. They built that thing to last. To withstand hurricanes, and it has."

Streeter paused and looked at his plate of ribs. "These are very good. Where's Martha?" he looked around and caught her attention and motioned her over. "Martha," he said, "these are very good ribs. If I become mayor of Groton again, I'm going to appoint you Head of Ribs." Martha laughed and wandered off.

"Where was I?" Jim asked.

"The lighthouse building," said Irma.

"Right. The Hamilton Douglas Company, a general contractor in New London, was subcontracted by T.A. Scott to build the lighthouse dwelling. It's three stories, has thirteen rooms, not counting the light tower. It's built of brick and granite."

Irma chimed in: "The design of Ledge Light is unique. There's no other lighthouse like it. Two wealthy men whose mansions overlooked the light used their influence to get a design that reflected the elegance of their homes. They didn't want to look out at a metal can, which was what would have been built at that time. So the designers ending up with a mongrel design that combined elements of both Colonial Revival and French Second Empire architectures."

Jim continued: "The lighthouse was completed in 1909. It was originally named Southwest Ledge, but to avoid confusion with a lighthouse of the same name in New Haven harbor, the name was changed to New London Ledge.

"It should have been Groton Ledge Light," the former mayor said grumpily. "You can still find postcards identifying the lighthouse as Southwest Ledge," he added. "The lighthouse was originally equipped with a fourth-order Fresnel lens and a kerosene lamp. The characteristic of its beacon is three white flashes followed by a red flash. In the mid 80s, the Coast Guard replaced the original lens with a newer electric one. The old lens is on display at the Maritime Museum in the Custom House over in New London."

"You ought to go see it," said Irma. "It's beautiful. A glass jewel. The new one is just a plastic cylinder."

Jim had finished his ribs. He finished the story.

"Ledge Lighthouse became operational on November 10, 1909. It was manned by civilian light keepers through 1939. Then the Coast Guard took it over and manned it until it was automated in 1987. In 1988, the New London Ledge Lighthouse Foundation, a non-profit group, got a thirty-year lease from the Coast Guard to take care of the place. I'm on the board. Especially in the last five years or so, we've done a ton of work out there restoring the building, putting up a museum, and guiding tours."

"You should go on a tour," Irma told Scott." See for yourself."

Through the tag-team narrative of the history of Ledge Light, Scott had listened and munched his burger. The Streeters had given him a good, concise background of the place. Now he wanted to hear about Ernie. He was about to ask, when Jim spoke.

"You like apple-cinnamon cobbler? With whipped cream and ice cream?"

It sounded good and Scott said so.

"Good. Because they make it really well here. But it's a lot. Too much for just one or two. For three, it's perfect. Martha!"

Martha came over and Jim ordered the cobbler.

"Trust me," he said. "This may be the best dessert you will ever eat!"

Irma rolled her eyes. "Jim probably agreed to meet you for dinner so we could order it." Jim feigned annoyance.

"What about Ernie?" Scott asked.

"Ah, Ernie! Good old Ernie! He's very popular around here. He could get elected mayor if he wanted. I've done a lot of research about Ernie," said Jim. "Historian that I am, I wanted to see what I could find out. See if I could find any truth to the myth."

"And have you?"

"Well, judge for yourself." As they waited for the best dessert ever, Jim began the story of Ernie.

"Okay. According to legend, sometime in the 1920s or 1930s, a light keeper named Ernie was assigned to Ledge Light. Some accounts say he might have been named John Randolph. His wife didn't like the isolated life out there or, in another version, got lonely ashore while Ernie was out at the light. Whatever version you believe, she met and eventually ran off with the captain of the Block Island Ferry."

"Which sailed by the lighthouse a couple of times a day," Irma added, "and Ernie could see it."

"Rubbing salt in the wound," Scott commented.

"Exactly," said Jim. "Well, poor Ernie brooded and became so depressed that one night he jumped to his death from the roof of the lighthouse. A gorier version has him cutting his throat with a razor then jumping. Overkill, if you ask me. His body was never found. But his ghost is said to haunt the place. The stories of hauntings mostly began when the Coast Guard keepers were out there after 1939. According the reports, doors open and close, books fall off shelves, there are strange sounds, the lights go off and on, boats become mysteriously untied, and most notably, the foghorn comes on even when it's sunny and clear."

Martha arrived with the cobbler, plates, and spoons. It was a huge pile of apple and cinnamon and pastry buried under a mountain of ice cream and whipped cream. Jim smiled at it.

"If you die and go to heaven, Scott, this is what they serve," he said. "Dig in!"

The cobbler was, indeed, heavenly, and as they ate, Jim told Scott more about his research on Ernie.

"Here is what I've found. You can decide if it's fiction or nonfiction. According to official records, the keeper assigned to the New London Ledge Lighthouse from 1926 to 1939 — when the Coast Guard took over — was a Howard Beebe. In fact, no one by the name of John Randolf or 'Ernie' is on any list of light keepers assigned to the lighthouse from 09 to 39."

"There must have been lots of assistant keepers out there in all those years," Scott interjected. "Maybe there was a last minute fill-in who didn't get reported. Couldn't Ernie be one of them?"

"I thought of that angle. So I looked at the official records from the towns of New London and Groton. I found no mention of the death of someone named Randolph or Ernie in all those years. Furthermore, the lighthouse logs in the National Archives make no mention of a suicide or even accidental death at the lighthouse."

"So nothing official at all?" asked Scott.

"Nope."

"What about the reports of hauntings?"

"Beebe never reported any paranormal occurrences or anything eerie taking place while he served out there, a lucky 13 years. Beyond him, quite a few paranormal investigators have been out there. Many haven't found any real proof of hauntings. Others, though, have felt energies and cold spots or recorded electromagnetic field anomalies. Some investigators have reported odd shadows, sounds, and other paranormal stuff. And there are plenty of people who get the chills out at Ledge Light. Who say they feel spirits. Some folks avoid the place. They get a bad feeling from it."

Streeter savored a spoonful of the cobbler. "To die for, isn't it?"

Scott thought about what Streeter had told him. Then asked:

"So, Jim, you don't think it's haunted because there's no record of Ernie, or Randolph, or anyone dying out there? And because there's no conclusive proof of a ghost?"

"Well, just because he's not in the records doesn't mean there wasn't a keeper named Ernie who jumped to his death off Ledge Light. Lots of records get lost. I deal with criminal cases all the time. You'd be amazed at what falls between the cracks.

"But if you want my opinion, this is more likely what happened: when the Coast Guard men started serving at the light, at some point there were two experienced guys and a young wet-behind-the-ears guy who got assigned to the light. Some night, just to kill the boredom, as a prank, the old guys started dragging some chains across the floor and making weird noises. Maybe they rigged up a spooky light or something. Whatever happened, the young guy got scared. The older keepers told him the place was haunted by 'Ernie' and concocted his story.

"After he's done out there, the young guy tells his buddies back on shore that Ledge Light is haunted by Ernie. So the next guy who goes out is expecting strange things to happen. So a moth flying by a light and casting a shadow or a draft blowing a door closed or a rat squeaking or a boat carelessly tied up that drifts away are all signs of Ernie's misdeeds. The Coast Guard guy finishes his time at the light, goes back, and adds to accounts of ghostly mayhem. The stories build; the legend takes hold."

"But, Jim, don't legends usually have their basis in some truth, some real events?"

"Sure. I'm not saying that everything you hear about Ernie couldn't be true. Who knows? All I'm saying is that the records don't support that story. Doesn't mean it isn't true. Just not proved. As a forensics guy, I want proof."

Streeter smiled and finished: "You know, in the end, Ernie is as real as we want him to be. That's how legends are born and how they endure. And the legend of Ernie adds a lot of color to the story of Ledge Light. So as a scientist, I may not have proof, but as a resident of Groton and lover of lighthouses, I'm all for the legend."

Streeter raised his wine glass in toast: "To Ernie," he said. They toasted the ghost who might or might not haunt Ledge Light.

"Hard to separate fact from fiction," Scott said.

"Exactly," said Streeter. "That's what makes it interesting. Tell me, Scott: have you been out to Ledge Light?"

"No. Not yet."

Irma chimed in: "Well, there is a lot to see out there. You should go out and get a feel for the place in person. The space. The location. The isolation. There's a lot to see. Exhibits about the building of the light, the life of the keepers, hurricanes — all sorts of stuff. There's even a keeper's room with a figure of Ernie in it."

"Really?"

"Yes," said Jim. "He's very creepy. He's just a mannequin, but scary. Very lifelike. He's frozen at the moment he's reading the letter from his wife. He looks pretty angry."

"And hurt," Irma added. "He's in shock. His heart is broken."

Scott tried to imagine the scene. He'd have to go and see for himself. He brought the conversation around to Fine.

"Do you remember a paranormal guy named Everett Line Fine? He worked with a group called the Groton Paranormal Group based here in Groton. He spent the night at Ledge Light about 5 years ago."

Streeter thought for a moment. "Yeah. Everett Line Fine. Strange name so it's easy to remember. He went mad, didn't he?"

"He did," said Scott. "During his night on Ledge Light."

"Do you know why?" asked Irma.

"No. That's part of what I'm trying to find out."

"What ever happened to him?"

"I'm not sure, Jim. His partner wouldn't tell me exactly. He said I should talk to the people at the Miskatonic Mental Hospital."

"Well, let me know what you find out. Might be something to add to my history of the lighthouse," said Streeter. "Or my story of Ernie."

"Everett also thought there might be some connection between Ledge Light and the big obelisk sculpture at Avery Point."

"Really? That's a new one. But it might not be so far-fetched. Like I said, there is a lot of history around here and a lot of ghosts, or so folks think. So maybe Ernie has some friends on shore."

"What are some of the other paranormal stories?"

"This area is loaded with ghosts and hauntings," Jim said. "The massacre at Fort Griswold, for starters, seems to generate a lot of paranormal energy. The battle was during the Revolutionary War. 1781. It was after the British overwhelmed the fort's defenders and killed the American commander with his own sword, after he handed it over in surrender. Not very sporting of them.

"The British were loading wounded soldiers on a big cart to take them down to the waterfront. They were going to put them on their ships as prisoners of war. The soldiers lost control of the big cart, which went careening down the steep hill and crashed in an apple orchard. To this day people hear the screams of the wounded soldiers, as they realized their imminent doom, and the final crash of the cart."

"And what about the Avery Copp House, Jim?" Irma prodded.

"Right! On Thames Street there is a beautiful old Victorian home. The Avery Copp House. People hear footsteps in deserted rooms and also get the feeling they're being watched."

"And at the Bill Library," Irma said, "they hear footsteps and things get moved."

"There are lots of ghosts around here, according to local lore," Jim said. "Because there is so much history. Ghosts and legends are the residue of history. The echoes. And it's not always big, dramatic stuff. Simple everyday life seems to have resonance, to create ghosts."

"Yeah," said Scott. "I got a haircut at Danielle's, and she said her barbershop was haunted. I may have even seen the ghost — a guy in a white smock with a razor."

"You know, now that I think of it, I ran for mayor of Groton a few times. And won. But hell, if I'd gotten out the ghost vote, I would have had some landslide victories," Streeter chuckled. "They're a big demographic around here."

"Works in a lot of places," said Scott.

Over coffee, they chatted about Groton and New London. Since Scott and Anne were fairly new to the area, he picked the Streeters' brains for recommendations of all sorts. It had been a nice dinner together, tended to with determination and humor by Martha.

As they were finishing, Scott had a final question for the Streeters.

"Have you ever spent the night on Ledge Light?"

"As a matter of fact, we have," Jim said. "A group of us went out years ago on a work party. We were patching walls, sanding, cleaning up a bit — hoping to start fixing the place up. We stayed over."

"What is it like out there at night?"

"Spooky," said Streeter. "Very spooky. The rooms are small. It's dark. Plenty of strange sounds. And I don't care if you believe in ghosts or not, you can't help but wonder what's around the corner waiting for you."

"And you're isolated," said Irma. "If you decide you want to leave, you can't. You're surrounded by water, a mile out to sea. No place to run."

"Did you want to leave?" Scott asked them both. Irma answered.

"Not at first. But late at night, you bet."

"Why?"

"Because I was scared."

"What scared you?"

"The thought of ghosts being there. Like Jim said: knowing the place is supposed to be haunted by Ernie, your imagination goes to work. You can't help but wonder what you'd do if you opened a door and there he was."

"What about you, Jim," asked Scott. "Were you scared of Ernie?"

"Ernie? Yeah, maybe a little. But that wasn't what scared me the most."

"What did then?"

"The shadows. I couldn't shake the feeling that there were things in the shadows."

"What sort of things?"

Streeter laughed nervously. "Things I really didn't want to meet."

7

LEDGE LIGHTHOUSE
1936

Ernie was stunned.

Ernie was not his name at all. At the time he served on Ledge Light, the journalist Ernie Pyle was gaining fame as a roving correspondent telling tales of out-of-the-way places in America. This keeper had a flair for storytelling that enthralled his comrades on the long nights at the light. So they had started to call him "Ernie" after the journalist. And the nickname stuck. So much so that they only called him Ernie and all but forgot his real name. Nobody off the light called him Ernie. Just the guys he served with out there.

So Ernie he was. He was in his room on the third floor. His room was at the base of the spiral stairway that rose to the light tower. It was a crisp fall day in 1936, and he stood in his room holding a letter.

It had been delivered just that morning by the weekly Lighthouse Service boat that dropped off mail, coal and other supplies and picked up one of the keepers for his rotation ashore. After morning chores that included painting the basement stairs and front door, his assistant keeper Thompson had left on the boat. Ernie was alone until the next morning, when the boat would return with Gilmore, Thompson's replacement for the next two weeks.

After lunch and some midday chores, Ernie had gone to his room to open the letter. It was from his wife, Frances, and it was a shock.

"*My Dear Husband,*

I do not know how to start this letter, nor how to convey my feelings adequately in words. My nerves are on edge; my emotions in turmoil; yet my resolve is firm. We have been married six years now, yet we have spent little time together. Your work as a keeper — noble, necessary and all-consuming — has taken you away from me for long days and weeks on end. I have often walked the beach and gazed out at the lighthouse, knowing you were there. Just a few miles away, yet so far from our home, so far from my side where I wanted you. Needed you. How strange to admit that I have been jealous of a building that seems to have stolen your heart. What I fear most in life is being alone. I simply cannot face it. I need a strong man by my side.

Over time, my loneliness has forced me to seek companionship, and I found it most truly in Captain King. Though as captain of the ferry to Block Island he, too, is a man of the sea, he returns to shore every night. I won't torment you with stories of how our friendship blossomed in your absence. Suffice to say it did. It took hold and grew, and now it is he who I love with all my heart, not you.

I don't know if you can understand my loneliness, but I am a young woman who does not want to spend her days waiting for her husband to return from his lighthouse, only to return there again. Captain King and I are leaving New London. We will never abandon the sea, just this town with all its lighthouses, with Ledge Light out there at the mouth of the river, its light and horn reminders of our failed marriage. Know that though I may no longer love you, there will always be a place in my heart and my memory for you. I know this will be painful, but with time you will forget me. I pray you will find love that will, like your lighthouse, guide the way to happiness.

I hope you will forgive me. I wish you luck. Be well and be safe.

Affectionately,

Frances

Ernie stared at the words on the paper. They were as sharp as daggers to his heart. Frances did not love him anymore. Frances was leaving him! She was running off with the captain of a ferry that passed by his lighthouse several times each day. A ferry that relied on the light *he* lit and the foghorn *he* sounded to make it safely home. Home to *his* wife! His dedication to Ledge Light had cost him his marriage. He had betrayed himself.

It was too much to bear.

Ernie stood in his room, clutching the letter, angry, heartbroken, the emotions tumbling over one another like the waves that slapped against the base of this accursed lighthouse.

He stood for a long time, reliving the memories of his life with Frances, like watching an old film. He felt hollow, as if all that he was had been emptied from him, leaving a shell. He dropped the letter onto the chest at the foot of his bed. He turned and picked up his razor from the shelf. He walked slowly out of the room, dazed, not thinking of where he was going.

Ernie went down the stairs to the second floor and then down to the first and made his way to the room at the southwest corner of the lighthouse. He opened the heavy metal door to the basement stairs. They were steep, concrete, painted red. They went down and then turned to the right, down past the cistern door on one side, a red handrail on the other side. There were seventeen steps, the last few hidden in the dark shadows of the basement.

Ernie descended slowly.

At the foot of the stairs, he switched on the basement lights. Though the light itself was fueled by oil, the rest of the building was illuminated by small electric lights. The power came from a cable on Avery Point that ran underwater to Ledge Light. It rose up the side of the building and connected to a high voltage transformer in an alcove carved into the 9-foot thick walls of the basement. The transformer that reduced the high voltage hummed with the power contained within it — 13,800 volts. Occasionally, a bright blue spark jumped from the transformer, illuminating the alcove like a lightning bolt. The alcove and high voltage apparatus was secured behind a locked mesh steel door, painted bright blue. It was like a cage, containing the electrical power as if it were a beast. A sign on the mesh door warned:

DANGER
KEEP OUT
HIGH VOLTAGE

And the keepers did. They left the maintenance of the menacing electrical apparatus to the guys from the Lighthouse Service who knew how to handle the deadly voltage.

The basement was small, divided into three areas. A cluttered utility room was filled with oil tanks, a furnace, auxiliary fuel and water tanks, and other gear. Pipes ran everywhere, making getting around the room difficult.

In the middle space, just a few feet from the base of the stairs, the main support column of the lighthouse rose from the brick floor. At ceiling level it connected to a wheel-like spread of steel beams that fanned out to support the first floor and connect to the exterior walls to help keep the building plumb. Another room housed the steam boilers for the foghorn. The basement was a hot, noisy place, just at sea level, full of machinery. It was where electricity, coal, oil, and steam all kept the building, the horn and the keepers going.

Ernie stood outside the high voltage cage. He pulled off his wedding band. He would show her. He would hurt her for life by taking his own life. She would have to live with the guilt. Even if she had lost her love for him, she could not deny there had been love, that they had shared a life. Now, the end of his would haunt hers. And this isolated lighthouse — this prison out at sea — would be his home forever. All those who came here or lived here would be subject to his will. He would remind future keepers of his time on Ledge Light. If he sensed someone was intruding on his world, he would make them pay dearly. From the moment of his death, Ledge Light would be his domain. HE would decide whether the lighthouse was a place of peace or terror.

As Ernie turned the ring in his hand, it slipped out. It bounced on the brick floor and rolled under the mesh door and disappeared into the shadows at the back, somewhere near the humming high voltage transformer apparatus. He bent down on one knee, mocking his pose when he had proposed to Frances. He tried to reach under the door to retrieve it. He pressed against the mesh, his hand searching in the darkness for the thin gold band.

Then he stopped.

What did he care? She was done with him, and he was done with her. With no love left to connect them, their marriage was over. The ring, the symbol of their union, meant nothing.

On his knees, his bulky coat pressing against the mesh door, the humming of the high voltage apparatus was loud — a menacing presence. It seemed to grow even louder, as if perhaps his anger and his heartbreak were being absorbed, adding to the energy that was the heart of the building.

He stood up. He reached into his coat pocket and took out the straightedge razor and flicked it open. It glinted in the light of the basement. He looked at his reflection in the blade, grey hair flowing from under his hat, glasses framing sad eyes, his lined face set in a mask of fury.

Ernie placed the blade at the edge of his throat.

8

AVERY POINT, GROTON
2014

L edge Light floated out at sea like an apparition, a mirage. The Ledge Light Foundation had been working on the light, and it looked great. The railings were a crisp white, two flags flanked the door, and some of the red brick had been newly repaired.

It was a hot September day. The white sails of countless boats dotted the waters near and far. Powerboats churned by, leaving wakes behind them. Fishermen in boats of all sizes drifted or were anchored, many around Ledge Light. The ferries on their way to Orient Point, Fishers Island and Block Island came by on schedules as regular as busses. In the distance, the Mystic Whaler, looking like an old pirate ship, rounded Race Rock lighthouse. The blue Project Oceanology boat headed out from its nearby dock to a tour of Ledge Light.

Joggers and mothers with babies in strollers and couples holding hands made their way along the path through the sculpture garden. Many stopped to read the engraved bricks of the memorial pathway. Some walked around the Avery Point lighthouse, peering up its granite sides. A photographer bent down behind a rock to shoot the coastline and the light.

Scott took in all the activity from the top of the rock where the Mythic Mystery sculpture was perched and pointed skyward like an accusing finger. He turned his attention to the steel obelisk. Fine had mentioned it in his notebook. During a sudden, violent storm, it was hit by lightning, according to Fine's narrative. One of the steel letters bolted to the sculpture had been blown off. A "K." Scott could see where the letter had been. He could also see the rusty outline of the "A" below it. Fine had found significance in the positioning of those two letters. They spelled "Ka," and Ka, according to Fine's notes, had something to do with spirits. Scott would find out more when he talked to the curator at the museum. Fine seemed pretty certain that the obelisk and Ledge Light were somehow connected.

Scott had to admit that the geography of Avery Point had a definite sense of relationships and affinities. Engraved bricks on a memorial path that lead to a lighthouse. Strange sculptures, including a monolithic pylon covered with mysterious letters. Ledge Light, New London Harbor Light, and Race Rock forming a path from the sea to the harbor. The huge Branford House mansion across a wide sloping lawn. There was a geography of meaning here. Scott just had to figure out what that meaning was. Maybe he could uncover some proof of Fine's theory of proximal affinity.

Things were slowly coming together in the story of Everett Fine and his night on Ledge Light. Scott had some context now, for both Fine and the lighthouse, and for the ghosts that seemed to drift through the area like clouds. There were still pieces of the puzzle missing, but Scott felt they were there, like things in the fog that are sensed before they are seen. And like someone sailing in the fog, Scott had a direction and a destination: Ledge Light. He just wasn't sure what he might encounter on his journey to it.

Scott wanted to know more about the cryptic obelisk. He had scheduled an appointment with Charles Roby, a curator at the Alexey von Schlippe gallery inside the Branford House. Roby was known as a philosopher. If anybody could find meaning in the jumble of letters, he could.

Scott made his way slowly across the broad lawn to the mansion. The lawn had once been gardens and statues and fountains. But they had all been bulldozed into the sea years ago. The memorial path and the sculptures that dotted its sides were the only modern concessions to decoration and memory.

The Branford House was an imposing granite building, its castle-like appearance more fitting to England than New England. With its steep roofs and tall, thin chimneys it was a bit forbidding. It had been the summer home of Morton Plant, one of the wealthy gentlemen who had influenced the design of Ledge Lighthouse. Now, it hosted weddings, lectures, and concerts, and was the home of the von Schlippe art gallery.

Scott strolled to the mansion and through the portico to two huge wooden doors. They opened into a big empty room. Marble fireplaces with ornate carvings and dark wood, also carved, graced this room and the others that branched off it. Scott could only imagine what it must have been like in a different time when Plant lived here and the rooms were richly furnished. When lavish parties were held. Plant had eschewed the elite social life and ostentatious mansions of Newport for his own coterie of wealthy friends and his own ostentatious mansion. Unlike Newport, the Branford House had no nearby competition. Plant was also a very generous philanthropist who did much for Groton.

As Scott walked through the rooms, his footsteps echoed. He climbed the broad staircase to the gallery. He was a bit early, so he browsed the current exhibit — a series of photographs by Maine photographer Richard Moore. They were titled "Twice Seen Scenes," and were fascinating. Moore found photographs, usually about 100 years old, and determined exactly where they had been taken. He'd go to the spot, and if a building hadn't been torn down or a shopping mall erected, he would get to work. He would match the exact vantage point of the old photo and the camera lens as well. Using a transparency of the original photo, he would line up his modern-day shot to match it.

Moore favored photographs that included people, whose outfits spoke of a specific time and culture. Looking through his lens 100 years later, he would wait until people entered the frame or, if it was a document of an event, for a similar event to unfold. It could be a parade, some men dragging a boat up a dock, painters with their canvases — whatever.

Once he exposed his modern picture, he'd put both in the computer and merge them. Moore created a new reality that was part old photo, part new one. The resulting images were dream-like and haunting.

Scott studied one of a parade in Deerfield, New Hampshire. There, in a single frame, were people from 1911 and 2011. Women in heavy bustle dresses and men in three-piece suits and hats stood side by side with people in jogging sweats or blue jeans. A man on an old-fashioned high-wheeler bike kept pace with a girl on a sleek modern racer. A girl with an iPhone and earbuds stood next to the bandstand where a military brass band oom-pah-pahed its way through patriotic marches.

In another of his creations, Moore captured a woman and her grandmother both painting at easels on the same porch — 80 years apart. Yet another showed two fishermen in 1900 dragging a dory up a beach while sunbathers in 2012 strolled by hand-in-hand. The more he studied the photographs, the more Scott saw in them, and the more they made him wonder about time and place.

"Intriguing photographs, don't you think?" asked a man who had quietly entered the gallery behind Scott.

Scott turned and smiled. "They're amazing. You must be Charles Roby, curator of the gallery?"

"I am," said the man, shaking Scott's hand. "And you are Scott Edwards?"

"Yes." Scott turned back to the photo. "It's mind-boggling to see the same scene a hundred years apart. To see people of both times sharing the same space, yet unaware of each other."

"I know," said Charles Roby. "The photographer took great pains to find the exact spot the early photograph was taken from. The scene matches perfectly. He overlaps the two shots and then erases parts of one and makes other parts transparent to merge the two eras. I find them very evocative. I look at the people in them and try to imagine how different their lives are. How different their worlds are...."

"Yet, there they are in the same place." Scott finished his thought.

"Like two blind men, facing different directions, each totally unaware of the other."

"This room we're in is a hundred years old," said Scott.

Roby picked up on his thought. He smiled. "So maybe there are 'others' here in this room with us? We can't see them, and they can't see us. We are their future; they are our past."

"Ghosts?" asked Scott.

"Maybe. Maybe the past and present live together in a space, on different planes or in parallel dimensions, but simultaneously nonetheless. That's what I see in these pictures: people from 1908 side by side with people from 2008. I want to ask: don't you see that person from the past? Don't you see that person from the future next to you? They are there together, separated not by a wall of plaster but by a wall of time."

"A transparent wall. A window," said Scott.

Roby smiled. "The more you look at these photos, the more you see in them. The more they make you think." The two men looked at the Twice Seen Scenes a while. Then Roby asked: "What did you want to see me about, Mr. Edwards?"

"The obelisk out on the sculpture path. Mythic Mystery. I want to know more about it."

"Why?"

"I'm writing a book about a paranormal investigator and Ledge Light."

"Fiction or nonfiction?" asked Roby.

"I'm not really sure, yet," said Scott. "The more I uncover the more intriguing the story is."

The two men wandered around the gallery of photographs taken 100 years apart, their narratives discreet yet overlapping. As they walked, Roby spoke. "I don't know a lot about Mythic Mystery. Not sure anybody does. Penny Kaplan created the sculpture in 2004. It was part of an installation, and later UConn bought it."

"What about the letters on it? Some meaning to the jumble? Maybe a code?" Scott asked.

Roby smiled. "Nobody knows. Ms. Kaplan has never told what the letters mean, if anything."

"The paranormal investigator I am researching saw it hit by lightning. A letter — a K — was blown off during a storm. It was above an A. The investigator thought that these letters, that together spell 'Ka', might have a connection to the ghost that haunts Ledge Light."

Roby chuckled. "That's quite imaginative. Why did he think there was a connection?"

"Proximity," answered Scott. "He was developing a theory about paranormal entities sharing locations in close proximity. You can see Ledge Light from the obelisk. They're only a mile apart. They do seem to connect somehow."

Roby thought it over.

"Who knows? Maybe he's right," he said. "I've heard a lot of different interpretations of those letters. Some more far-fetched than that. I remember one guy who thought the letters were a message to aliens. They would come some night and send a little green man to write down the letters and they would figure out the message. And then it would be the end of the world or something. Another guy thought they were the initials of the members of some secret cult. I've heard theories that they were city abbreviations like the airlines use, a coded religious tract, or the molecular structure of a magical new element."

"What do you think they mean?" asked Scott.

Roby was silent a long time. He was staring at a photo of a clambake. Men in overalls and suspenders tended the smoking pit, while people clearly from the present stood on a rock and looked down at them. Roby gazed at the photo as he spoke.

"I think folks take those letters too literally." He laughed a bit at his own pun. "They think the letters are a code. Maybe they are. But I have a different interpretation. It's not what the letters mean that is the message. It's our wanting to know what they mean. Our need to understand. THAT'S what the obelisk is telling us. That's why Kaplan called it Mythic Mystery. It's asking us to look at our own need to understand, to find order in the jumble, meaning in the mystery. When you stand back a ways from it, the letters disappear against the black steel. You see this powerful shape. It looks like the number 1 or the letter I. It's a singularity. Like you and me. Like the instant in these photographs. Our mysteries become our myths. Like half of the lore of this area. We want to unravel our mysteries, but sometimes they defy us. Like those letters. Like lots of things, really.

Life is full of mysteries. Well, anyway, that's MY interpretation of the thing. It's not about what the letters mean at all."

"That's quite philosophical," said Scott.

"Well, I'm an old guy and old guys philosophize. We spend so much of our lives mired in the details. It's like standing a few inches from a painting and looking at the little brushstrokes. With age we step back and see the big picture. That's philosophy."

"Seeing the forest for the trees," said Scott. Roby nodded. The two men roamed the gallery together a few minutes longer.

"I have to go now, Mr. Edwards. I have some cataloging to do. I may philosophize, but I still have lots of details to tend to. We never seem to outgrow that. I wish you luck. I hope you figure out your mysteries. Tell me if you do." He left Scott alone in the gallery.

Scott would have to keep in mind what Charles Roby said. He'd have to try to see the big picture. Scott realized he was prone to getting lost in details. Research was like that. You fall into a topic, and one thing leads to another. It was good to become immersed, but not to drown. He'd have to try to change that. Scott also knew that change is our least efficient behavior. Or so he'd heard from another philosophical old guy he'd once met.

The curator had not solved the mystery of the obelisk. Instead, he had just added another layer of questions and possibilities to it.

Just like Twice Seen Scenes.

a Richard Moore
"Twice Seen Scene"

Grandmother and Grandaughter
painting on the same spot
85 years apart.

9

Scott's mind was full of thoughts of photography and the mystery of pictures when he got home that afternoon. He checked the phone messages, but nothing from Dr. Falk yet about Anne's tests. He wondered when it was exactly that the phone ringing had taken on such ominous importance. They had reached the age when a phone call might be news that someone had died, or was about to. They'd experienced both. Now when the phone rang they immediately started to unbundle their worries and fears.

So far, he had not uncovered much about Everett Line Fine or the obelisk, but he certainly had found out quite a bit about Ledge Light and the paranormal. He rummaged through the field box again, taking out its strange assortment of items. Was any one item in the box the key to what had happened to Fine on Ledge Light? So far, Scott didn't know. But he sensed the story was in all these objects, somehow. And he sensed it was a fascinating and dramatic story. He had a few details, a few of the minute brushstrokes. Yet the bigger picture eluded him. Scott knew he had to keep at it, to keep digging. Though at times frustrating, it was also fun. He had met interesting people and sometimes stumbled into unexpected adventures.

He looked through Fine's stuff: his field journal of notes and ideas and theories. His exotic invention, the Phanoptiscope, with its even stranger set of goggles. The tape recorder without a tape. The metal letter K blown off the Mythic Mystery sculpture. Morgan, his little carved sailor good luck charm. The ACME EMF meter. And his decidedly retro film camera. Yes, it all added up to something — to a man gone mad.

But how? And why?

Scott picked up the camera and looked through the viewfinder. He turned a few knobs and was surprised when the film rewind knob showed resistance. He knew that feeling. He had shot a lot of photographs during the days of film. The resistance meant there was film in the camera. Suddenly excited, Scott looked at the frame counter. It was at 19. Eighteen shots had been taken on this roll of film. Maybe they were pictures Everett had taken on his visit to Ledge Light! He didn't know why nobody had bothered to check the camera, but perhaps in the confusion of getting Fine off the light and to the hospital, the camera was the last thing anybody cared about. Perhaps the pictures would fill in some of the puzzle.

In the digital age, finding a lab to process the film would be all but impossible. Wondering what to do, Scott remembered his friend David, a serious amateur photographer in Portsmouth who still shot film. He was one of a vanishing breed who loved the look of film, who mixed chemicals and retreated to the red-lit world of a darkroom to process and print photographs. If anybody could process the film, it was David.

Slowly, Scott rewound the film back into its canister. He opened the camera back and popped the rewind lever to free the roll. He read the label: "Kodak Tri-X Pan Film. 135-36." It was a roll of black-and-white negative film, 36 exposures. Everett had shot half the roll.

Scott took out his iPhone and checked his contacts and found David's number. A quick call and it was all arranged. Scott would drive up over the coming weekend for a visit, and they would process the roll of film and see what it showed.

For the next few days, Scott found himself staring at that roll of film and wondering what the pictures would show. What had he shot? Where? Had Everett captured the image of a ghost?

Ding! Ding!

Anne: How is the investigation going?
Scott: Okay. I went to an art gallery down at the Branford House. That big mansion down by the sea. Amazing exhibit. We'll go when you get back.
Anne: You are certainly getting around.
Scott: I'm off to Portsmouth Saturday to see David. I have a roll of film he agreed to develop.
Anne: Film? Who shoots film these days?
Scott: Nobody I know but David. This is an old roll. Found it in the camera of the paranormal guy I'm investigating.
Anne: Does he have a name?
Scott: Yes, Everett Line Fine.
Anne: Strange name.
Scott: Strange guy. I think I'm just getting started on uncovering his story.
Anne: Complicated?
Scott: Well. The plot thickens, as they say. I miss you.
Anne: I miss you too. I hate being away this long!
Scott: I know what you mean. Well, only a little while longer.
Anne: Yeah.
Scott: When do you give your talk?
Anne: Day after tomorrow.
Scott: Nervous?
Anne: Naw. I hope to knock 'em dead!
Scott: Like you did me!
Anne: Sigh.

There was a pause before her next text came in.

Anne: Scott, this stuff is easy. I'm much more nervous about my test results. I wish we'd hear already. The waiting is killing me.
Scott: You'll be fine.
Anne: Well, maybe. Let's hope. We both know the odds.
Scott: Think positive.
Anne: I'm trying. Say hi to David and Nike. Wish I could be with you.
Scott: In a dark room?

Anne: Always! :)
Scott: Love you!
Anne: Love you too.

Scott looked at the phone. It defaulted to Anne's photo on the home page. The texts let them communicate, but it was not like being together. He really missed her. This was the kind of adventure they usually shared together. Like everything. He put the phone away. He had been nervous about the tests, too, but didn't want to let on. She'd be okay. She had to be. He could be without her for a few weeks, but he couldn't imagine a life without her. Scott was glad he had his research to keep him busy. Better than pacing around the house, looking at the phone. It could ring any time. What news it would bring had them on edge.

* * *

Saturday, Scott had a pleasant drive to Portsmouth and caught up with David and Nike over lunch. They had recently traveled to the Amazon, where they met a shaman in a village who performed a purification ceremony on David. With smoke and chanting and a sprig of some sort of plant, he cleansed David of any spirits that might have crept into him, like viruses on a computer.

"Did you feel any different afterward?" Scott asked.

"Not really," said David. "Just a little congested from the smoke."

After lunch, Scott and David went to his studio, which was an area of the house past his record collection, his telescope collection, and his kaleidoscope collection. He was a man of many hobbies, photography being just one.

"So where did you get this film?" David asked as he mixed the chemicals in his darkroom, a state-of-the-forgotten-art affair in a room off the room that showcased his camera collection.

"It was in the camera of a paranormal investigator I'm investigating. I think it's about five years old. Will it be okay?"

"If there was no light leak in the camera and nobody opened the back, it should be fine. You think it has pictures of ghosts?"

"I have no idea. I don't know if you can shoot pictures of ghosts."

"I don't know either."

"Well, David, in a way you can," Scott said a moment later. As David turned out the lights and loaded the film from the canister onto the reel of the developing tank, Scott told him about Moore's evocative Twice Seen Scenes. They were images that seemed like photographs of ghosts.

"They sound interesting," David said. "But I'd call them 'Time Frames.'"

Once the film was loaded on the reel and safely in the light-proof stainless steel developing tank, David turned on the lights. He set a timer and, after checking the temperature, poured in the D76 developer. Every 30 seconds, he shook the can to make sure the developer did its job, then tapped it to get any bubbles off the film. Bubbles would block the developer and create spots. When the timer buzzed, David rinsed the tank out with stop bath and added the fixer fluid.

"So why are you interested in this guy?" asked David.

"It started when I found a box of his stuff in an antique store. A notebook, a tape recorder, the camera, some weird ghost-hunting apparatus, and a few other things. I was looking for something I could build a story around. And I think maybe I found it."

"Sounds intriguing. Where is he now?"

"I don't know. That's a part of the story I'm still trying to track down. He went mad on his night at Ledge Light. He wound up in a mental hospital."

"Not good," said David.

"That's all I know at this point," Scott continued. "I plan to go to the hospital."

David took that in for a moment and shook his head.

"Hopefully not as a patient. You know, Scott, you sure do get involved in some strange things writing your books. Hurricanes and boxes of jewels. People trapped on a lighthouse. Magicians and carnival freaks. Shackleton and meteorite hunters in Antarctica. Now a mad ghost hunter on another lighthouse."

"You're right. The research pulls me in and sets me off in unexpected directions. I go where the trail takes me. I learn a lot. Then I start to weave a story. Half of it is true; the other half exists only in my imagination."

"How do you keep track of which is which?"

"I don't. That's the fun of writing."

David nodded. Indulgently. David was a man of precision and facts, not wild riffs of the imagination. He liked his reality real.

"Okay," he said. "The decisive moment. Let's see what we have here."

He spilled out the last fluids from the tank and opened it. He took out the metal reel and started to unwind the film.

"Well?" asked Scott, looking over his shoulder, but not able to decipher the negative images of the film.

"You're in luck. It looks like some good images. No light leaks. Decent contrast. They look in focus. Let me hang the roll up to dry. Then we'll make a contact sheet so we can really see what's going on."

"How long will it take to dry?" Scott asked. He was very eager to see the pictures.

David smiled as he unrolled the film and clipped it to a hook inside a 6-foot tall stainless steel cabinet.

"This is a Clearlight 1400 Filtered-Forced-Air Thermo-Regulated Safety Drying Unit," said David. "The best made. In 10 minutes, the film will be dry. No embedded dust. No curling. No degradation of the emulsion."

Scott nodded and said, "I hope it works better than the 1200 did."

David frowned. He didn't know if Scott was kidding or not. He cleaned up the darkroom and mixed the chemicals to process the contact sheet: Dektol, wash bath, and fixer, each in their own tray — one red, one white, and one blue, and each with plastic tongs in a matching color. It took him just 10 minutes to get everything ready. He put on white cotton gloves to handle the film. Scott had to suppress a laugh. Now David looked like either a magician or Mickey Mouse.

He carefully cut the film into strips, each 6 photos long. Since there was only half a roll exposed, he had only 3 strips. He put these in a frame, then turned out the room lights and turned on the darkroom safelight. It was red, and Scott felt like they had journeyed to hell. Maybe David was the devil?

He opened a box and took out a sheet of paper and put it in the frame, beneath the hinged glass lid that held the strips of film. He lowered the lid and latched it closed so that it was tight to the paper. He put the frame under the enlarger, set the timer for 8 seconds, and pushed the start button. The enlarger beamed light down through the strips of film onto the paper.

David opened the frame and took out the paper. "Excuse me," he said, gently moving Scott aside to get to the Dektol tray. He slid the paper into the fluid and began to gently rock the tray.

Very slowly, the faintest image began to appear. This is the magic moment in the darkroom, when a blank sheet of paper becomes a photograph, as gently and mysteriously as an apparition materializing. In this case, it was a contact sheet of 18 images. When the images got no darker, David took the paper out with tongs, shook it, then placed it in the stop bath. After half a minute, he moved it to the fixer tray. He turned on the white lights, took the paper from the final tray, and clipped it to a wire hanging across the side of the room to dry.

Both David and Scott moved to the glistening sheet of paper to see the photographs. Scott was excited. There were images of the obelisk, Ledge Light from a distance, the exterior, and various interiors.

"Bingo!" Scott said excitedly.

David smiled. "Looks like your ghost hunter shot some pictures when he was out at the lighthouse."

They peered at the images as the paper dried, which only took a few minutes. David cleaned up the darkroom. He unclipped the paper from the wire.

"Let's look at these upstairs," he said, leading the way.

David took out a huge magnifying glass. Through it, the images Everett had shot were a window onto his investigation of Ledge Light. Eighteen frames that chronicled his journey to and through the building.

And maybe more. Maybe the photographs were way stations on his journey to a much darker destination.

"Fascinating," said Scott. "The roll starts ashore, at the obelisk at Avery Point. Look: there is the letter K he said was blown off by lightning. And there is Ledge Light. Looks like he kept shooting on his visit to the lighthouse."

"Some interesting details," said David.

"Maybe they will tell the story of what happened to him out there."

"Let's have some lunch," said David. "Then I'll make you some enlargements of these. If I can hold on to the negatives a while, I can scan them so you'll have them digitally. You can do a lot to enlarge and enhance the photos on a computer. Might help you uncover some things."

"Fine," said Scott. He was staring through the magnifying glass at the photo of a closet door.

"Find something?" David asked.

"Just wondering about this shot," said Scott.

"Looks like a closet door."

"Yeah, it seems to be. I'm not sure why he was interested in it, or some of these others, either. He seems to have found the doors at the lighthouse interesting. I wonder why."

"Maybe it wasn't the doors," said David. "Maybe it was what was behind them."

Everett Line Fine's 18 Photographs

**Frame 1 - Mythic Mystery sculpture on Avery Point.
Ledge Lighthouse in distance about a mile offshore.**

Frame 2 - Letters on sculpture. Ledge Light in distance

Frame 3 - Letter K blown off sculpture by lightning

Frame 4 - Ledge Lighthouse

Frame 5 - In the shadow of the light

Frame 6 - Lantern room and door to catwalk

Frame 7 - The lantern room tower, catwalk and roof

Frame 8 - Ladder to light, window, strange stencil

Frame 9 - The long room on the third floor

Frame 10 - The closet in the room on the second floor

Frame 11 - The main stairway

Frame 12 - The light, window, ferry passing by at dusk

Frame 13 - Mullion, light, lantern window reflections

Frame 14 - The door at the top of the basement stairs

Frame 15 - Looking down basement stairs. Cistern on right

Frame 16 - Looking up the basement stairs

Frame 17 - Metal door to high voltage transformer alcove

Frame 18 - Basement. Utility room & HV Alcove on left

10

LEDGE LIGHTHOUSE
1936

No, it was not the way to go. Too gruesome. Too much a burden for Gilmore to come to the light and find him. And too clear. He wanted his death to be more ambiguous so that people would wonder what happened to him. He had another idea. With luck, his body would never be found. He would just disappear.

Ernie put the blood-tinged knife away. When his hands touched the small cut on his neck, they came away bloody. It was not a deep cut, but a sharp one, one that would bleed easily.

No matter.

He walked to the bottom of the basement stairs and grabbed the red handrail to steady himself. When he took his hand away, it was even redder — the paint was slightly wet! Yes, Thompson had just painted the banister that morning in the bright red paint they used down there. He had forgotten. Red blood. Red paint. He walked up the stairs, ducking under the pipes that cut across them. He put his hand against the white plaster wall next to the cistern. When he took it away, a red handprint showed brightly. Ernie looked at it. It reminded him of when he was a kid at school, and they would do finger painting. Sometimes they would dip their hands in paint and make a print just like this — and giggle. Nothing funny now. This print was his final signature, something to remember him by. He wondered how long it would remain on the wall.

Ernie opened the little hatch to the cistern. It was full of water that came to just below the edge of the hatch. He dipped his hands in, washing away the blood and the paint. He closed the hatch and continued up the stairway.

Ernie made his way through Ledge Light to his bedroom on the third floor. He looked at the letter again. Seeing the words just deepened his anger and his heartbreak. He shook his head and mumbled "Frances."

She had betrayed him. He had worked so hard and with such dedication to help others, and she had betrayed him. If she were here, he would kill her.

But she was not.

"Damn you, Frances!" he said. And then shouted: "Damn you to hell!"

Ernie left his room and climbed the ladder-like stairway into the lantern room. A stencil on the wall caught his attention: "018." It marked one of the access points to the pipes of the fire protection system. It needed a fresh coat of paint. The lighthouse was full of stenciled signs and numbers and labels — a visible manifestation of the Lighthouse Service's penchant for order and precision. Keepers were that way, too. They lived lives of strict daily routines and took pride in doing so. They were methodical men.

As he climbed through the lantern room, the numbers, the cold steel of the stairs, the bright brass of the handholds and vents, the sky through the portholes of the light tower — everything seemed vivid to him, as if he was experiencing it for the first time. Or maybe because it was for the last.

Up he went to the lantern room at the very top of the lighthouse. It was a small circular room about 5 feet across, steel at the bottom and glass windows from the waist up to allow the light to shine out to sea. The round fourth order Fresnel glass lens sat atop the apex of the center column and filled most of the space.

Even in his anger and hurt, Ernie was a keeper of the light. He had a duty to perform, and he would do it this night as he had so many others.

Ernie checked the glass and wiped a few smudges and bits of dirt from the lens. He pumped the fuel to fill the reservoir tank. He opened a small hatch in the lens and checked the wick of the light. It was just the right length, clean, and saturated with oil. Ready to be lit, ready to shine through the Fresnel lens where it would be focused and beamed out into the darkness. It could be seen for 19 miles.

Ernie closed the little hatch and gave the lens a gentle push with his finger. The big light turned smoothly. He watched as three clear sectors of the lens floated by, then a blacked out sector, then one of red glass. It was these panels that gave Ledge Light its unique signature of three white and one red light blinking in the darkness.

He wound the crank, pulling the weights up the center column until they stopped at the very top, just under the light. He engaged the brake. When darkness came and he lit the light, he would release the brake, allowing the weights to slowly descend, their drop measured and timed by a series of gears that translated their fall into the turning of the light. It would take them four hours to descend all the way to the basement. At that point, he should wind them back up, repeating the process every four hours, ensuring that the light would turn and flash its white and red pattern.

Unfortunately, this night, the blinking would stop after four hours. By the time that happened, he would no longer be the keeper of Ledge Light. It would not be his worry.

His preparations done, Ernie sat down at the base of the light and waited.

11

New London
2014

The Lyman Allyn Museum sits atop a hill at the edge of town above a humming highway. It looks like a Greek temple with its pediment and columns. Like Ledge Light, which was surrounded by sea, the museum is adrift in a field of grass.

Scott Edwards parked his car in the circular driveway in front of the museum and went inside. At the reception desk he asked for Fuzzy and was told she would be down from the attic in a few minutes. He thought about texting Anne, but decided against it. As much as he liked to hear from her, every exchange circled back to the damned test. Why get her focused on it if she were happily preoccupied? He'd wait.

He wandered into the Glassenberg gallery on the main floor where there was an exhibit by a local photographer, also an architect, who specialized in shooting the architectural details of New London. Patterns of brickwork, etched stone faces and birds, ornately carved wood, eerie weathervanes — the photographs revealed surprising and beautiful details that were generally overlooked. If, as Charles Roby said, it was easy to get lost in the details and miss the bigger picture, these photographs showed that with an observant eye, one could also find fascinating details hidden in plain sight.

Scott wondered if that was the case with his investigation of Everett Line Fine. Were the objects in Fine's box, or the letters on the obelisk, or the photographs he took, all full of obvious meaning? Was he standing too far back, or too close? Where would meaning become apparent?

He heard footsteps on the marble floor. He turned to see a short pretty woman making her way toward him. She looked to be in her 70s, though he could not tell.

She entered the gallery with an incandescent smile, and her persona seemed to add energy to the small room. She had black hair, thick wide black glasses, slightly tinted, a bright red sweater, and a huge necklace of a pre-Columbian head carved in jade and interspersed with large beads. Her lipstick matched her sweater. Fuzzy made an entrance, and she was a presence. She extended her hand to shake his.

"Fuzzy Glassenberg," she said.

"Scott Edwards," he said, noting that the gallery bore her family name.

"Welcome to the Lyman Allyn," she beamed. "My home away from home."

"Looks like a nice museum," said Scott. "Though I haven't gone any further than this gallery."

"I'll show you around, if you like," she said, then added: "You said you wanted to learn a bit about Ka."

"Yes, I'm researching a book about a paranormal investigator who thought that Ledge Lighthouse might house the Ka of a keeper who committed suicide out there."

Fuzzy took a moment to process all that. "Wow!" she exclaimed. "That sounds like one of the horror movies my kids love to watch. Actually, WE watch. I love them, too."

"I don't know much about horror movies," said Scott. Though thinking about it, with Mary Angela Lenska's dissertation research, Chuck Freedman's having been a monster in a movie, lightning hitting Mythic Mystery, Fine's going mad at Ledge Light, and the legend of Ernie, Scott felt he was slowly sinking into a horror story. The dark fragments were piling up, like coal in a bin.

"Let's go upstairs to the Egyptian exhibit," said Fuzzy, "and I'll tell you what I know about Ka. As it happens, I love ancient Egypt. When I went to Wellesley, they let me create my own little department to study hieroglyphs. Can you imagine that?"

As they walked, Scott noted the variety of art on display. Impressionist paintings, models of whaling ships, colonial furniture, medieval tapestries, African masks, modern art, and a dollhouse that spanned an entire wall. Noticing Scott swiveling his head, Fuzzy explained.

"We have a bit of everything, as you can see. I say our collection is pyramids to Picasso. It gives the community a taste of a lot of different art. And it's great for kids. You never know what might resonate with a kid, so I think it's good to expose them to many different eras and styles. We have changing and traveling exhibits, too, of course. And the occasional blockbuster single-theme show like 'The Artist Sees New London' I curated a few years ago."

They wound their way up a broad marble staircase to the second floor, then down the hall to a gallery. It was an amazing room with custom designed wood and glass cases of amphorae, ushabti figures, fragments of glass bottles, some inscribed cuneiform tablets, and a small mummy dramatically glowing beneath a spotlight.

"Is that a mummified bird?" asked Scott. He had never seen a mummified bird. Actually, he had never seen a mummified anything. But it sure looked like a bird, even through the dusty old bands of cloth wound around it. He could see the shape of the bird, and its beak poked up and out of the wrappings, a dead giveaway.

Fuzzy smiled as she watched him gazing at the bird in awe. "Yes, it is. It's a mummified falcon. The falcon was a symbol of protection in ancient Egypt. The bird was a fearsome hunter, so it could protect the Pharaoh. If another spirit was coming after the spirit of the Pharaoh in the afterlife, the spirit of the falcon would be there to swoop in and help."

"An afterlife bodyguard," suggested Scott.

"Sort of," Fuzzy said with a laugh. "Falcons are beautiful birds, but aggressive and deadly. You don't want to mess with a falcon in any life."

She looked at the mummy and smiled. "Getting this was a triumph for me. It took a lot of searching and negotiating to get a real mummy. And I had to pry the money out of the board. The kids love it. Kids love mummies. I know. My boys never tire of watching the old mummy movies with Boris Karloff."

"That's where the mummy comes to life, right?" asked Scott.

"Yes. Which leads us to Ka, actually. Ka is not the easiest thing to explain. Let me start with these." She led him to a case with a collection of small figurines of people.

"These are ushabti figures. They were funerary figurines used in ancient Egypt. They put ushabtis in tombs. If the deceased had to do manual labor in the afterlife — kind of puts a damper on paradise, don't you think? — these figures could step in for them. Paradise reclaimed. See: this one has a hoe and a basket. Ready for the field. The mummified falcon would protect the Pharaoh, and these guys would do the chores. Even after death, the Pharaoh lived a pretty good life.

"Now Ka is a bit different. Ka is the life given to a man by the gods. When he dies, his Ka lives on, preferably in the body itself. Which accounts for mummification. But the Ka could also find a surrogate home other than the actual body." She moved on to another case where there was a small stone statue. It was an intricately detailed seated figure of a Pharaoh, about a foot tall.

"This is a Ka figure," she said pointing to the ornate little sculpture. "Ka figures were also put in tombs. They were meant to be vessels for the spirit of the dead to return to and inhabit. So if there was no body, or the body had turned to dust, a statue would work. In fact, anything that resembled a human could be a vessel for the Ka.

"Some scholars, and probably paranormal investigators, believe the spirit of a dead person might not be content with a stone figurine. It might go after a living person to inhabit. At least for a while. Crawling into a living person would give the deceased a chance to taste the sweet elixir of life again. This is all theory, of course. Nobody really knows. But one could imagine that given a choice, a Ka spirit might prefer a living person to a ceremonial figurine."

"Would a person know the Ka was after him?"

"I'm not sure. Who knows? I have read that for a Ka to inhabit a living person, that person would have to be fragile, weak — susceptible to possession. If this paranormal guy was scared, he might have been vulnerable."

"So it's possible that the Ka of Ernie, the dead keeper, possessed him?"

"It's possible." Fuzzy paused and looked at the Ka figure, then turned to Scott.

"When he went to the lighthouse, were there any figurines, statues, mannequins, or any other human forms?"

"No. The building was empty. A mess. No exhibits. Just junk and..." Then Scott remembered Morgan. "No, wait! Everett brought a figure of a sailor with him. A small figurine carved of wood. But only 5 inches tall."

"Hmmm. Well, size is not important for Ka. The ceremonial figures, as you can see, weren't big either. You can't get too picky about all this stuff. I mean ... how big is a spirit?"

"Yeah," said Scott. "How many angels fit on the head of a pin?"

"Exactly," said Fuzzy. "This is all way beyond our comprehension. You can't take it too literally. Think spiritually not physically. I suppose it's possible that the little figure of Morgan would have worked as a Ka figure. But with a real person around, my guess — and that's all it is, by the way — is that the spirit would try to inhabit him instead."

"So long as he was scared and weak."

"Probably so."

Scott tried to imagine the scene at Ledge Light. Everett. Morgan. The spirit of Ernie coming out of the shadows, maybe even trying Morgan out, but then leaving him. Watching. Waiting. Maybe he did something to soften Everett up a bit? To weaken him. Make him fragile and susceptible.

"You ever see the original *Wolfman* movie?" asked Fuzzy.

"A long time ago."

"Well, poor Lawrence Talbot, played by Lon Chaney Jr., gets bitten by a wolf and thereafter turns into a werewolf. He's a tormented soul who doesn't *want* to be a werewolf, but he has no choice in the matter. The villagers know the score. They even have a little verse that describes his plight, I now it by heart — every time there's a full moon, my boys chant it ominously:

> *Even a man who is pure in heart*
> *and says his prayers by night,*
> *may become a wolf when the wolfbane blooms*
> *and the autumn moon is bright.*

"It's not Ka exactly, but the same idea," Fuzzy said. "A dark night. Full moon. A frightened man overcome by supernatural powers. Half himself, half a savage wild animal. A wolfman. The only way you can kill him is with a silver bullet! Great stuff!"

"A movie script," said Scott.

"True. But who really knows? We only know what we know. We don't know what we don't know."

Fuzzy looked around the gallery, at the mummified falcon, the ushabti figures, the carved Ka sculpture. Her face glowed with wonder. Appreciation. Pride. "That's the beauty of art. It helps teach us things we don't know."

Scott looked around, too — at the figurines, the falcon mummy. They all spoke of life after death, of spirits coming back and inhabiting human-like figures. Or desiccated birds.

Fuzzy said: "Some say that if you have been inhabited by a ghost, even if just for a few hours, you will be the worse for the wear and perhaps altered for the rest of your life. Maybe Mr. Fine had just such an experience. Whatever happened to him?"

"He wound up in a mental hospital."

"Yes — definitely worse for the wear."

She paused and looked at Scott, her face etched with concern. "So you are planning to go out to the Ledge Light?"

"Yes. I want to experience it at night, just as Everett Fine did."

"And end up mad?"

"I hadn't really thought about that."

"I would," she said. After a moment she continued: "Is it still deserted? Empty? A mess?"

"No, not at all. From what I've been told and seen on their Facebook page, they've fixed it up a lot in the past few years. Really transformed it. There is a museum out there now. There are exhibits in the rooms. A theater with a film. A gift shop." Scott chuckled. "They even have a keeper's room with a spooky life-size figure of Ernie."

Fuzzy's eyes widened. "Really?"

"Yes. I haven't seen him myself, but I've heard he's very life-like. Very scary."

"Brother!" exclaimed Fuzzy. "A perfect Ka figure!" She shook her head. "Bring a silver bullet!"

12

LEDGE LIGHTHOUSE
1936

Ernie sat at the base of the light looking up at the windows as the sky turned from blue to red to the deep cobalt blue of twilight. He was a lonely man in a lonely spot. He had been reliving his life with Frances and his life on Ledge Lighthouse. His mood had constantly vacillated from sadness and hurt to anger. The thin cut on his neck had stopped bleeding, but his crisp white shirt collar was stained red. His whole world felt stained by Frances's betrayal.

As darkness descended, Ernie checked the fuel and the wick again, then lit the lamp. He disengaged the brake to the weights. The weights dropped. The gears turned. The big glass lens began to rotate, casting its colored light on him. White. Black. Red.

Turning from the light, he unlocked and pushed open the heavy door. It was half curved metal and half curved glass, a panel of the lantern room that swung open to the narrow catwalk that encircled it. Ernie stepped out into the embrace of the night. He slowly and carefully closed the heavy door behind him. He stood on the catwalk, more than fifty feet above the ocean waters. It was a magnificent view. The night was clear and the stars were out. To his left, New London Harbor light blinked. A white flash. Then three seconds of black. Then the white flash again. Over his shoulder, Race Rock off the point of Fishers Island blinked red every thirty seconds. All around him, the lights of buoys and other nearby lighthouses blinked. On shore, the industrial heart of Groton was ablaze with hundreds of lights on smokestacks, cranes, docks, and buildings. Looking up the Thames River, ahead due north, both shores twinkled with the lights of homes, cars, and shoreline facilities.

When the wind kicked up some waves, the straight-line streaks of the lights on the black water were slashed into a jumbled chaos of bright shards. Ernie felt his ordered world had been shattered to pieces as well. Frances had ruined everything.

Ernie walked around to the south side of the catwalk, all of five paces. He turned, pressed his face against the window, and looked back into the lantern room. He watched a few revolutions of the spinning lens. It seemed to be working smoothly. The wicks were trimmed perfectly. The light was steady and bright. How many nights had he trimmed those wicks, lit that light, made sure it sent its beacon out into the darkness?

And at what price?

He turned to look out to sea. Fishers Island and Gardner Island were black humps in the darkness, and Long Island was just a dark stripe on the horizon. Though Ledge Light was a solid brick and stone building, it seemed small in the vastness of the sea and sky in which it floated. It seemed as if all the heavens and the seas were revolving around him. Ledge Light was the center of the universe. He could see the beams of the light turning — three spokes of white and one of red, made visible by the water vapor that drifted up from the seas.

As Ernie watched, a brilliant full moon rose over Groton and chased the stars away. It laid down a bright path on the dark waters of Long Island Sound. He walked around to the east side and gazed at the moon and its path across the water. So beautiful! Ledge Light might be isolated, but its isolation afforded unobstructed views that were spectacular. A keeper might be adrift from the flow of everyday life on shore, but that remove fostered an appreciation of the water, sky, and light that made up his world.

Mesmerized by the moonbeam which seemed to beckon him, Ernie crawled under the railing onto the lead-covered copper roof. It was about 20 feet square — the size of a boxing ring. He took a step toward the edge of the roof, then looked back to the light tower to make sure the door was closed.

Ledge Light's lantern spun slowly, and he was alternately bathed in bright white light, then darkness, then blood red light. White, black, red. Over and over. His moods seemed to change too, from clarity to sadness to anger.

He took another step toward the edge.

White.

What did the beauty of this spot matter anymore? He had shared his love of the view with Frances, telling her about sunsets and moonlight and storms, about snowy days when it seemed the lighthouse was inside a snow globe. She had always loved his descriptions. And they had shared so much more, hadn't they? He had bright memories of things they had done, memories they had made. But no more.

Black.

Ernie took another step toward the edge.

He realized that it was not enough. The memories they had made together had been overshadowed by the emptiness they felt when they were apart. Their life together as husband and wife was a life lived in short chapters. The story of their love was always interrupted when he headed back to Ledge Light. The flames of passion doused just as they had ignited. He had kept one light lit at the expense of another.

Yet many wives remained faithful when their husbands went away. Ship captains and soldiers, salesmen and hunters, railroad engineers and pilots, all left home often. And many remained happily married. Absence makes the heart grow fonder, they say. But not with Frances. Absence had given her license to cheat on him, to give her love to another. What was wrong with Frances that she could not adapt to his life? Yes, Ernie thought, the problem was really with Frances. She was weak. She was self-centered. She did not know how to love. His anger surged.

Red.

He took another step.

White. Black. Red. Ledge Lighthouse flashed in the darkness, a beacon of hope to those at sea, a flame to the emotions of the keeper who tended it.

Ernie looked to the southeast and saw the lights of a ship heading toward the lighthouse. He knew what ship it was. It was right on schedule. It was the Block Island ferry, heading home to New London on its final trip of the night. Was Captain King at the wheel? Was he looking at Ledge Light and smirking? Was he whispering: "She is mine now"?

Ernie's jaw tightened. He watched as the boat drew near. Damn him! Damn Frances! He would show them both what they had done.

He stepped forward. He was at the edge of the roof. He peered down and saw the concrete apron surrounding the building, about 7 feet wide. At its edge, a metal railing. Below the railing, the big blocky base to the lighthouse dropped another 18 feet to the water, where a 3-foot wide landing lip circled it. From the edge of the roof to the water, it was 10 feet out and fifty feet down.

The moonbeam came across the water all the way to the lighthouse, a bright silver path. He would walk that path, follow it to eternity.

And back. Back to Ledge Lighthouse. He would never really leave. He would always be here, hidden in the shadows, behind the doors, down in that humming box of high voltage.

He would show Frances that she could leave him, break his heart, drive him mad, but she could never conquer his spirit. Ernie vowed to haunt Ledge Light forever.

White. Black. Red.

White...

The ferry turned north and headed up the Thames River to its dock in New London. The moonbeam beckoned.

Black...

Ernie bent his legs and then uncoiled, jumping up and out, away from the lighthouse, out into the darkness.

Red...

The moonbeam was shattered when he hit the water, broken like the man who hit it. The ripples his splash created spread out. Gradually, the beam came together again until it was once again a solid path on the calm waters. The sea had swallowed up the keeper.

Ernie was gone. Ledge Lighthouse was abandoned. No one remained to tend its spinning light.

White. Black. Red.

13

Arkham, Massachusetts
2014

The Miskatonic Mental Hospital in Arkham, Massachusetts, was hidden in a secluded wooded area at the edge of town. It took Scott a while to find it down a country road. He was surprised when he rounded a corner and saw a complex of stone buildings of Gothic style, with steeply pitched roofs and ominously pointed gables. They formed a sharp, zigzag silhouette against the cloudy grey sky. As Scott drove up, the hospital loomed, dark and forbidding. It projected a brooding aspect, as if expressing the tormented psyches of those it housed.

Though many of its patients were transient, several dozen were there permanently. The most dangerous or delirious were housed in buildings with barred windows. These buildings looked like prisons, which they essentially were.

Scott stopped his car and looked out the window. He shuddered involuntarily. He had never been to a mental hospital. He had only read about them and seen them in movies. They were never presented as anything but ominous and disturbing. He had arranged a visit with the head of the hospital, a Dr. Sigrid Markhal. If not exactly eager, she was at least willing to discuss Everett Fine.

The September day was gloomy and raw, befitting the location. The first fallen leaves of the season swirled in the wind, rattling as they flew by. Scott pulled his collar up as he made his way from the parking lot to the main building. Letters carved in the stone archway above the main entrance read "Miskatonic

Mental Hospital. Founded 1924." The front doors were massive and wooden, with big iron hinges and locks. They looked medieval. In fact, the whole building looked like a throwback to an earlier, harder time. Scott guessed that though the hospital was founded in 1924, the buildings that housed it were much older. Perhaps from early colonial times, when European architectural influences were still prevalent. It might have been a monastery, an armory, or even a prison.

Stepping inside, Scott found himself in a long dim hallway with doors on either side and a stairway halfway down on the right. It appeared to go both up and down. The place seemed deserted.

It took his eyes a moment to adjust, then he saw a small reception desk. A man sat behind it, reading a book. Scott saw the cover: *"At the Mountains of Madness."* It was by H.P. Lovecraft. As Scott approached, the man put the book down. His face was gaunt, his head bald, his eyes sunken.

"May I help you?" he asked, looking surprised, as if he did not expect visitors.

"Yes. I'm here to see Dr. Markhal."

"Do you have an appointment?" the man asked.

"Yes. At three."

"Name?"

"Scott Edwards."

The man consulted a scheduling book a moment, then looked up.

"Please take a seat and wait," the man said, gesturing to three small chairs in the corner, to the side of the desk. A patient sat in one. Or at least Scott assumed he was a patient. He had a hospital bracelet on. He was dressed in green pants, a white shirt, and a teal cardigan sweater. The man looked to be in his 50s, a bit heavyset, with dark bags under his eyes. His thin hair was unkempt.

"So you're here to see Dr. Markhal," the man said as Scott sat down, leaving an empty chair between them. "Dr. Markhal is the head cheese here," the man said. "She's a very prominent psychiatrist."

"So I've heard. I've never met her."

The man nodded. He folded his hands in his lap and looked down at them. Scott noticed the man's long fingernails and scab-covered knuckles.

"My name is Lukas," he said quietly. "I've been here six hundred seventy-two days, nine hours, and fourteen minutes."

"Uh, oh," thought Scott. "I hope not waiting to see Dr. Markhal," he joked.

"No. I'm her patient."

Scott nodded. He wasn't sure what to say, but he need not have worried. Lukas needed little prompting.

"I came here six hundred seventy-two days, nine hours, and fifteen minutes ago to get treatment for extreme obsessive-compulsive behavior. Along with paranoia, eight phobias, and two other incipient personality disorders, which I am not presently at liberty to discuss," Lukas explained. "And consti-pation," he added. "Also psychological."

Scott was at a loss for words. His awkwardness was saved when the man at the desk leaned forward and said to Scott: "She can see you now. Go to the stairway down the hall and up to the second floor. Hers is the fourth door on the left. Please do not open any other doors." He returned to his reading.

Scott stood up. "See you later, Lukas," he said to his new friend.

"Watch out for telephones," Lukas whispered. "They can ring any time."

Scott walked down the hallway, his footsteps echoing on the ancient stone floor. Between branching hallways and doors, dark oil paintings hung on the walls. They were portraits. Glancing at one, Scott read a small identifying plaque: "Dr. Michael Greene. Attending Chief of Psychiatry 1957 – 1971." Scott ascended the stairs to the second floor and passed by sev-eral doors whose labels hinted at the dark corridors of madness: Catatonic Ward. Criminally Insane Confinement Cells. Night-mare Clinic. He could only imagine what was behind those doors.

He passed some offices on his way to Markhal's, each with a small name plaque: Dr. Gordon Rowbotham. Dr. Artemis

Hale. Dr. Harrison Kat. He found Markhal's office, opened the door, and stepped in.

"I'll be with you in a minute," came a disembodied voice from another room.

Scott took the opportunity to look around.

Markhal's outer office was a small area with two chairs, a hat rack, and a lone decoration on the wall. It was a cartoon animation cel of Wiley Coyote. It was brightly inked, the acetate layer with Wiley on it superimposed on a background drawing. The cartoon showed Wiley furiously jumping on a small rock that was clearly plummeting earthward. Behind him was a typical southwest scene of mesas and red rock mountains.

Dr. Sigrid Markhal came out from her inner office. Scott turned to meet her. She was in her 60s, Scott judged, tall with curly hair. She had an open, friendly face, with sparkling eyes. She smiled and held out her hand.

"Dr. Sigrid Markhal."

"Scott Edwards," he said, shaking her hand.

"Do you like it?" she asked, gesturing at the animation drawing.

"I've always liked Wiley Coyote," said Scott. "I can kind of relate to him."

"Hmmm, interesting," said the doctor, looking at the cartoon. "Wiley is a supreme example of obsession. He will do anything to get the roadrunner. Anything! He keeps buying contraptions from the ACME Company even though they never work and usually cause him great suffering. You know, one definition of obsession is doing something long after you have forgotten why you are doing it. That's Wiley. He is compelled to chase the roadrunner. He has no choice. And he has no chance. He'll never catch him."

Scott was startled. He had no idea his fondness for a cartoon character betrayed such personality problems.

"Well... I... uh... maybe I don't identify with him that much."

Markhal laughed. "Relax. Sometimes a cartoon is just a cartoon. I identify with him, too, and I'm not obsessive. Well, maybe a little. Wiley may be obsessed, but he's also quite lovable. We root for him. Because, like you say, we all identify with his wacky determination. We all chase after things we have no hope of catching. He's just a metaphor."

"Or just a cartoon character," said Scott, hopefully.

"Yes. Just ink on plastic." She looked at the cel a moment. "Talk about obsessiveness: each second of an animated film takes twenty-four of these drawings. That's over seven thousand drawings for a five-minute cartoon! Imagine how much patience and focus that takes!"

"That's a lot of drawings," Scott said. He could not imagine it.

"Let's go into my office," said the doctor.

Markhal's office was dark and made of dark wood. A few lamps with cozy amber shades lit the gloom. It was lined with bookshelves. Piles of books, reports, and loose bundles of paper lay on a couch, a small table, and on the floor. Her desk was awash with papers piled high. A few paintings and photographs hung in the shadows, and some diplomas, too. She sat at her desk, and Scott took a seat opposite her.

"So how can I help you?" she asked.

"I'm trying to find out about Everett Line Fine," said Scott. Markhal frowned for an instant, then recovered a more neutral look.

"So you said when you called. May I ask why?"

"I'm writing a book about paranormal investigations. Maybe about Fine, since he had such a remarkable experience at Ledge Lighthouse."

"Fiction or nonfiction?"

"Everyone asks me that, and the truth is, doctor, I'm not quite sure. I'm trying to figure out if what happened to Fine at Ledge Light really happened or was all in his imagination. Or perhaps some combination of the two. If what happened was imaginary, my story would be a nonfiction account of one man's personal fiction. If what happened to him was real, that's a different story. It gets complicated."

"I can see that," said Markhal. "How did you happen to become interested in Fine?"

"It was totally random. I bought a locked box at an antique store. I had no idea what was inside. It turned out to be some of his stuff. That started me on this journey through his life."

"I see. Maybe it was fate," she said, then took a moment to stack up some reports and papers on her desk. Scott could tell she was weighing what she wanted to say, or perhaps if she wanted to say anything at all. She sighed and looked up at Scott.

"Well, I guess there is no point in not sharing what I know. Everett Line Fine was a patient here."

"Was? Not anymore? Where is he? What happened to him?"

The frown returned to Markhal's face. This time, it stayed.

"He died," she said quietly, in almost a whisper. "He committed suicide. Jumped off the roof of the hospital."

Scott was shocked. "My God! I had no idea. I was hoping to meet him."

"Not here."

Scott sat back. Everett Line Fine — dead! He had assumed he would meet the man at some point. And even if he wouldn't or couldn't talk, Scott would be able to put a face on the enigmatic ghost hunter whose story he had been uncovering. The news threw him off balance, and it took him a few minutes to recover. Markhal gave him time.

Finally, he asked: "Did he ever recover from the trauma of his night on the lighthouse? All I have heard is that they found him inside, on the basement stairs, curled up, in shock, saying his name over and over."

"That's the way he was when he arrived here. I treated him. Until he jumped."

"So he never got better?"

Markhal looked at Scott a minute without speaking. Then she said: "Let me show you something. Come with me."

She stood and walked around the desk and out of her office. Scott followed. They walked to the stairs and down to the first floor. Markhal stopped and turned to Scott.

"You don't have sciaphobia, I hope?"

"Sciaphobia? What's that?"

"Fear of shadows. Like you find in a dark basement, which is where we're headed," she said.

"I don't think so."

"Good. Just thought I'd ask. Basements tend to be creepy places, full of shadows, especially in old buildings. Freaks some people out."

They continued down to the bottom of the stairs. Scott could barely make out a doorway in the darkness of the stairwell. Markhal took out some keys and found the one to unlock it. She did so, reached in, and flicked on the lights. They did little to illuminate what lay beyond.

"Storage," she said. "Patient records." She stepped inside and Scott followed. It was a long room full of shelves full of boxes. Scott could only imagine what stories were contained in all the records. Given they were the stories of the mentally ill, he imagined they might be quite fascinating. Or disturbing.

Markhal made her way down the center aisle, then turned and headed down another and then another. Scott followed. The room was larger than he had initially thought. The corridors created by the shelves created a maze. And Markhal was right: even with the lights on, the place was mostly shadows. He didn't feel fear, exactly. It was more of an uneasiness. Then he thought to himself: "Well, after all, you are walking around the shadowy basement of a mental hospital."

Markhal was looking around. She seemed a bit lost. "Our file system is in transition. Actually, I think it's always in transition. We've tried filing things alphabetically by patient name, by year, by type of illness, by referral path — you name it. No matter what system we try, it all ends up kind of jumbled. At the moment we are back to by the year. If I recall, Everett Fine came here about five or six years ago?"

"Yes. 2009. In the fall."

"Okay, let's see: '07... '08... '09. Good! Now let me see if I can find Fine." Markhal looked up and down the shelves for the year 2009. Then for a box with his records.

"Ah! There he is." The box labelled "Everett Line Fine" was up high, out of her reach. "Can you get it, please?"

Scott took down the box. It was the second box he had held related to Everett Line Fine. The first one had started this strange journey. He wondered where the second one would lead him.

"Let's bring it back to a table where we can spread out," Markhal said. They headed back to the center aisle. As they walked, Scott thought how much like a human memory the storage room was. We know something is there, but finding it can prove elusive.

Markhal put the box down on the table. She took off the lid. Inside were some charts and narratives. There were also three notebooks. All were standard size, bound in handsome leather. And there was a small plastic bag.

"Take a look," said Markhal, handing Scott a notebook.

Scott opened the notebook. The first page read: "Everett Line Fine. Journal 1." Scott turned to the first lined page. It was filled with writing. Three columns of careful, precise handwriting. "Everett Line Fine" was all that was written. Over and over, line after line, column after column. Scott turned the page. The exact same. Fine's name written over and over, about eighty times per page. The third page was the same, and so was the fourth. Letting the pages flip quickly, Scott saw that the entire notebook was filled with pages with nothing but Everett Line Fine written on them. Obsessively.

"The second notebook is the same," said Markhal. "And so is the third, at least until the end. Here, take a look."

She handed the third notebook to Scott. He thumbed through it and saw the same precise writing, over and over and over again.

"Go to page 279," said Markhal.

Scott turned to the page. It looked like all the others to him.

"Look closely," Markhal urged him.

Scott did so. It took him a while to spot it. But sure enough, about forty lines down, one entry was different. Instead of "Everett Line Fine," it read "Ernie Line Fine." Then it switched back to "Everett." A few lines later, there was another "Ernie." Scott turned the page. The change from "Everett" to

"Ernie" became more frequent down the page. On the next page, even more so. It seemed that Fine was in the midst of a battle between himself and Ernie. The last few pages told the outcome. The "Ernie" entries took over; only a few with "Everett" to be found. The final page, which stopped halfway down, was even more shocking. Here the name had changed to "Ernie." No "Line Fine." There were only a few "Everett"s. The writing stopped. The fragment "Er" was the last entry.

"He was fighting," Scott murmured. "Trying to hold on."

"He left his room abruptly in the middle of that last entry. He made his way to the roof and jumped," said Markhal.

"He lost his battle," said Scott.

"Yes, he did. Fine lost everything because of his night on Ledge Light. First he lost his mind and, finally, his life."

In silence, Markhal put the notebooks back in the box. She held on to the small plastic bag. She put the lid back on the box and walked it back to where they had found it. Scott put it back on the shelf for her.

"Let's go back to my office," she said quietly.

Scott followed her down the long aisle and out of the room. She flicked off the lights and locked the door. They were again in the gloom of the bottom of the stairwell. Scott felt a deeper darkness. He felt the despair and desperation of Everett Fine, fighting a losing battle to save himself. And he felt some of Markhal's regret at being unable to help him.

As they went up the stairs, Scott noticed that Markhal hugged the wall, walking as far from the banisters as she could. And she walked quickly.

Back in her office, she poured them coffee. She took a long sip from her cup. She seemed distracted. Lost in memory. After a moment, Scott asked:

"Doctor, did Everett ever talk about his night at Ledge Light?"

"No. He never said a thing about it. He was here almost six months."

"He spent his days writing his name in those books," she continued. "He'd stop long enough for a therapy session. I tried everything I knew to get him to talk, to open up, to get inside his trauma so I could lead him out of it. Nothing worked. He would just sit and look at me, maybe say his name, then go back to writing. Truth be told, he was too far gone by the time he got here. I couldn't put Humpty Dumpty's pieces together again, sad to say."

"So you never learned what happened to him that night at the light."

"Not exactly. Not from him directly." Markhal opened the small plastic bag and took out a tiny cassette tape. "But we had this."

"A tape?"

"Yes. A recording of some of his time at the lighthouse. I have a transcript of it, but you'll understand more when you listen to it. You'll get a much better feel for his emotions — his fear — than from words on paper. Do you have something you can play this on?"

"Yes, doctor. I have the actual recorder he made it on."

"Of course, you have his field kit. We had it a while. Someone else went through it when he was admitted. The only thing forwarded to me was the tape. I guess they thought that was the only thing that would interest me."

"Why didn't you hold on to his box of stuff?" Scott asked.

"Mr. Edwards, we get a lot of stuff that comes along with our patients. We keep what might be useful for therapy. When a patient leaves us, if there is no family or anyone to claim the rest, we send it off to secondhand shops or antique stores. We can't hold onto it all. You saw how cluttered our records room already is with just paperwork."

"Everett had no family?"

"No one ever came here to see him. We couldn't track down a next of kin once he took his own life. I tried very hard to do that, believe me. So we had no choice but to turn his body over to the state. I imagine they arranged for burial or cremation. In any event, you should listen to the tape. I can remember it even after all these years. It's quite something."

Scott took the small cassette.

"Dr. Markhal, they found Everett at the top of the basement stairs mumbling his name over and over. That was all. From what you say, he continued that, at least in writing, while he was here. What was going on? Post traumatic stress disorder?"

Dr. Markhal picked up a paperclip and idly began twisting it into abstract shapes. "In broad terms, it was. But it was really worse than that. Everett Fine suffered personality disintegration. As the name implies, the very structure of his personality, his identity, came undone. He lost himself in his fear. His repeating his name was a desperate attempt to hold on. To take the basic building block of who he was — his name — and use it as the foundation for his sense of self. But it didn't work. Everett thought Ernie was taking him over. If you believe something strongly enough, it might as well be true. Fine was engaged in a fierce psychological battle to save himself. Sadly, he lost that battle, and when he did, he took his life. Or Ernie took his life. Or maybe it was Ernie taking his own life again, if he had possessed Fine."

"Do you think there was really a ghost that possessed Everett?"

"I don't know. Ghosts and the paranormal aren't my realm, Mr. Edwards. I deal with the human psyche. There are enough dark corners in it without ghosts."

"Fine was scared of something out there at the lighthouse."

"Undoubtedly. The tape shows that. You can listen to it and draw your own conclusions. But I can tell you this: there is no fear so great as those we hatch and nurture in our imaginations. That's why the best writers and directors know to keep things vague, hidden in the shadows. What you don't see is often much more terrifying than what you do see. What you see might shock you for a moment. But what you don't see can grind at you and erode away your will. It's much more corrosive. And much more personal. We fill the darkness with demons of our own design.

"That's why kids are afraid of the shadows under their beds or a dark closet. No telling what monsters might lurk there. A lot of us never outgrow those fears. At least not completely. I still keep my back to the wall when I go up the dark stairway at my mother's house. I've never outgrown my childhood fear that something will reach through the banister and grab me and pull me down into the darkness."

She gave a brief chuckle that had an edge to it. "Actually, my older brother *did* reach through the banister once and grab me. That didn't help."

"Scarred for life," Scott said.

"Well, yes, actually," she replied with a laugh.

"So, is that your worst fear, doctor?"

"Oh, no! It's just one."

Scott remembered Lukas with his eight phobias.

"So what *is* your worst fear, if I might ask?"

Dr. Markhal picked up a snow globe and looked at it. Inside, a little figure of a mermaid floated. Markhal turned the globe in her hands and watched the mermaid drift about. She sat back in her chair, still holding it. Whether it was a window to her memory or something to calm her down, Scott didn't know.

"I grew up in Philadelphia. It's the home of the Mütter Museum. Ever heard of it?" she asked.

"No," said Scott. "What kind of museum is it?"

"It's a museum of medical horrors, a place of nightmarish exhibits. It was started around 1860, I think, by a guy named Mütter. He donated his collection. There are all sorts of pathological specimens. Misshapen skeletons. Aberrant fetuses pickled in jars. Grotesquely deformed body parts floating in tanks. There are endless exhibits of real bodies, bits and pieces of bodies, skulls, bones, tissue samples, and wax models of others things. It's a place the Elephant Man could roam and seem almost normal. If I recall, the museum's motto was 'prepare to be disturbingly informed.'

"When I was a kid, around twelve or so, I was a tomboy. I hung out with a bunch of kids in a kind of gang. Not what you see these days. No violence. We did a few pranks but, back in the 60s, they were pretty tame. Now as it goes with these things, if you wanted to be truly accepted — you know, part of the inner circle, one of the cool kids — you had to prove yourself. There was a rite of passage. A ritual to show your bravery."

"And that's where the Mütter Museum came in?" Scott asked.

"Yes. I'd been there a few times, and the exhibits were indeed very disturbing. The monsters there weren't the phony stuff of movies. You couldn't laugh them off as guys in costumes. You couldn't say to yourself they were just special effects. The abominations at the Mütter were real. And all them were shocking.

"It's pretty amazing how badly wrong the human body can go. Most of us never see double-headed babies or faces twisted and distorted by giant tumors. We don't see the ravages of advanced syphilis or exotic jungle diseases. Well, you see all that and a lot more at the Mütter. You can check your imagination at the door because the Mütter has stuff beyond your imagination."

"What's the point of a museum like that?" Scott asked. "Who would want to go see it?"

"Well, the original purpose of the collection was to help medical students do research. It offered some very unique things for them to study and think about."

"And to have nightmares about," added Scott.

"No doubt about that. It would be a rare person who didn't get nightmares after a visit to the Mütter. Anyway, even the Mütter has its boundaries, limits to what it freely exhibits.

"There was one room, tucked at the end of a hallway. It was a small, dark room that had only one exhibit. There was a sign outside warning that it might not be for everybody. It was so disturbing, so horrific, that the museum basically warned you to stay out. When you looked in the doorway, there was an enormous glass jar. It rose about seven feet from the floor. It was tall enough to hold a whole man. An overhead spotlight shown down into it so the fluid inside glowed. The side of the jar facing the door was painted black so you couldn't see what was in it. You had to go in and walk around to the front to see this particular abomination.

"The rite of passage was simple. The boys would gather at that door and the kid who was trying to show bravery had to walk in and around and look at the thing. Then come out. That was it."

"Why not just go in, keep your eyes closed and come out?"

"Because at least one kid, the leader of the gang, had kept his eyes open. You'd have to whisper in his ear what you'd seen. So he'd know if you really had."

"So did you go in and look?"

"I went to the museum with the boys. We went down that dark hall. I remember Ralph with his round face and bright red hair, standing at the doorway to that forbidden exhibit, smiling at me. I remember his words: 'You gonna go take a look, or are you chicken?'

"I went in. I started to go around the front of that glowing jar. But I stopped. I couldn't do it. I just couldn't look. I ran out screaming. I ran out of the museum, the boys laughing at me. I don't know how many of them had been able to do it. I don't think many. I didn't care. They teased me and a little while later I drifted away from the gang. Life went on."

Markhal kept turning the little snow globe with the mermaid in her hand, lost in memory.

"Funny how your imagination works on you. I always wondered what was in that jar. I even went back years later when I was a medical student at Jefferson. I'd dissected cadavers by then. I'd seen some pretty nasty stuff in the ER. I went back down the hall and to the doorway of that room. The jar was still there. But I couldn't bring myself to look at it. I was too scared."

"So you still don't know what's in that jar?"

Markhal looked up at Scott.

"Sure I do: my worst fear. It's a horror beyond any I've seen or imagined. It's taken on a kind of mythic status in my mind. What could possibly be in that jar that was so bad the Mütter discouraged you from looking at it? Whatever it is, I'm too terrified to look. So it's my worst fear, the fear I can't face. I believe we all have a fear that is singularly disturbing for us. An ultimate demon of our own design."

Markhal put the snow globe down. The mermaid drifted to the bottom. The spell cast by her story dissipated. She looked at Scott and asked:

"What about you, Mr. Edwards? What's your worst fear?"

Scott had been imagining the museum, the rows of display cases and cabinets and a huge glowing jar in a dark room. He had to turn away from those thoughts at her question.

"I'm terrified of electricity, doctor. I'm electrophobic."

"It's a logical thing to have a healthy fear of."

"Well, my fear goes beyond being healthy."

"Why are you so afraid of electricity?" Markhal asked.

Scott told his story: "When I was sixteen, there was a hurricane. I went out in our yard to grab a trash barrel that was blowing around the yard and banging into things. It was raining hard, very windy, and I couldn't see very well. I picked up what I though was a garden hose. It wasn't. It was a downed high voltage power line. A live wire. 13,800 volts.

"I remember the feel of the shock, that sizzling pain starting in my hand and going up my arm. It was like fire running through me. An electric shock isn't like anything else. It's nasty. As sharp a pain as you could imagine. It hurt like hell, yet I couldn't let go. My hands seemed paralyzed. I felt the shock spread through me, and then I blacked out. They rushed me to the hospital. I almost died on the way. An EMT saved my life by giving me CPR. It was a close thing."

"You were lucky to survive," said Markhal.

"I was. I was pretty scrambled for a while. My hands were burned and my nerves damaged. Physically, I recovered. But the permanent aftereffect is that I'm terrified of electricity. Just plugging in a lamp or a computer — anything — makes me sweat and shake. I hold the cord in my hand, and I just can't do it. I remember the shock I got when I had the line in my hands. I'm scared of that instant when I plug something in and the electricity surges from the wall into the cord while I'm still holding it. It's something I can't overcome. Plugging something in. Such a simple thing. People do it all the time. But I can't. I was almost electrocuted, and ever since my worst fear has been electricity."

"With good reason."

"I guess. I've seen doctors, and they've tried to help me get over it, but nothing's ever worked."

"Are you scared of lightning? That's electricity."

"No, not especially. It's just holding a cord full of juice that terrifies me. Our fears come from experience, don't they? I've never been hit by lightning. But I did pick up that high voltage line."

"So what do you do?"

"I have my wife plug things in."

"A sensible solution."

"We manage. It's not a big deal." Scott chuckled nervously.

"We work around our fears," said Markhal. "That's often all we can do. If we can't overcome them, we can at least try to avoid them."

"Easier for you, doctor. You don't ever have to go back to the Mütter Museum."

"True. My worst fear can stay in its jar in the shadows of that room."

"But there are those dark stairways," Scott said, remembering how she had stayed close to the wall when they went up the stairs from the basement.

"Yes, hard to totally avoid them in life. But dark stairways aside, you see that both our worst fears are a mix of real experiences and how they fester in our memories."

"So, doctor, do you think that what Everett saw and what caused him to go mad was some fear of his? That it was all in his imagination?"

"Possibly. Fine was stressed. He might have started to project some of his fears into the darkness of the lighthouse. He spooked himself into a terrifying waking dream. They are very vivid even when they are total hallucinations. The person experiencing them lives them as if they are real. Which, subjectively, they are. His dream became a nightmare, and he never really woke up from it. The nightmare became his world. His reality. Ultimately, his madness. That's certainly one explanation," said Markhal.

"Is there another?"

"Yes. There could have been a ghost."

Scott gave Markhal his phone number in case she thought of anything else to tell him about Fine. She gave him the micro-cassette to listen to.

"It's a fascinating tape," she said. "And chilling. It's not easy to listen to someone becoming unglued. It's not easy to know what's going on. Listen closely. I'd like to know what you think."

"Thank you, doctor. You've been very generous with your time, and very helpful."

"You're welcome, Mr. Edwards. I feel badly about what happened to Everett Fine. I always wished somebody had come by to talk about him. But nobody did." She paused, then added: "Helping you helps me."

Scott left Dr. Markhal's office. He bid Wiley Coyote good luck and went back down to the first floor. On his way out, he passed Lukas, who was standing rigidly against the wall, his eyes fixed on the cracked ceiling.

"Keep watching the skies," Lukas whispered.

Scott looked at him a moment, then left the Miskatonic Mental Hospital.

14

Scott had become immersed in this project. He sat alone in his study, his desk full of notes about paranormal investigation, psychological conditions, the history of Ledge Lighthouse, ghost stories, Egyptian Ka figures, and other bits of research. He had created a kind of master diagram with ideas in little circles connected by arrows and question marks. Lots of question marks. What had started as a simple flow chart of Everett Line Fine's story now looked more like a Jackson Pollack painting. The little wood figure of a sailor, Everett's mascot Morgan, stood beneath his desk lamp, as if overseeing the work. Everett's camera, notebook, and the Phanoptiscope were also on the desk, half buried beneath papers.

He looked at the microcassette Dr. Markhal had given him. Written on it in neat lettering was a label: "Everett Line Fine. Investigation of New London Ledge Lighthouse. July 10, 2009."

Scott put the tiny tape in the player and hit play. He heard some fumbling noises and then the voice of Fine. The voice was unremarkable. A little nasal, a bit rushed. Probably just excitement. The tape was real-time documentation of Fine's experiences aboard Ledge Light. What he saw, what he heard, what he felt. His curiosity, his excitement, his confusion, and his fear were all recorded. Scott sat back, closed his eyes and listened to Everett Line Fine's narrative.

Everett Line Fine's Tape Recording

"Test. Test. 1-2-3. Testing. Okay, this is the field recording of Everett Line Fine, investigator for the Groton Paranormal Group. The date is July 10, 2009. And the time 6 p.m.

"I'm here at Ledge Lighthouse at last. Russell, Chuck, and Jerry dropped me off. Russell unlocked the front door and told me to obey the signs and be careful. They'll pick me up tomorrow morning. I'm alone out here. I'll do an in-depth investigation of this place. I'll see what I can find out about Ernie, the keeper's ghost that legend says haunts this lighthouse. Maybe I'll find out. Maybe not. I'll keep an open mind and be as scientifically rigorous as possible.

"It's a beautiful spot, that's for sure. I have to say, it's not a bad place to investigate! I feel pretty lucky that this is my work and that it can take me to someplace as unusual as this. Ledge Light is an imposing building. It seems small from a distance, but it's big once you're on it. It's quite solid; quite massive. Has to be, I guess, to withstand hurricanes. And it's seen its share in over a century. Must be something to be out here when all hell is breaking loose!

"The building shows a lot of exterior deterioration. I see some big cracks in the bricks. All the railings and a big crane on the west side are a mess — they are full of rust spots like open sores. Standing at the north rail, I can see Avery Point and the Mythic Mystery sculpture I saw hit by lightning. It knocked one of the letters off. A "K." I think it has something to do with the Ka of Ernie. Maybe I will find out tonight. Maybe something here will confirm a proximal affinity. I'll see. While I have some daylight, I'll do a visual inspection of the exterior, maybe take a few photos, then go inside and see what I find."

At this point, Fine gave a detailed and rather tedious description of the outside of the building. He was determined to document with care and precision. Scott listened to lengthy descriptions of every detail of the lighthouse's exterior, from missing railing spans to faded signs, from examinations of pipes and wires to a count of the windows. Fine even paced off sections of the deck to give rough measurements. Fine paused at times to note passing boats or to line up a landmark with something on the lighthouse. Scott marveled at the man's ability to resist going inside. He clearly took his job as an investigator seriously.

Scott listened as the tape went on.

"7 p.m. I have completed my inspection of the exterior. Nothing particularly noteworthy in terms of potential paranormal activity. If there was an Ernie and he jumped, he had to go out a good ways to clear the apron and landing lip around the building. But since they never found a body, I guess he did. The main outside features are the big rusty crane. There is a hatch to the basement. There are bars on the windows on the first floor to prevent vandals from breaking in. Or, for that matter, someone getting out if the doors are locked.

"The views of New London, Groton, Fishers Island, and Long Island Sound from here are spectacular! I can't wait to see them from up top. There are lots of boats going by, especially ferries. I saw one to Block Island. Ernie's wife ran off with the captain of the Block Island ferry, they say. I saw the Mystic Whaler under sail out by Race Rock, and a lot of pleasure craft and fishing boats. I'm a happy camper out here by myself in this beautiful location. It seems to me it wouldn't be too hard to be a keeper here.

"Well, enough of the outside of Ledge Light. Time to take a look inside.

"Okay, I'm walking inside now. It is 7:10 p.m. Up a few steps and into the front entryway. My first impression is that of a dark corridor. Lots of paint chips on the ground in this front hall. To my right is a bright blue door with a sign: "Danger: Battery Charging Area. No Smoking." The door is secured with a big lock. The Coast Guard certainly doesn't want anyone screwing around in their battery room. Off limits. I guess they are the batteries for the solar panels that power the light and foghorn. All the rest of the lights, according to what I've been told, get power from a cable that runs out here from the shore. Jerry told me the fuses are old and the circuits frail so I shouldn't be surprised if the lights go off. Well, I have a flashlight if they do. It won't bother me. The darkness will just add to the atmosphere — perfect for someone hunting for ghosts."

Fine laughs. Sound of footsteps.

"Okay, to my left is another doorway to a small room with wood on the walls and a linoleum floor, cracked and peeling here and there. Looks like 60s stuff. It was probably the kitchen. It's empty now except for a beat up folding metal chair and a small wood table. I think I'll make it my headquarters. Back in a minute."

There are the sounds of him puttering about, mumbling to himself as he unpacks his backpack.

"I'm back! I've unpacked my bag. My little ghost hunting buddy Morgan is on the table, ready to give me luck. He is dressed in a sailor's outfit, so he should be right at home. I've unpacked the Phanoptiscope and goggles. I have my bottled water and sandwiches and candy bars. My thermos of coffee and bag of donuts, too. I didn't bring much. This tape will be my main documentation, along with some photos.

"This room leads into a bigger room with some built-in benches. They're padded, so maybe I can use one to sleep on if I want to catch a few winks. There are some built-in bookcases. There are a couple of old charts on the wall, and a few chairs. Otherwise, it's an empty room. My guess is this was either where the keepers ate or hung out."

Fine roamed around Ledge Light, reporting on every room. Except for some chairs, boxes of junk, brooms, old cans of paint, wood, and a faded poster of lighthouses, the place was empty. Fine dutifully described the decrepit, empty rooms. He described the peeling paint, the grimy windows, hanging wires, rust, the wood floors stained from leaks, the general rundown condition of the lighthouse. It seemed the Coast Guard — or somebody — had stripped away sinks and showers, stoves, light fixtures, and even sections of molding. There were big silver cast-iron radiators in every room, but most were no longer attached to the plumbing. At one point, Fine waxed a bit philosophical:

"I can't help but think of all the men who served out here and spent countless hours fixing things, cleaning, polishing the brass, painting the walls. Almost eighty years of care. Of pride. Now, no one cares. The place is a mess. All that work is slowly coming undone. Ledge Light is dead. It's sad. If this lighthouse is haunted, it's a ghost being haunted by a ghost."

Fine's tour took him to the basement. It was full of old machinery and scraps of wood and pipes, doors, paints, oil cans, and so on. He commented on the main column that went all the way up to the lantern room and through which the weights descended turning gears to spin the light. He opened a small hatch on the column in the basement to see if the weights might still be there, but found nothing but spiders. He wondered aloud how spiders found their way to the lighthouse. They were, he declared, Ledge Light's keepers now.

Fine was fascinated by an alcove in the basement that was closed off by a blue mesh door. It was secured with a big brass lock. It housed the high voltage cable and transformer. Its loud hum could be heard on the tape. He noted a sign on the door: "Danger. Keep Out. High Voltage."

He snapped photographs as he toured the desolate, abandoned lighthouse. It took almost two hours for Fine to roam the building, looking at and reporting on each of the rooms. Occasionally he stopped to do some basic EMF readings. He had been everywhere accessible to him but the light tower.

"It is now 9:10 p.m. and I have completed my initial inspection of Ledge Light. I have only the tower to see.

"I want to pause and say that so far, Ledge Light seems pretty benign. It is a bit creepy, especially the basement. I think the overall sense of gloom comes from its being deserted and decaying. Additionally, the lighthouse's isolation adds to the feeling of being alone and helpless. I expect it will seem a bit more forbidding late at night when there are more shadows, but so far I have little to report in terms of paranormal sensations. All my EMF readings have been nominal, with expected spikes near known electrical sources.

"I'm back in the first room on the first floor, with the wood and the linoleum. I... hmmm ... uh, oh ... Morgan is on the floor. I wonder how he got there? Maybe the table is tippy and he fell off.

"'You okay, little buddy? Don't get hurt: you have to watch out for Everett.' Mary Angela would laugh if she saw me talking to a carved wooden figure. But Morgan and I have been a lot of places together. He keeps me company. And we've been in a few tight spots. She should talk, anyway. I've seen the rabbit's foot she keeps in her field kit. And Chuck has his special ring he wears around his neck. We all have our good luck charms. Okay, Morgan is back on the table, no worse for the wear. 'Now you stay put! No wandering around. And don't let Ernie's Ka possess you!'"

Fine started humming the Twilight Zone theme as he fiddled with something.

"I'm hungry. I think I'll eat my sandwich and then resume the investigation. It's pretty dark now. The light in this room works, though the fixture has a lot of dead moths and flies in it so it's kind of dim. Dim and disgusting! So I'll be back in a while. This is Everett Fine, signing off from Ledge Light!"

There was a click on the tape as Fine stopped it. Scott did the same. He got himself another cup of coffee. There was a long way to go. Even though nothing much had happened, it was fascinating listening to the audio recording. He felt like he was right there with Fine. The man was calm, rational, even amusing at times. There was no sense at all of an impending mental crisis. Yet Scott knew that it was coming. He knew that somehow, as the tape inexorably unspooled, things would take a turn for the worse. The methodical, calm man on the recording would not remain so. Scott had the urge to warn Fine, to tell him to leave right now, before whatever happened to him happened. It was a silly notion. Though it seemed immediate and in the present, the drama unfolding on the tape had played itself out five years earlier. It was just an echo of the events of that night.

Scott found his palms sweaty with anticipation as he started the tape again.

"It's 9:15. I'm on the third floor. Lights up here are off. I flipped the switch a few times. The lights flickered on but went off again. Well, Russell warned me they might do that. So I don't think it's Ernie. All I have for light is my flashlight, and it won't last all night. But there is a full moon, and some bright light from it is coming in.

"I have the Phanoptiscope and goggles with me. They need a name, too. I've been toying with 'Phantocculars.' Not bad. I'll see if they work before I decide. I figured it was time to try out the scope and goggles for real, outside my lab. 'My lab.' I like the sound of that. Makes me sound like a mad scientist. Maybe I'll call it 'my workshop' instead.

"Oh, I forgot to mention: the front door is closed and I can't open it. A gust of wind must have hit it. I heard it slam shut when I was coming up the stairs. I went back down and that door won't budge. The windows are barred on the first floor. So, I'm trapped inside. Not happy about that. It might be the first sign of some paranormal activity out here. No, wait, come to think of it, it might be the second. When I was checking on the door, I want back to my headquarters and Morgan was on the floor again. That's the second time. Maybe I bumped the table when I left the room and he tipped over. And maybe when the wind blew the door closed it created a vibration that tipped Morgan over. All possible. I have to consider simple, rational explanations and not jump to the conclusion that the spirits are doing these things. Then again, they might be. Morgan might make a good little Ka figure for Ernie. I warned him. Well, I have no proof of anything yet.

"Actually, I owe my inspiration for the Phanoptiscope to Morgan. One day I had him perched on my windowsill. I had the sheer shade pulled down, so he was sandwiched between it and the window, just a silhouette. When the sun set, it cast his shadow on the shade. So there was Morgan, the real object, and his shadow, like a phantom, behind him. I got to thinking that spirits might be this way, that they cast phantom shadows. With luck, the Phanoptiscope will let me see them. If so, it would add some credence to all that stuff about shadows the ombralogists wrote. Angie would be happy about that.

"Speaking of shadows, I probably shouldn't even mention this, but a few times it seems... well ... it seems as if the shadows are following me. Of course, when I use my flashlight, it hits doors and the edges of walls and the stairway railings. They all create shadows. And as I move they move. But it really gives the sensation that I am being followed by dark shapes. Just nerves, I suppose.

"Right now I'm in the big long room on the third floor. The walls are really a mess. Looks like they've been working on scraping the paint away. Lots of layers. Some of the blobs of paint look like shapes. That one looks like a butterfly. That one a man's profile. You could make a Rorschach test out of them. There are dormer windows and little ledges you can stand on to look out. I can see the moon and its reflection shimmering on the water, and lights ashore."

There was a long silence on the tape of about a minute. Apparently, Fine was in the dark room looking out the window, thinking. Then his voice was back, sounding strained.

"I have to confess, I'm a little uneasy. I really feel the isolation now that it's dark. And not being able to open the door and get out doesn't help. I think it's better that I keep busy. Time to try out the Phanoptiscope. I'm excited. This will be its first test. In theory, it should work. We'll see.

Sounds of Fine fiddling with things.

"It's 9:40 p.m. I'm firing up the Phanoptiscope. I put the tape player in my pocket — I need both hands. Hope it records okay. The scope is on. The iridium energy pack powered up okay and seems to be providing a good strong energy source. All six flux circuits are on. Closing the lid. I'm getting the projector unit locked in place and adjusted. High energy cable connected.

"I wish my hands weren't shaking. It's hard to attach things and it will be hard to set it up."

For the next few minutes, Fine just mumbled some numbers and settings as he calibrated the scope.

"Okay, I'm back. Hope this is recording okay. I still need both hands. Took me a long time to set up the scope. It's dark and I had to work by moonlight. Saving my flashlight as best I can. I powered up the scope. I set it to do a wide sweep and eighty percent conversion to start with. I did a preliminary set up of the goggles. I have one lens set for basic enhanced low-light vision with the plus 2 diopter in place. The other lens has the auxiliary enhancer unit in place with the IRX filter dialed in. I think I will try it out in this room first. What a moment! At last, I am using the scope on a real investigation. I really want it to work."

There is the sound of a gentle hum. Fine moving. His shirt pocket scraping over the recorder's mic, causing thumps and static.

"I think I saw something move, but maybe it was just the light leaking out of the scope casting a shadow. I should log this test. This is Everett Line Fine. It is 9:52 p.m. and I am on the third floor of Ledge Lighthouse. Going to test my new device, the Phanoptiscope. The lights are out and I am working mostly by moonlight. The Phanoptiscope is set to project the UV and IR light in alternation, with a gamma light overlay superimposed in a cycle of 6 seconds. Slow sweep of 180 degrees. I set the goggles to do a far range wavelength enhancement of eight, filtered at plus 2. Resolution at medium. Here we go. Projecting now. I'm getting solid transmission lights. Receiver is working. Okay, okay — first images coming in."

There is a pause of about ten seconds.

"What the...? Good lord! What?"

Fine's voice drops to a whisper.

"It's hard to describe what I'm seeing! It's incredible! The scope works! The room I am in is empty. But not when I see it processed through the Phanoptiscope. I am seeing images of people and furniture. They are dim and keep fading in and out, but I see them. Everything is washed out, slightly blue, blurry, and transparent. Low res. Not very sharp. Yet I can make out faces. There's one group of guys playing cards. Then they kind of turn into mist and fade and then there's a single guy working on making a model ship. He's sitting right where the middle of their poker table is. He doesn't seem to see them and they don't seem to see him. And now there are another two guys arguing. They are all dressed differently.

"It's incredible! Wait: another guy just walked in smoking a pipe. He walked right through the guys playing poker. The room is full of guys, some interacting, but the groups are oblivious to each other! I think what I'm seeing is different eras. The same room over time. I'm going to push the scope to full power and adjust the goggles to twelve. I'll move in the other filter.

"Wow! I can't believe this! The same guys are still there, fading in and out, but now I can see into the shadows, and there are even more guys from the past in this room. One is sitting reading; two more are listening to the radio; and there is one looking out the window. And even weirder, there is a guy standing fooling around with a deck of cards, and the cards are in the same spot where my hands are holding the scope.

"The Phanoptiscope is seeing phantoms! It works! How can I describe this? It's as if I am in a theater. And I'm seeing on stage — at the same time yet unaware of the other — ten different plays and several solo performers. It's as if the rooms have a memory of what has happened in them. And I am able to glimpse them all at once.

"I am seeing ghosts! This place is full of them! They are the shadows of the men who served here for all those decades. I wonder if they are here now or if the scope is picking up the building's memory traces of its occupants. There's a difference. Ghosts would be active; memory traces passive.

"They don't see me, whatever they are. I must be in a different realm altogether."

Sound of Fine walking.

"I'm walking down the hall toward the head keeper's room at the end. I see more guys going up and down the stairs, and one climbing up the ladder to the lantern room. I... whoa... one of the guys just walked right through me. Now *that* is strange! Man — this is very weird! Très bizarre!

"It's 10:04 and I just walked into the keeper's room. Through the scope I can see there is a bed, a shelf with some books, and some other stuff. The bedside table has a radio and a flashlight. There are a few pictures on the walls and a calendar. There is a chest at the foot of the bed. A table with a lamp and some family photos. A chair and some clothes hanging on hooks on the wall. There is also a... I... wait... wait... someone is coming in here!"

Fine's voice is back to a whisper.

"He's walking in the door. He's wearing a keeper's coat: a heavy thing with six brass buttons. He has a hat with the Lighthouse Service symbol. He's maybe in his 50s. Big spooky eyes behind glasses. Long grey hair. Looks like he has a letter. I... it may be Ernie! He's gone over to the window. Looking out. Watching something through his binoculars. Now he's turned back. Picking up the letter. Reading it. Looking up. Right at me. Doesn't see me. He looks angry. Hurt. He put the letter down. He's just standing there. Crying maybe. This is tough to watch. Poor guy. Boy, it's cold in here.

"Now he's picking up something from the table. I'm not sure, but it looks like one of those old fashioned razor blades, like the barbers use. Now he's walking out. He seems in a hurry. Down the hall. Down the stairs.

"I've been holding my breath! I have to breathe! I'm sure that was Ernie. The Phanopticsope showed me when he got the letter. I don't know if it was his ghost or not.

"Maybe I'll follow him."

Sound of Fine walking briskly.

"Going down to the second floor. I'm going to pop my head in the room at the top of the stairs. Let's see what the scope shows.... Okay, there are two guys in there. One is playing the guitar. I can't hear it, but I can see them. Let me try something.

"Incredible! When I take off the goggles, I am alone in an empty room. No life at all. It's hard to wrap my mind around this. I am sharing Ledge Light with crowds of spirits and, at the same time, all alone in the empty rooms of a deserted building.

"Goggles back on. Across the hall, in another room, a guy is talking to a pretty girl. She looks college age. I bet she isn't supposed to be out here. Now they're kissing. But there is another figure in the room, from another time. A guy lifting weights. Strange. Now the girl ... wait ... she's fading. They all are. Now they are back ... shit! ... gone again. I think the scope is losing power.

"It seems the iridium crystal that powers the Phanoptiscope drains quickly. I should have turned it down. I'll need to find a way to modulate and amplify the energy better. I've only been able to use it for a few minutes. It works well, but the strain of generating, converting, and projecting the light drains the power much more quickly than I thought. And processing the signal through the goggles must drain it even more. I should have tested it longer in the lab. Maybe the beam's interaction with the spirits causes the scope to expend more power. I had it set for feedback enhancement. Need to have more control over it. It will be a great tool for our paranormal research. Maybe if I can figure out a way to record the images, I could take pictures of a ghost and prove they exist. That would be a big breakthrough!

"Now I'm back in the dark. I should head down and see if I can find any trace of Ernie.

"I... what is that? I think I hear something down the hallway. In that little room at the end. A faint scratching sound.

Not sure if the mic on this thing will pick it up. It's pretty crappy. Maybe when I get closer. Probably just wind blowing some old wire against a window."

Sound of Fine walking down the hallway.

"I'm at the room. The door is closed. Scratching sound faint. Can you hear it? It's quiet now. Not sure if I should, but I'm opening the door. The room is very small. Empty except for a radiator, some scraps of sandpaper, and an empty spackle can with dried up spackle on a trowel.

"There is a closet in the corner. This room is pretty dark. The moon is on the other side of the building. I'm putting the Phanoptiscope and goggles down in the corner.

"There! I heard it again. Scratching. Something is behind the door of the closet. It's an old varnished wooden door. I'll take a photo.

"Yes, I'm sure it's coming from the closet! There's something behind that wooden door. Jesus, what could it be? Wait, there it is again. And again. More than one. Is the tape getting it? Something is scratching. Maybe a bunch of things. Maybe I shouldn't open the door. Whatever is in there can stay in there. I'm scared. There is definitely something behind that door. Could it be Ernie? Did he go in there? Is he trying to trap me? Get me to open the door? Then what? Shit — he has a razor! Maybe he wants to cut my throat.

"Damn I'm scared. Get a grip, Everett. But ... I don't know what to do. What to do. I'm supposed to be an investigator, right? Of the paranormal. Shit like this is what I am supposed to figure out. But I don't want to get my throat cut. I don't want to bleed to death on a deserted lighthouse all alone.

"Okay, stay calm. Breathe. Maybe I should ... Jesus! I swear I saw something move in the crack at the bottom of the door. I should get out of this room. But I can't seem to back up. It's like there is something in the shadows — or maybe it *is* the shadows — pushing me toward the closet. I have the flashlight. There, it's on. Nothing in the shadows. Just my imagination. I can't let my imagination run away with me. I have to stay calm. Calm? How the hell am I supposed to stay calm out here in a building full of spirits? And a ghost with a razor? And with something — somethings — behind the door?

"Gotta be professional. Focus on the investigation. Log this.

"The time is 10:18. I'm standing in front of a closet door in a small room at the end of the hall on the second floor of Ledge Lighthouse. I believe I hear something scratching at that door. It will probably be a mouse.

"Flashlight on. Beam all over the place. Hands shaking. Putting the recorder in my shirt pocket again. I feel like I'm in a dream. I'm watching my hand reach out and turn the door-knob.

"I'm opening the door...

There is a long loud scream on the tape. Confused sounds of Fine bumping around. A lot of static and scratching of the mic against his shirt.

"No! Shit! ... How many? ... Get away ... Get off me! GET OFF!!!"

The sound of Fine's feet and him bumping the wall. Then the slamming of a door and Fine running down the hall, breathing hard, mumbling to himself. After about a minute, Fine spoke, gasping, obviously completely terrified.

"Jesus! Jesus! It was rats! Dozens in that closet. Maybe hundreds. I had no idea when I took a picture of it. Flashlight hit their eyes. Red eyes. Demon eyes. They started to come out of the closet. Swarmed at me! A big writhing mass of mangy rats! Ran across my feet. I kicked them away ... slammed the closet door. Some got caught in it. I could hear bones crunch! I ran out of the room ... slammed the door shut. I don't know if any followed me out. I can't be sure in the dark. I hate rats! Ever since that time when I was a kid. Just like tonight. Surrounded by hundreds of the filthy things! Dear God! Just my luck to encounter the thing I fear most!"

Sound of Fine panting. Moaning.

"I have to calm down. I'm shaking so much I can barely hold this recorder. I can't imagine how they live out here. Maybe they eat each other. What a horrible thought! I can imagine them now, in the darkness, filling the room. Okay, okay, okay. Calm down Everett! Get a grip! Forget that room. Note to self: don't open up any more goddamned doors out here!

"Damn … I left the Phanoptiscope and goggles in the room with the rats. I think I kicked them when the rats came at me. I hope I didn't ruin them. They're very fragile. Well, I sure as hell ain't going to go back in there to get them! No way. The power was about drained anyway. I'll get them in the morning."

Silence for a moment except for Fine's heavy breathing.

"I … what was that? I heard something. Upstairs. Footsteps. Now what? I should go see. Why not? Can't be worse than a closet full of rats! God, I feel like there is one on my back. Silly. But who knows? Maybe there are some in the shadows. I have to worry about that, now. And just to add to the fun, my flashlight is fading. It's pretty dim.

"It feels like my heart is going to break out of my chest. Just like that scene in *Alien* … no, Everett, don't go there. Don't start thinking about stuff like that. Not now, not here! Maybe I didn't hear footsteps. Maybe it was just the beating of my heart.

"Okay … what the hell. I haven't been up to the light tower so I might as well go. At least it will be bright up there with the light and the moon. Maybe I can get some fresh air, too. Clear my mind. Yeah. Gotta clear my mind. The doc told me when I get stressed to slow down. Breathe. Clear my mind. Think good things. Yeah, well, she wasn't here in a room full of damned rats!

Sound of Fine climbing the metal stairway.

"These stairs are really creepy. The banisters cast shadows on the walls that move as I go up. I think I said that before. I don't like the shadows here. Don't trust them. I'm on the third floor. Back down to Ernie's room. The ladder to the tower is right outside it, so the head keeper didn't have far to go if he needed to get to the light. I'm not going back in there. I'm not going back in Ernie's room, and I'm not going back in the rat room.

"Wish those rats weren't down there. Really creepy thinking of them filling a room. Right below me, too. I hope they don't get the door opened. Or don't find a pipe or hole in the wall to crawl through. I really do not want to be alone out here in the dark with rats swarming all over the place. Hell, I'll jump off and swim home.

"Okay, back to business. Keep busy. It's midnight. I'm heading up to the light tower. I have my camera and flashlight.

Sound of footsteps on the metal ladder.

"12:05 and I am in the first stage of the light tower. There is a stencil here that says DIE. At least that's what it looks like it says. It's on a wall with cracked paint so it's not that clear. Why would someone stencil DIE on the wall? Maybe it's meant for me. A warning? Or a promise? I don't know. I don't know anything. I wish my dad was here to help me. My hands are shaking and my flashlight beam is all over the place so maybe it's just making it hard to see clearly. It could be a number, "018." I'll take a picture and show it to Chuck and Angie. See what they think. They should be here. I never should have come out here alone. Bad idea! Note to self: do not do this alone!

"I'm going to climb up the ladder now. Into the top part of the lantern room where the light is. The ladder is narrow and there are a bunch of stiff wires hanging around the edges. I have to go through a narrow hatch."

"What if Ernie is up there? And as I come through he grabs my hair and pulls my head back and cuts my throat with that razor? I'm defenseless. Maybe that's what DIE means? It *is* a warning! Maybe I shouldn't go up. I can take one more step and maybe see what's up there.

Sound of Fine taking another step on the metal ladder. Long pause.

"Okay. I can see the curve of the glass. It's a small room, maybe five feet across. The light takes up most of it. And there is a door to a catwalk that circles the tower. I... shit... something grabbing my ankle! I'm going up!

"I'm in the lantern room. All clear. No Ernie, thank God. Not sure what grabbed my ankle. I hope it wasn't a rat.

"It's bright up here with the light spinning. I'm glad to be here with it. I'm tired of the shadows. The room is white metal to about three feet, then big, thick diamond-shaped windows all the way around. A dark cupola overhead. The light is like a great big eye. The thing turns and goes from white to black to red. Three whites and a red — that's Ledge Light's pattern.

12:10. I'm in the lantern room. The light's spinning. White. Black. Red. And the door is open! The goddamned door is open! How can that be? It's bolted. It's heavy. How did it get open? The wind? I don't think I came up here earlier and left it open, but I can't be sure. It's like trying to remember a dream. I'm getting confused. I'm going to sit down right here at the base of the light and try to calm down. Okay: try to breathe and compose myself. Someone else could have left the door open. Or ... no, don't start thinking that! I'll shut up and shut off the recorder for a bit. I wonder if there are spirits in here with me?

Sound of rustling and the recording stops. Then it starts.

"It's about 12:30. I'm in the lantern room at the top of Ledge Light. I feel so small inside this big empty building in the middle of the water. No one can help me. I have to get through this on my own. I'm pretty wired up and jumpy. I just remembered I have that pill the doctor gave me. She said it was a drug that helped with fear. Well, I'm afraid. But I don't want to take it yet. She warned me there could be side effects. She said to only take it if I am so scared I can't function at all. I'm scared but I am still functioning. I know who I am. Everett Line Fine. Everett Line Fine. Everett Line Fine. That's me. So I'll wait.

"I've decided to go out on the catwalk. If nothing else, I'll get some fresh air."

Sound of the lantern room door creaking and then banging into the railing of the catwalk. Footsteps on metal as Fine goes out. A little wind hits the mic and rumbles.

"12:35. On the catwalk now at the top of Ledge Light. What a view! I can see New London Harbor Light blinking to my left, and over there is Race Rock. There are lots of ships. There goes a ferry. I can see Avery Point where I was during the thunderstorm. The harbor is ablaze with light. The moon is full and bright — sparkling on the water. And I ... wait! What was that? It sounded like footsteps.

"Shhhhit! I think there's somebody out here with me! Is that ... no ... well, maybe ... damn light ... I think ...

There is a pause in the tape. Sound of Fine breathing. Then his whispered voice, a little obscured by wind across the mic.

"I see a vague shape through the glass on the other side of the walk from me. Hard to see because the light is so bright when it comes around! And these windows are scratched and pitted. And there are a lot of reflections. But I see something. It's a man! I don't need the Phanoptiscope to see him. But he doesn't seem real, exactly. It's like he can't quite keep his shape, like he's made of smoke or mist and his edges kind of blur and drift. I can just make out his face. It's Ernie! He's looking through the window and past the light at me. I'm sure it's him. Or his ghost. His damned ghost!

"I'll try to take a shot. Probably be blurry. The glass is thick. Everything is distorted. And my hands are shaking."

Faint sound of the camera clicking and Fine winding the film.

"I took a picture. I'm too scared to go around. It's hard to see, but he's still there. Now he's moving around toward me. I've got to get away … wait … he stopped. Wait. Wait. He's climbing down to the roof. Now he's on the roof. In the shadows. Just a shadow. Now taking shape. Getting clearer. I can see him in the moonlight now. It's Ernie alright."

Fine lowers his voice to a whisper.

"I'm whispering 'cause I don't know if he can hear me. Ernie is on the roof. Crouched under the catwalk. I don't dare walk around near him. He might reach up and grab me and pull me … wait … wait … he stood up. He's walking across the roof. Slowly. He's looking around. He's at the edge of the roof now. He's staring down at the water. What? No! He's turned toward me. His face is shadowed by his hat, but I saw the moon glint on his glasses. Long grey hair. Brass buttons on his coat. What's he doing? He's raised his hand. It looks like he is motioning to me. Can he see me? Maybe he can. Maybe he's waving at the light. Does he want me to come out on the roof with him? No way! I'm not … he turned away. Looking down at the water. Turning back again. Motioning again. No way! He turned away. He's so close to the edge. He's looking around. His shoulders are … is he crying? He might be sobbing. I can't tell. He … Oh my God! Oh my God! He jumped! He jumped off the roof!"

Sounds of confusion and bumping and steps and a door slamming. Breathless:

"This is Everett Fine. I am back inside the lantern room. It's … it's about 1 a.m.. I just saw what I think is the ghost of Ernie. He jumped off the roof. That's how he killed himself. Chuck told me about this. It's called a 'residual haunting.' It's when a ghost repeats something over and over. I'm not staying around to see it again. He was motioning me like he wanted me to jump with him. The hell with that! I'm not jumping from anywhere. I'm going back downstairs. I'll take my chances with the rats"

Sounds of Fine climbing down ladder.

"I'm back on the third floor. I wish I could get off this lighthouse. I've seen enough! I'm scared. I ... a light. A light came on in the long room on this floor! Let me see who's there ... going into the room now. Nobody here ... wait. A figure in the corner. I ... I ... Dad? No, can't be. Dad? He's gone, but I swear I saw him. What *is* this place?

"Too many shadows. I see things in them. Moving about. I can't tell what exactly. I just see shapes moving. Shit! I hope there are no more rats! One room full is enough. But some might have gotten out. They might be waiting in the shadows. Or they might come after me.

"I can still hear them in that room. Gotta stay away from that room. Maybe I'll go to the first floor. I'm heading down. I hate these stairs. I don't like the open banisters. There's a chill in here.

"I may ... what's that? Something at the top of the stairs. Small. A rat? No, it's not moving. Something small ... Oh my God! It's Morgan! Just standing there at the top of the stairs! How the hell did he get up here? Did I take him? I don't remember taking him, but I must have. Maybe when I brought up the scope. Lot's has been happening so maybe I just forgot. Shit! I'm going to take Morgan back down to the first floor. You okay, Morgan? Did I take you up here or are you possessed by Ernie's spirit? But Ernie jumped. Well, don't let him get to you. Just keep repeating to yourself: 'I am Morgan. I am Morgan.'

"I'll bet Ernie won't settle for a wood carving. I'm here and that could be more tempting for him. Nothing like living flesh and blood for a spirit to crawl into. I know now. I'm right about proximal affinity. That freak cloud and lightning knocking the K off was a warning. I should have heeded it. It was telling me,

Everett Line Fine, that Ernie's Ka was out here and looking for
a host. Waiting for someone. For me, Everett Line Fine! And
the letters on the obelisk ... I bet they spelled out a warning,
too. I just needed to figure out how to read them.

"I gotta be careful. I know how all this happens. You let
your guard down or fall asleep and they take you over. Fall
asleep? That's a joke! Like I could calm down enough to fall
asleep."

Footsteps on stairs.

"On the first floor now. Morgan back on the table. He better stay there. I ... SHIT! The foghorn just came on! It's loud.
Scared me big time. I jumped and bumped the table and Morgan fell off. I'm putting him back and I'm laying him down.
Stay there! There goes the horn again. Loud! Hear it? The
voice of the lighthouse. It sounds like a huge animal. What a
sound! How the hell did guys sleep out here with that thing
blasting away? Maybe it's better in the basement. It's isolated
down there. Thick walls. Nine feet I think they said.

"Okay, Everett, be professional. A status report. It is 1:30
and, as you can hear, the foghorn is on and loud. I don't know
why it's on. It's a clear night. Full moon. No reason for it to be
on, but it is. No reason for there to be a closet full of rats, but
there was. It's so dark out here! The lights are off and my flashlight is up in the tower. I'm a bundle of nerves. Just one thing
after another: Shadows. Those spirits I saw through the scope.
Rats. Ernie. Morgan. I've never been in a building like this.
Never. Nobody's lived here for thirty years so there's been
plenty of time for the ghosts to gather. In the darkness. Maybe
GPG can come back as a team. Well, maybe not me, Everett
Line Fine. I'm never coming back here.

"I'm tempted to take that fear pill.

"I gotta get away from that horn. I'll go down to the basement. Get away from it. It's really dark down there but it would
be quieter I think. Did I already say that? I'll leave Morgan up

here in case Ernie wants a Ka figure to inhabit. Better Morgan than me! Everett Line Fine. Everett Line Fine. Pathetic, huh? I'm trusting my soul to a five-inch carved wooden figure I bought at an antique store for seven bucks. He may already have been taken over by Ernie, actually. He's been tipping over. Then I found him on the second floor. Twice. Or did he tip over twice? Did I mention that already? And the foghorn? I don't know. I'm getting confused."

Sound of Fine walking around. Then he starts to speak again, the fear in his voice evident.

"1:45 a.m. I'm at the top of the basement stairs. There is a big steel door here. It's open. There is a sign on it: "Watch Your Step." Okay, I will. I'm looking down the stairs, and they are very steep. Concrete. Part of the foundation. Painted a blood red. There is a red railing. There are seven steps down, and then they take a sharp turn to the right. I can't see any farther. The stairwell wall to my right blocks my view. Moonlight is coming in the window at the top of the stairs to my left. I can hear the hum of the high voltage transformer. Okay. Here I go. Everett Line Fine heads down the rabbit hole. Maybe into Dante's inferno."

Footsteps on the cement stairs.

"One step. Two. Three. Four. Five. Six. Seven. I am at the bend in the stairway now. It continues on another seven steep steps to an arched doorway that leads to the basement. Some pipes cross over the bottom few steps. And there is a small hatch in the right wall labelled "Fresh Water." That would be the cistern. From here the basement is just a dark doorway. The moonlight doesn't reach into it very far. I can hear the hum of that high voltage transformer. It's in a cage, like a dangerous beast. It seems like the only living thing out there. It and the horn.

"Down a step. Down a step. Down a step. At the cistern. Damn! What's that? Hard to see. Looks like a handprint on the wall. Red. Blood or paint? I don't know which. Could it be

Ernie's after all these years? Maybe it's a fresh print. Maybe he jumped and hit the base and is all broken up and bloody and he came down here and ...

"Shit! Stop! Stop thinking! I know who I am: Everett Line Fine. Investigator for the Groton Paranormal Group. Ernie's not down here. He's not going to surprise me. That damned horn! I can't think straight! I feel it going through me. It's cold down here. Very cold.

"1:50 a.m. Heading down the final part of the stairs into a dark doorway.

Down a step. Down. Down. I had to duck under the pipes at the bottom of the stairs. Just a trickle of moonlight from the top of the stairs."

Sound of his footsteps on the stairs. Foghorn. Humming electrical sound gets louder.

"I ..."

There was silence for a few seconds. Then with a click, the recorder "play" button popped up. The tape had reached its end. The small machine sat on the desk, silent. Scott stared at it. He had just heard a chilling real-time recording of a man tilting into madness.

The recording had ended just as Everett had gone into the basement. He probably kept talking, unaware the tape had stopped. Nobody would know exactly what happened to him down there. He had had a rough night already. The stress and strain were evident in his voice. So was the fear. From what Scott had heard, he was already losing his grip on reality. Whatever happened in that basement, it had pushed him over the edge and caused his final, complete mental breakdown.

It was tantalizing. As Dr. Markhal had said, exactly what was happening at times was open to interpretation. But it added a lot of details to flesh out Scott's portrait of Fine. What Fine reported, and how he reported it, had started to connect pieces of the puzzle.

And yet the tape also raised new questions. How much of what Everett had reported had really happened? How much of it was just his growing fear projecting itself into the shadows that surrounded him? Had the ghost of Ernie, his Ka, poked around in Everett's memories to find his fear of rats and made that a waking dream? Or had there really been rats?

Did Scott hear the scratching that Everett had heard? Could he make out a second set of footsteps out on the catwalk? Or was it just his imagination, too, fired by Everett's vivid descriptions and genuine fear? The sounds on the tape were like the shadows through which Everett moved: evocative, suggestive. Maybe they were full of menace. Or maybe they were innocent — absent any deeper darkness.

The tape was compelling. And ambiguous.

Scott sat and replayed Fine's tape in his mind. He tried to imagine the night as it unfolded for the terrified man. Scott realized that to understand what Fine had experienced, to answer some of his questions, he would have to spend the night alone on Ledge Light, just as Everett Line Fine had. Only then would he know — really know — if the tape was a diary of madness or a chilling documentation of a place of paranormal menace.

Or, perhaps, like Twice Seen Scenes, something that merged them both.

15

NEW LONDON HARBOR
2014

The bright sunshine hit the white sails of the Mystic Whaler as it sailed out of its pier in New London and headed south to Ledge Light. The sails were almost blinding in the morning sun and were beautiful against the sky. Scott held a cup of coffee in his hand as Captain John gave a safety briefing and then explained the day's itinerary. He introduced the guides from the Ledge Lighthouse Foundation, Wayne, Bruce, and John, who preferred to be called by his nickname "Zook," derived from his last name, Mazzucchi.

The Whaler was a beautiful wooden schooner that plied the waters of the Thames River, New London Harbor, and Long Island Sound during the summer. It offered sunset lobster dinner tours, day sails around the area, and longer voyages to Block Island and Newport. And in recent years, it had added stops at Ledge Light to some of its day sails. It was a beautiful boat, 110 feet long, laden with lines, pulleys, belaying pins, brasswork, and heavy canvas sails. It harkened back a century and a half earlier when ships of its kind set out from New London on whaling voyages to distant waters, sometimes as far away as Antarctica. Though regular tours to Ledge Light were offered on the sturdy blue boat of Project Oceanology out of Avery Point in Groton, those with more time to spare and a yen for the quiet of a sailing ship took the Mystic Whaler.

So it was for Scott. He had seen the Whaler gliding by from shore — a few times not far from an incoming submarine — and he wanted to sail aboard her to Ledge Light. Scott had booked the tour to see for himself the domain of Ernie and the place that had unhinged Everett Fine. He knew a lot about the lighthouse's history and lore. But nothing except a visit could convey the feel for the actual place. For its spaces, its moods, its character. He wanted to see what it was like to be out on a solid building surrounded by water. He wanted to sense its isolation. He wanted to hear what the tour guides had to say, roam the building's rooms. He wanted to be where Fine had been. And Ernie, too.

He hoped he could convince the Ledge Light Foundation to let him stay overnight, alone, but wasn't sure he could arrange that. So this daytime visit might be his only chance to see Ledge Light with his own eyes and touch it with his own hands.

As the Mystic Whaler made its way out of New London harbor, Scott had time to think about Everett's tape yet again. The tape had been chilling. Even difficult to listen to at times. It was hard to hear a man lose his grip on reality, to descend into madness. And to not hear the final act — whatever had happened in that dark damp basement to completely unhinge him — was frustrating. Had Everett encountered Ernie down there? Or, in that ultimate place of shadows, with the foghorn wailing and the high voltage cage humming, had Fine simply let his imagination defeat him? Had a single rat so frightened him that he lost his mind?

There was a gap between 1:50 a.m., Fine's last timed entry, and 5:30 a.m., when Russell and Chuck found him at the top of the basement stairs, behind the door, curled in a ball, desperately saying his name over and over. He had been in shock when they took him off the light. And according to Dr. Markhal, Everett Fine took the truth of what happened in that basement with him to the grave.

Scott wondered if he would ever have all the pieces to the puzzle he was trying to solve. The mystery of Everett Line Fine was not giving up its answers easily.

After a leisurely sail out of New London, the Mystic Whaler headed southeast toward Race Rock. Ledge Light was about a half mile to starboard. They would stop at it later. Zook sidled up to Scott at the rail.

"It's quite a place," he said, pointing toward Race Rock Lighthouse. It was a castle-like stone building perched on a cylindrical stone base that rose out of a man-made island created from huge boulders.

"It's very mysterious looking," said Scott.

They both gazed at the lighthouse. "Hard to land there, so no tours yet. They hope to work on it. There's a good book you should read if you haven't."

"Yeah?" Scott asked.

"Yes, *Legacy of the Light.* A thriller that covers two generations of lighthouse keepers and the hurricane of 1938. It's a real page turner. It'll keep you up all night reading it," said Zook.

"I'll check it out," said Scott.

"Lighthouses are good places for stories," said Zook. "They're isolated, storms roll in, and the few people on them have to cope with whatever comes their way."

"A real pressure cooker."

"Exactly. And no place to run. Something happens and you may be trapped. You read *Legacy* and you'll see."

Ding! Ding!

Anne: Hi, Sweetie!

Scott: Hi, my love. How are you? How is the conference?

Anne: I'm fine. The conference is intense. Some good stuff. Some not so good. More bad PowerPoints.

Scott: I know what you mean. Half the time at Rotary if a speaker starts one, I leave. I can't take the slides of teeny tiny print and someone saying: Sorry you can't read the text. Let me read it for you.

Anne: LOL. Exactly.

Scott: Good to see you laughing.

Anne: Yeah, today, I'm feeling okay. I feel like maybe I will beat this thing yet.

Scott: So far, you have. You'll see. The test will prove it.

Anne: Let's hope. Anyway, I just wanted to tell you how much I love you. And thank you for being there for me.

Scott: No place else I'd rather be. I love you, too, you know. You're my life.

Anne: Where are you now?

Scott: On a big old fashioned schooner heading out to Ledge Light.

Anne: Come on! Where are you really?

Scott: Really. I'm on the Mystic Whaler, on a tour to the light. We can go together sometime.

Anne: Well, hell! Sounds better than a dark, cold hotel ballroom. This book is sure taking you places.

Scott: That it is.

Anne: Have you unraveled the mystery of your ghost guy?

Scott: Not yet. Some mysteries are stubborn. Seems every time I answer a question it raises another one.

Anne: So it goes. Well, good luck.

Scott: Thanks. I may need it on this one.

Anne: Did I tell you I love you?

Scott: Maybe. And I love you. No mystery there.

Anne: Have a good sail! Enjoy the lighthouse!

Scott: Good luck with the PowerPoints. You're allowed to sleep during them. Love you.

Anne: Love you more. Bye!

Scott was happy to have chatted with Anne. She had a lot of strength. She sounded better today. Day at a time. It seemed like a long time since their lives had been any other way. Maybe someday they'll get back to planning things in the future.

After a spin around Race Rock and a wonderful lunch, the Whaler heading north to Race Rock's sister lighthouse, Ledge Light.

Onboard was a sea shanty singer. As they sailed, he sang the "Ballad of Ernie."

Tell me a tale of New London's Ledge Light
Sing it clear and sing it bright
A tale of men who served out at sea
A story of betrayal and mystery.

In the 20s or 30s according to lore
A keeper named Ernie lived far from the shore.
His wife could not take his life on the light
So she looked for new love to make her heart right.

She met a ship's captain of the ferry to Block
While strolling along the waterfront dock.
O'er time their love blossomed and she came to see
Her marriage to Ernie could no longer be.

So she sent him a letter, a heartfelt farewell
That arrived at the lighthouse like a message from hell.
Ernie could not believe what he read
It stung his heart and it spun his poor head.

Broken and lonely, Ernie was sad
And seeing the ferry drove the man mad.
He could take it no more and so one moonlit night
He climbed to the roof and jumped from Ledge Light.

But though he was gone from this mortal life
Ernie swore vengeance because of his wife.
So as a ghost he came back to the light
To give all the keepers a terrible fright.

According to legend Ernie is there
On Ledge Light he waits to give you a scare.
So beware of the shadows where Ernie may loom
The ghost of the lighthouse who haunts every room.

The ballad was a big hit with the tourists on the boat. It got them excited about seeing Ledge Light and especially Ernie.

"Does Ernie really haunt the lighthouse?" a boy asked Bruce, one of the guides.

"That's for you to find out."

They drew near Ledge Lighthouse. Its style was completely different from Race Rock, though its function was identical. Captain John approached slowly then cut the motor and let the Whaler drift alongside the lighthouse. His crew threw lines out, and one hopped onto the landing lip to secure them. It was all masterfully done with a minimum of engine work required. In five minutes, the Mystic Whaler was securely tied alongside Ledge Light.

Passengers climbed down a small set of stairs onto the light's landing lip then up a metal stairway that ran along the huge concrete base whose top was the foundation for the lighthouse building.

Scott Edwards climbed the stairs and, at last, set foot on Ledge Lighthouse. Bruce and Zook, two of the guides, disappeared into the building to get things ready. The Mystic Whaler bobbed alongside. Captain John sat on a bench puffing a cigar. Looking around, Scott had to agree with Fine — it was a spectacular spot.

When everybody was up, they crowded in front of Wayne, who stood atop the three steps that led to the door of the lighthouse. Flanked by flags flapping lazily in the breeze, he began his briefing. As Wayne spoke, Scott wandered over to the corner, squeezing around a curved pole that poked up from the deck about 7 feet. It was near the rail. A big wooden pulley hung from short ropes tied to the end of the metal hoist. Wayne continued his brief history lesson.

"On shore there, you can see the white tower of the New London Harbor Light, the first lighthouse built on Long Island Sound. It was the fourth of the original twelve colonial lights that the young United States government managed under its newly established Lighthouse Board. Originally built in 1761, it was rebuilt in 1801. It's the fourth oldest working light in America.

"Around the corner, off the point of Fishers Island, is Race Rock lighthouse, built in 1872. It was quite an engineering feat. First, they had to build an island on the rock, then the lighthouse on top of it. Someday, we hope to run tours there, but it needs some work first.

"This lighthouse, Ledge Light, was built in 1909 to augment the other two. The three work together to provide a pathway of safety into New London harbor. All three are now owned by the New London Maritime Society. The Ledge Light Foundation has been steward of Ledge Light since 1987. It will lease the building from the Maritime Society and continue its work of restoration, expanding the museum, and providing public tours.

"The Foundation is all volunteer. We welcome your help, and hope you will come out someday with a work group to help us preserve this unique and beautiful piece of our maritime heritage."

Wayne told the visitors more about Ledge Light and how the tour would be run. Scott learned that oversight of the keepers job had passed from the Lighthouse Board to the Lighthouse Service, both civilian, and then, in 1939, to the Coast Guard. Three keepers manned the building until 1987. At that time, the light was automated, and the keepers left for good. Unless you believed the legend of Ernie, of course. If you believed in Ernie, the ghost of one keeper remains at Ledge Light for eternity.

"What about Ernie?" someone shouted to Wayne.

"You'll see him," Wayne said with a smile. "I guarantee it." With that, he led folks inside.

"First fifteen in go on up to the theater on the second floor, at the top of the stairs. You can see the orientation show. Everyone will get a chance to see it. Everybody else: roam where you like. You can join Bruce down in the basement or let Zook and me show you around the second and third floor exhibits. Or head up to the lantern room for the best view in town. The door is open. There is plenty of time for everybody to see everything.

"Where's Ernie?" a boy asked, impatient to meet the ghost.

"You'll find him," said Wayne, then added in a stage whisper: "Or maybe he'll find you!" Everybody laughed at that and started to disperse around the lighthouse.

Scott stayed by the front door. Bright light flooded the building. It was alive with the sounds of the film, of people talking, of the guides explaining history and the workings of the lighthouse. Scott wanted to take his time. He wanted to roam around the rooms as Fine had, gauging for himself if they seemed full of menace.

The empty room to the left of the doorway, where Everett had set up his headquarters and where Morgan had repeatedly tipped over, was now a gift shop. It had cases of T-shirts, mugs, postcards, posters, pins, books by a local author, miniature lighthouses, and other Ledge Light themed souvenirs. A table and a guest book beckoned. Scott signed his name and added: *In the shadow of Everett Line Fine.*

The gift shop led into a long briefing room adorned with charts and a mural of the lighthouse painted by the last keepers to man it. There were shelves of model lighthouses, a small lens and bulb system to demonstrate how the light worked, and a TV showing clips of lighthouse films and picture galleries. Padded benches lined two walls.

Scott circled back toward the front door and up the wide metal stairway. He remembered from the tape Everett's frightened description of the shadows these banisters created as his flashlight raked across them.

On the second floor were a theater, a history room, and a small room at the end of the hall of exhibits and photographs. It was the room where Fine had heard and then encountered a closet full of rats. The room's door was open. Scott waited as two girls looked at the exhibits and snapped a few selfies. When they left, Scott had the room to himself. The varnished closet door was handsome, and latched closed. Scott recognized it from the photographs and from Fine's terrified description of the rats. Scott stood in front of the door. He didn't hear scratching, yet he hesitated to open it. The thought that behind it might be hundreds of rats that would swarm out and over him gave him pause.

Scott shook his head. "No rats," he said to himself and opened the door. There were no rats. There was an old shag carpet, two space heaters, some fluorescent bulbs, and paint chips on the ground. On a shelf, a jar was barely visible in the shadows. A pipe ran from the ceiling through the floor with plenty of space around it. Nothing else.

As he closed the door he noticed the bottom edge. There were streaks and gouges along it. Were they scratch marks? Scott knelt down and felt with his fingers. They were real. But from rats or from people bumping in and out with the space heaters?

In the hall, Zook announced that the second showing of the orientation film was about to start. As Scott made his way to the theater, he asked Zook where the pipe in the closet of the small gallery room went.

"To the cistern in the basement," Zook said, then added: "You better get to the theater. Show's about to start."

Scott parted the thick black velvet curtains that hung in the doorway. They helped keep the light out and the air conditioning in. He took a seat. The film was dramatic and informative. Riveting. It gave Scott a very good feel for the history of the building, the life of the keepers, the remoteness and beauty of the location, the terror of the hurricane of 1938, and the sad and chilling story of Ernie.

After the film, the history room across the hall filled with people, so Scott worked his way up to the third floor. It was busy, too. He went down the hall to Ernie's room where a family was crowding the small area. Busy taking pictures, they were in no rush to leave. So Scott climbed the curved metal ladder that gave access to the two-staged light tower. He went through a metal hatch and found himself in the lower stage — an octagonal room about 5 feet across. It had two porthole-style windows and another curved metal ladder of 7 steps that went through a hatch to the light itself. The same old electrical wires Everett had mentioned in the tape dangled near the edges of the ladder.

On the white wall beneath one of the portholes, near an electrical relay box, Scott saw a stenciled number: "018." Both the left edge of the 0 and the right edge of the 8 were worn away, so the 0 looked a bit like a D and the 8 a bit like an E. Squinting a bit, Scott could see how, in the dancing beam of a flashlight, 018 could be read as DIE. But the more he looked at it, the more Scott began to wonder if, in fact, the stencil didn't spell DIE? Why would someone paint that? As a joke? Or had someone scraped away the paint to create a message? A warning? A promise? Who? And why? People were coming from below, so Scott climbed up into the light room.

The light room housed Ledge Light's beacon. The original fourth order Fresnel lens, a glass work of art, had been removed in the 1980s and replaced with a utilitarian and totally uninspiring plastic cylinder. It had three clear panes, one black pane, and one translucent red pane inside. As these panels turned around the fixed array of bulbs — only 35 watts — from any given spot outside the lens, the light appeared to blink three white and then, after a short pause, one red. It was Ledge Light's unique signature at night. On a chart, next to the exclamation point that signified a lighthouse, the legend "3W 1R" told mariners that a light they saw that blinked 3 white and 1 red was Ledge Light. Every lighthouse was different. Neighboring Race Rock blinked red every 30 seconds. New London Harbor light blinked white every 3 seconds.

The lantern room's walls were metal to about waist height. Then big trapezoidal glass panes were held in place by thick metal mullions. The room had brass vent mechanisms and was topped by a cupola. One whole section of metal and glass turned out to be a heavy thick door that swung outwards onto a narrow catwalk the encircled the lantern room. Scott stepped outside. More than 50 feet above the water, the view was magnificent! The top of Ledge Light gave a bird's eye view of Groton, New London, and Long Island Sound. Boats were everywhere, their arrow-shaped wakes slowly spreading out and fading away behind them. Birds swooped around the light. The roof was small, its grey color almost obliterated by a dried white coating of bird droppings. The catwalk was about 5 feet above the roof. A sign warned: "No climbing on the roof." Scott looked back through the window, through the small room, past the spinning lens, to see Zook on the catwalk opposite him. His face was distorted by the double windows of scratched and wavy glass. Scott wondered what someone or something would look like seen this way at night.

After looking at Zook and thinking about Everett's tape a moment, Scott turned back to look out to sea. As lonely and remote as duty at Ledge Light might have been for the keepers, they could not complain about the drama of the location. The keeper in the orientation film had told how the building seemed to shudder when the huge waves of bad storms hit it. That was hard to imagine. The place seemed so solid — a manmade mountain in the sea.

But the keeper had also spoken poetically about being out there when it snowed. He described the silence and how the lighthouse seemed to be inside a snow globe. The descriptions, the photographs, and the music had created a dream-like scene in the film. Whatever might lurk in its shadows, Ledge Light was undeniably a place of beauty and wonder.

Scott left the tower and climbed back down the ladders to the third floor. On the way, he had to coax a little boy who was paralyzed with fear by the lower span of the ladder, which crossed above the stairway. Looking down between the iron steps, the boy had seen the stairs dropping away below and froze. He was afraid of the sudden sense of height after the claustrophobia of the tower.

"It's okay," Scott said. "Don't look down. Just put your left foot on the step ... good ... now your right ... and you're almost there." The boy made it down the last few rungs to the third floor.

"Thank you," his appreciative mother said. Seeing the boy's fear, she spun him gently away from Ernie's room and marched him down the hall. He was scared enough.

At the base of the tower ladder, back at Ernie's room, Scott found it still crowded. He went down the hall to a room at the top of the stairs. It was where Everett had seen a man playing a guitar while another listened. And, from a different era, some guys sitting around the radio. Now it was filled with tourists from the present all studying exhibits. Across the hall, the long room where Fine had first tried the scope held more exhibits and tourists.

Scott recalled Richard Moore's Twice Seen Scenes photos and how eerily they had come to life when Everett had used his

Phanoptiscope and goggles. As Scott watched people milling about Ledge Light, he could not help but wonder how many unseen people were there with them at that moment. How many keepers from how many years went about their daily routines, oblivious to the tourists from the future come to see their world? It was an unsettling thought. Scott had a different perspective from all these other visitors and even the guides. To him, Ledge Light was both the place he saw with his own eyes — the sunny rooms, the colorful exhibits, the fresh paint — and the place that lived in his imagination, defined by Fine's tape. That Ledge Light was empty and decaying, a place of phantoms, menacing shadows, a closet full of rats, and Everett Fine, lost in a nightmare.

A sudden loud shriek indicated that someone had encountered Ernie.

Scott walked out of the long room and back toward Ernie's room. He waited for a few people to clear out. Finally, Ernie's room was empty. Scott walked in, past a short jog of wall and along a wooden barrier that divided the room. He turned to his left and jumped in shock. There was the mannequin of Ernie. It was, indeed, creepy. Even scary. He stood by a window in the furnished keeper's room. As Scott looked over the barrier and took in the scene, a shadow in the corner near Ernie suddenly grew to over 6 feet tall. It took on the form of a man and came at him.

Scott flinched.

Then smiled. It was Zook.

"Oh!" Zook said, startled when he saw Scott. "You scared me."

He had been kneeling in the corner, in the shadows, turning on a light. He had squeezed his way past the mannequin of Ernie, by the chest at the bottom of the bed, and was set to clamber back over the barrier.

"I like to turn on the light on that table in the corner," he said a bit sheepishly. "It adds to the feel of the room. We don't like people seeing us going over the barrier. We don't want them getting back there and messing around with Ernie. I try to sneak over before the tour starts, but I didn't have time today. We have a big group to wrangle, and I had to start the show."

"I won't tell," said Scott.

"Thanks," said Zook. "What do you think of Ernie?"

"Pretty creepy," said Scott.

"That he is. I wouldn't want to be alone out here with him!" Just then a man came in and asked about the big metal hatches on the floor, and Zook left the room with him, going back to his tour guide duties.

Scott turned back to the mannequin of Ernie. It was about 6 feet tall. He was dressed in grey pants, a turtleneck, and a heavy keeper's coat with gleaming brass buttons with an anchor and rope design. He wore a cap with a gold Lighthouse Service insignia — a generic tower light surrounded by laurel leaves. Ernie's hands were very realistic. His left hand held a letter — no doubt the one his wife had sent telling the poor man of her betrayal. But it was Ernie's face that was so fearsome.

It was an older man's face — maybe in his 60s. Whoever had created this spooky figure had found a very realistic mask and embellished it. A shock of long grey hair came out of the back of the hat. Realistic glass eyes stared out from behind wire-rimmed glasses. And the expression ... how could Scott describe it? Anger. Hurt. Shock. Madness. They all played across the rubber features of Ernie's face. Somehow, the whole mannequin seemed alive, frozen in action like the single frame of a movie. No wonder people gave startled cries when they walked into the room, turned, and saw this apparition standing there!

The designers of this exhibit had created a lived-in room where a very realistic man stood at the moment when his life started to unravel. You could feel his pain. His anger. His resolve for vengeance.

This mannequin hadn't been there when Fine had visited Ledge Light. None of the exhibits were. A good thing. Had Everett encountered this thing that night ... but then Scott realized that maybe he had encountered something worse: a real ghost.

Scott shuddered. Whether from a frisson of fear or from the odd chill of the room he didn't know. Standing there staring at Ernie, who stared back at him, Scott wondered about

Everett Fine's tape. Its narrative of rooms alive with spirits, closets full of rats, and the ghost of Ernie was compelling. Maybe all of it was true. Or maybe Fine had encountered nothing more than empty rooms whose shadows invited his imagination to fill them with his worst fears. With demons of his own design.

Scott decided it was time to head to the basement where Everett had experienced something in the darkness from which he had never recovered.

16

The basement of Ledge Light was at the bottom of a steep stairwell that led deep into the building's foundation. It went down seven steps then took a right angle turn for another seven steps. High up on the wall above the angle of the stairs, a barred window let in daylight. It cast a glow through the arched doorway at the bottom of the stairs. The way the stairs turned and descended, there was no way to get to the window without scaffolding of some sort.

Scott stood at the top of the stairs, where a thick metal door had been opened for the tours. At this point in the visit, nobody was down in the basement. Scott would have it to himself. The stairwell walls were white and the stairs and banister a bright red. The paint was flaking. Scott headed down. He got to the angled portion of the stairs and saw pipes crossing above the bottom few steps, yellow warning tape signaling low clearance. Ledge Light was full of warning signs. On the right wall, a small hatch was labelled "Fresh Water." Scott descended another step and stood before it. It was a hatch to the cistern. He opened the latch and swung the small door open. It was pitch dark inside. He pulled out his iPhone and turned on its flashlight. The cistern was a cavernous chamber under the first floor. It was crisscrossed with pipes on top. The bottom portion was divided into several deep tanks that went down 10 feet or so. In the history exhibit room on the second floor, there were panels of photographs from the late 1950s taken by a keeper named Rick Bonanno. They were a charming look at life on Ledge Light. Guys sunbathing, eating dinner, listening to Elvis records, chipping ice from outdoor tanks, fooling around with a brood of puppies, helping a crew repair the underwater electric cable.

One photo showed a man inside the cistern, astride the tank dividers. Scott shuddered when he thought of falling into one of those tanks. The door could swing closed. You might drown in there. A weird thought: drowning inside a building in the middle of the water. The tanks were empty and dry now. Not much better. To fall in and break a leg, to die slowly in the pitch dark. Scott thought of the rats that Everett might have seen. Maybe they lived in the cistern. Scott cringed at the thought. That guy in the photo was crazy to be fooling around in there. Maybe you had to be crazy to serve on a lighthouse. Or maybe serving on one made you crazy. Scott closed the door and latched it.

He turned to the basement again. Four more steps and he would be at the bottom. The lights were on, but not much light came up the stairway. He heard the humming of the high voltage transformer. He descended into the gloom.

The first thing Scott encountered in the main area of the basement was the column that helped support the building. About 2 feet across and hollow, the column was where the weights from the lights used to descend and turn gears that turned the light. A small hatch at the bottom of the column provided access to them. The floor was brick. And moist. The main room was about 10 feet wide and maybe 15 feet long. Bruce had told him the walls were 9 feet thick and the basement floor was about level with the landing lip, a few feet above the water. Two doors led to two smaller rooms.

To the left, right at the bottom of the stairs, was a utility room. The museum label called it "the room of obsolete technology." Scott went in. It was a maze of tanks, boilers, pipes, a furnace, desalinization unit, and all sorts of panels and gauges. None of it worked anymore.

Scott exited the utility room and went into the other room. Though in the past it had housed the air compressors that had powered the foghorn, now it was a small workshop and storage area. A single dim bulb cast a yellowish glow on an old table saw. Behind it were shelves of paint cans. To the right was a jumble of brushes, wood and pipe scraps, ropes, jars, tools, and a mess of other junk from across the years piled in the corners and on an array of plastic shelves.

Not much to see. Scott went back in the main room and stood in the middle. To his right, about ten ladders were leaning against the wall in a jumble. The wall rose to a storm hatch at the height of the base — about 18 feet. Scott had heard Bruce, one of the guides, explain that it was so hard to get supplies and equipment on and off Ledge Light that things tended to stay out here "a very long time." That was why there were so many ladders. "Ledge Light is a lot like Las Vegas," Bruce had joked. "What happens on Ledge Light stays on Ledge Light."

The detail that was most compelling in the main room was a deep alcove about 4 feet along the wall from the door to the utility room. It was fenced off by a blue metal mesh door with a sign: "Danger. Keep Out. High Voltage." A loud hum emitted from the darkness behind the mesh door, which had a big brass lock on it. It was where the high voltage cable from the shore came in and was split and converted for use in the building. Scott's phone light showed a big black box with some cables coming from it. There was a faint blue glow emanating from the transformer, and every so often it sent out a blue spark of crackling electrical energy. The alcove was at least 7 feet deep in the 9-foot thick walls of the base.

Being so close to high voltage made Scott's hands sweat and his breathing grow quicker. It was an unconscious response as his worst fear kicked in. He was glad for the mesh door that separated him from that humming electricity. He didn't like being even this close to all that voltage. He closed his eyes and took a deep breath.

Standing there, Scott felt there was something ominous about that alcove and the box and the hum. He looked around. What had happened to Everett down here? What terror had befallen him in these three small, cluttered rooms that would push him to madness?

Scott looked at the column with its tiny hatch. At the black iron spider web of trusses at its top, supporting the first floor. He felt the dampness, saw the dim reflections of the bare bulbs in tiny puddles on the brick floor. He could smell old oil, and the ion-charged electrical smell wafting from the alcove. The high voltage transformer was the only old thing in the building that still worked. It seemed almost alive back there in the darkness, waiting. A beast in a cage.

"Danger."

17

The Custom House in New London is the oldest continually operating custom house in America. It is a handsome granite colonial building on Bank Street, at the edge of the Thames River. It has seen its share of history over the years. It was where the slaves who revolted in 1839 aboard the famed Amistad ship were taken ashore. The building now houses the New London Maritime Society's museum. One of the items on display is the original fourth order Fresnel lens from Ledge Light. It was taken from the lighthouse in the mid 1980s and eventually wound up in the Custom House where it now resides as the centerpiece of exhibits about lighthouses and New London's rich maritime history.

Scott opened the big wooden front doors and entered the building. He was met by Bill LaRue, the chief docent of the maritime museum.

"Hello. Welcome to the Custom House," said Bill. "Please sign in."

Scott dutifully signed the guest register.

Tall, soft-spoken, and avuncular, Bill was a walking encyclopedia of local history. He guided visitors around the building and could spin fascinating historical narratives about whaling, the battle of 1812, the Amistad slave rebellion, the history of New London harbor, lighthouses, or, if you had the time, all of them.

Bill led Scott into the main display room of the Custom House. He asked Scott what he would like to know about. "We have an orientation film in the making," Bill said, "but it's not done yet. Not sure it ever will be."

"I'm heading out to Ledge Lighthouse," Scott explained. "And I wanted to see what you might have to say about it."

"Well, the Custom House Maritime Museum owns the lighthouse now," said Bill. "Over here, we have some handsome informative display panels. But the main thing is the original lens. That's it over there." He pointed to a faceted lens, about 3 feet tall, perched on a pedestal in the corner. It glowed and cast streaks of light on the adjacent walls.

Scott walked over to it.

"Give it a gentle push with your finger," Bill prompted.

Scott extended his index finger and, as directed, placed it at the base of the lens and pushed. The massive, faceted glass lens began to spin slowly, quietly. Scott could not believe such a light tap would spin such an obviously heavy object.

"It rests on a bed of mercury," Bill explained. "Almost frictionless."

The lens was not solid. It was a series of curved concentric prisms with spaces between them, all shaped into a bulls eye configuration by gleaming frames of brass.

"You can see the bulb isn't very big. Neither was the wick when they used kerosene to create a flame. The arrangement of the prisms, invented by the Frenchman Augustin-Jean Fresnel, is extremely effective at gathering, focusing, and magnifying light. This lens could be seen for 19 miles."

"So what did the keeper do?" asked Scott as he walked around the slowly spinning lens, marveling at its beauty. It was like a huge jewel.

"Well, keepers spent a lot of time cleaning and repairing, oiling and painting. Routine maintenance. As you can imagine, a building out in the middle of the ocean, surrounded by water and assaulted by wind and rain and snow, takes a beating. Always stuff to repair. But they were called 'keepers of the light,' after all, and the light was their main business.

"They had to fuel the kerosene reservoirs in the lens and trim the wicks so they burned clean and bright. They spent so much time trimming the wicks they were often called 'wickies.' The mercury below the light sometimes evaporated a bit. The keepers would inhale it or absorb it through their skin if they had to fiddle with it. It's poisonous. Makes you crazy. So some of them ended up 'wacky wickies.'" Bill said this seriously, without a trace of humor.

Scott wondered about Ernie.

"Every night, the keeper lit the light. The lens was turned by weights that hung down the center column. The wire went all the way from beneath the light to the building's foundation. That's six floors. They'd crank the weights up to the top, throw a lever, and the weights would slowly drop. As they did, they turned a series of gears that turned the light."

Bill bent over and pointed to a small box that held a spool of wire and a slot for a crank.

"See, there, under the light. That's where the wire for the weights was wound up, and there's the crank handle. It took about four hours for the weights to descend the whole way, then the keeper had to wind them back up. All night. Every night.

"The keeper's whole life revolved around this lens. The whole lighthouse was built to support it and the tiny flame within it. It was the heart and soul of the building and the men who lived there."

Bill and Scott walked around the lens admiring it, their faces periodically bathed in red light. When they were on opposite sides, Bill's face was distorted by the curved glass.

Scott said: "Apparently there was a keeper named Ernie in the 20s or 30s who committed suicide by jumping off the roof of Ledge Light."

"That's the legend you hear," Bill replied. "Most lighthouses seem to have ghosts. But if you want to talk about the spirit of a lighthouse, I think it's the foghorn. It sounds so sad, so melancholy. Like someone or something crying, wounded and afraid, maybe. I think folks hear the foghorn, and they can't help but imagine some tormented spirit out at the lighthouse."

Bill was quiet a moment, and then said gently:

"I'll make a sound that's so alone that no one can miss it, and whoever hears it will know the sadness of eternity and the briefness of life."

He looked at Scott. "That's from a Ray Bradbury story," Bill said. "I think he captures it pretty well."

Scott touched the lens again. Feeling the slightly warm glass, he felt connected to Ernie, whoever he was. He, too, had touched this glass. Stared at his reflection in the gleaming prisms. Scott thought about what he had heard and read about shadows that held spirits. He wondered if the converse were true. Could a light — this light — also hold the spirits of all the keepers who had tended it? The keepers who had measured the days of their lives by its slow spin?

Scott thought about the keepers. About Ernie. About Everett Fine alone in the lighthouse, getting more and more spooked as the night wore on. He imagined how a rattling window, or a shifting shadow caused by the light of a passing boat or the wail of the foghorn could have been magnified into things of terror. Scott saw the lens metaphorically: just as it took a small flame and magnified it, so too could the lens of one's imagination take a small fear and magnify it.

Lost in thought, Scott drifted away from the lens and looked around at some of the other exhibits. Bill hovered a few feet away, occasionally remarking on something or telling a background story.

Scott wandered slowly. His route took him to the stairwell, where a pretty, grey-haired woman was working on a wall mural. She was painting a scene of an old clipper ship sailing into New London harbor, passing by the tall white harbor light.

"That's Bettie," said Bill in a whisper. "Both she and her husband are history buffs and work in museums. She's painted murals in a number of places. She's a wonderful artist. This mural will be her legacy to us. To New London." Bill drifted away to the front door where he politely met some new visitors. "Please sign in."

Scott watched Bettie paint. She was so absorbed in her work, she didn't even notice him.

"It's beautiful," he said quietly.

Bettie turned to him, her bright blue eyes sparkling. "Thank you. I love landscapes. Or seascapes, to be more accurate."

"You really capture the spirit of the harbor."

Bettie took a few steps back and looked at the painting, absent mindedly wiping her hands on a paint-streaked rag.

"I'm trying," she said, studying her mural, squinting and tilting her head. "That's what painting is all about, really. Capturing the heart and soul of something. Its essence. You think I've got it?"

"You do. It wouldn't surprise me if that boat sailed right out of the painting and across the wall. It seems so real, so energized."

"I'm not trying to make it real so much as true," she said.

"You have it. Really."

"Thanks. That's encouraging. And I need it. I have a lot of painting to go." She turned back to the wall, picked up her palette, dabbed a brush on it, and began to paint again in quick delicate strokes.

Scott watched, fascinated, as she painted a few black shapes on the beach. They didn't look like anything. Then she pulled her brush through the wet paint and gave the blobs some shape. Arms appeared, then legs, then the brim of a hat. Not too precise or fussy, but recognizable. Scott marveled at how with just a few strokes, Bettie had transformed the meaningless black shapes into a group of picnickers. He told her as much.

She smiled at him. "I suggest. You complete. That's art," she said.

Scott left Bettie to her mural. He thanked Bill for his time, made a small donation, and left.

While all the maritime displays were interesting, it was the original lens of Ledge Light that made Scott feel his visit to the Custom House had been worth the trip. In its glittering prisms he had glimpsed the spirit of Ledge Light.

As Scott crossed the street to his car, he realized he had parked just down the street from the New London Antique

Store. His strange journey had started there when he had spotted Everett Line Fine's field case almost buried beneath magazines and books. Strange how things work out. What was that quote he had read in that magic novel?

"You never go so far as when you don't know where you're going."

How far would this unplanned journey take him?

18

T hat night, David called.

"I'm going to send you a few digital photos, Scott."

"Fine's half roll?"

"No, I haven't scanned them all yet. I'm sending just one shot. Frame 13. I was scanning them and checking them. I usually enlarge them 200 percent, then as much as 600 percent to check for dust, sharpness, chromatic aberrations — that kind of thing."

"And?"

"Well, I'm not sure, Scott. I had scanned frame 13, the one of the light at night shot from outside the lantern room. It was one of the more interesting images."

"Yeah, I have the print here, along with the others you made. I've been looking at them. They give a good feel for the lighthouse. Frame 13 is pretty abstract. What about it?"

"Well, like I said, I usually enlarge the scans to check them. I enlarged that shot and was moving around in it, and I thought I saw something."

"Saw something? What?"

"I don't want to say, Scott. Because if I say, you will be predisposed to see what I see. No, I want you to see for yourself. I showed it to Nike who doesn't see what I see. So we showed it to some neighbors. We're split. Half see what I see; half don't. When you blow it up, it gets confusing. It might just be our minds trying to make sense of the streaks and reflections, and reflections of reflections.

Anyway, I'm going to send you three JPEGS. The first is the frame as shot. The second is a portion enlarged 200 percent. The third is the spot where I see something enlarged 600 percent. Take a look. You decide."

"David, you didn't fool around with these in Photoshop, did you? Add in something just to pull my leg?"

"Scott, I don't do that kind of thing. All I did was enlarge the frame and tweak the sharpness and the contrast. That's it." David sounded offended. He was a purist. He wouldn't be caught dead creating Twice Seen Scenes.

"Okay, David. Sorry. I can't wait to see them. Send them over."

Scott looked at the enlargement he already had of frame 13. It was a contrasty, confusing photo of the lantern room shot from outside on the catwalk. He didn't know what David could have seen.

The email came in a few minutes later.

David wrote: "Here are the shots, Scott. Let me know what you think when you've had a chance to take a good look at them. Best, David."

Scott pulled the three attachments off the email. They were labelled "Frame 013_As Shot, Frame 013_200%, Frame 013_600%."

The first file, Frame 013_As Shot, was pretty much like the print he had. Maybe a little more detailed and a bit sharper. David had used Photoshop to define the edges just a bit and to bring out some of the shadow detail. Looking at it, Scott didn't see anything.

The second file, Frame 013_200%, showed more noise, as would be expected from an enlargement. David had zoomed in on the far windows of the lantern room, to the left of the light. Since the photo was shot through two panes of thick glass with a very bright light source in the scene, there were reflections everywhere. The scratches in the glass also caught the light and appeared as hundreds of little comet-like streaks against the darkness of the night beyond the panes. The photo was a confusion of blurry shapes, dark blobs, and white streaks.

In a dark area just below a diamond mullion, Scott thought he saw something. It was vague, just the merest suggestion of — of what? He couldn't really tell. It was just some very faint shapes, suggestive, but no more. He moved on to the final enlargement.

The third file, Frame 013_600%, was a magnification of the area with the faint shapes. They were behind the outer pane of glass seen through the pane where Everett had stood to shoot the picture. The reflections and steaks again dominated the frame. They looked like comets. But then, squinting, Scott thought the random shapes became something familiar, just as the painter Bettie's dark shapes had become picnickers.

Could it be?

He squinted and thought he saw ... a face!

Yes, he could see it now! Two eyes. The hint of a nose. The edge of a cheek, catching the light. A dark curved line that could be a mouth. Perhaps the suggestion of a braided strand on the brim of a hat!

The face was so vague that as soon as Scott saw it, it seemed to dissolve away into a meaningless mess of dark and light. A chiaroscuro of confusion.

But then it came back.

Scott looked at the photo for long while. It kept playing a trick of perception on him, like an optical illusion. One second it appeared as a face, the next as just shapes. Scott knew we tend to find — or create — faces when we look at things. Chuck had had a paranormal term for this: a simulacrum.

Scott could not decide. Was the photograph a meaningless misfire? Or the image of a ghost? Was it a self-portrait, the reflection of a man descending into madness?

Maybe the picture would make more sense once Scott was out there at the light at night and could study for himself the reflections in the windows of the lantern room. He remembered how Zook had looked by day, how the thick glass had distorted his face. At night, a face might not be clear at all. It might be just a distorted simulacrum. As it was in the photograph.

Like so many other pieces of this puzzle, frame 13 was evocative but not conclusive.

He called David and told him so.

"We see what we want to see in photographs," said David. "We filter their objective documentation through our subjective interpretation."

"I thought photographs show the truth," said Scott.

"They may show it, but can we see it?"

Scott recalled what Bettie had told him about painting. The painter suggests, the viewer completes. Maybe photographs were the same. And Everett's tape, too. Maybe even Ledge Light itself.

The lighthouse suggests stories, and we complete them — colored by our interpretations, shaded by our fears.

Frame 13 - As shot

Frame 13 - Enlarged 200%

Frame 13 - 600%

19

This journey, kicked off by finding Everett Fine's case, had taken Scott to some very different feeling places: The cluttered chatterbox of Danielle's barber shop. The offices of the Groton Paranormal Group. The von Schlippe art gallery. The Egyptian room at the Lyman Allyn Museum. The eerie Miskatonic Mental Hospital. Each place had added its own layer to the story he was putting together. The people he had talked to had added their perspectives. His visit to Ledge Light had given him a firsthand sense of the place. A tape and a series of photographs — one in particular — had all added detail and texture. And yet, the central enigma remained. What exactly had happened to Everett Line Fine in the basement of Ledge Lighthouse that had caused him to go mad? Scott had to find out.

He was back at the Miskatonic Mental Hospital. Back in Dr. Markhal's waiting room. Back looking at the animation cel of Wiley Coyote, the poster child for obsession. Scott had come to understand a lot more about obsession as he teased out Everett Fine's story. He had, perhaps, dipped in it a bit himself.

Ding! Ding!

Anne: I just checked the home messages and there was a new one but it got cut off. Did you happen to listen to it? See the caller ID? Maybe it was Dr. Falk? I've been trying to reach you.

Scott: Sorry. I am in a bad reception area. I saw that message this morning. Not the doctor. Someone selling toasters.

Anne: Oh. Damn! I wish Falk would call already!

Scott: I know. Sorry.

Anne: Oh well. We wait. We wait. We wait. Where are you?
Scott: In a mental hospital.
Anne: Have I been that bad!?
Scott: LOL. No. Part of my research.
Anne: I won't even ask. See if they have a bed for me while you're there.
Scott: Will do. How about a king size for us both?
Anne: Deal.
Scott: Gotta go. Love you!
Anne: Madly in love with you!

Anne was back to being nervous. Not that he blamed her. Waiting for a doctor to call and tell you the results of a crucial test was very hard. The vast mechanism of a hospital, with all its bureaucracy and regulations, didn't speed the process along nor take in to account how excruciating the waiting could be. And HIPAA made it impossible for Scott to call and find out anything on Anne's behalf. They would just have to wait.

Dr. Markhal came out to the waiting room and greeted him.

"Doctor, I've been wondering about Wiley and his obsession with the roadrunner. Did he ever catch him?" Scott was really wondering whether he would ever figure out Everett Fine's story.

"Oh no! That wasn't allowed," she said with a laugh.

"Allowed?" asked Scott. "By whom?"

"Well, allegedly by the team of animators, lead by Chuck Jones. There was supposed to be a set of rules that governed the stories, believe it or not. One was that all devices and supplies Wiley buys in his pursuit of the Roadrunner must come from the ACME company. Another was that gravity should always be Wiley's enemy. And of course an iron-fast rule was that Wiley would never catch the roadrunner."

"Bummer," said Scott.

"Not that Wiley knew that, of course. He was doomed to keep trying, though he could really stop at any time. That's obsession for you."

Scott just shook his head and hoped he'd fare better. They went back to her office and settled in.

"So, you've listened to Fine's tape, and been out to the lighthouse?" Markhal asked.

"Yes, both."

"And?"

"Well, the tape is intriguing. But hard to tell exactly what was happening. It's like listening to someone talking on the phone. It's a one-sided conversation."

"Yes," said Markhal. "And there are times when he isn't talking when there is just silence or footsteps or other noises."

"Right," said Scott. "I listened to some of them over and over. Funny how sounds out of context can be so puzzling."

"I know. I was listening for clues that might have helped me determine if Fine was also having memory blackouts."

"Becoming unconscious?" Scott asked.

"No. When someone is having memory blackouts they are quite awake. And doing things. They just don't remember. It's not uncommon for people who are under stress, or really drunk or under the influence of drugs to forget what they did."

"How does that figure in with Fine, doctor?"

"Well, something like the little carved figure he had... I can't recall its name."

"Morgan."

"Right. Morgan. Fine put it in one room when he got there and, if I remember correctly, he found it somewhere else later."

"Yes, at the top of the stairs."

"Well, if it was inhabited by a spirit, that could account for its moving. But it could also be that Fine moved it himself, then did something else, then came back and found it and had no memory at all of moving it. So, to him, it was scary. It was possessed somehow. It was real."

"There's no way to know exactly what was going on?" asked Scott.

"Unfortunately not. You don't hear it on the tape, at least not clearly. But memory blackout was one thing that, clinically, I had to consider."

"It gets complicated, doesn't it, doctor? Determining what was real, what was imaginary?"

"It *is* complicated. And ambiguous. But whatever happened, on the tape, Fine is coming unraveled, that's for sure. I suppose it was inevitable."

"Inevitable?" Scott asked. "What do you mean by that?"

Sigrid Markhal spun in her chair and looked out the window. She reminded Scott of Chuck who did the same, as if the window were a window not to the outside, but to memory. He waited.

She sat there looking out the window close to a minute before she spoke again, subdued, her back still to him.

"Fine was a patient of mine long before he went to Ledge Light."

"Really?" said Scott, stunned.

"Yes. Some years ago. He was having problems. A mix of depression and some delusional thinking. Not all that uncommon in young men, really. He came here for a month or so for treatment."

"On his own, or did his family send him?"

"Well, let's just say he was encouraged to come to me. His father was alive back then. His mother had already passed away, sadly. He was an only child. His father couldn't seem to get through to him at that time, and some of Fine's behavior was a bit strange. His father found me, we talked, and eventually Everett came here."

"Did you cure him?"

Markhal laughed. "Cure is a relative term in this business, Mr. Edwards. Sometimes psychological problems resolve themselves. But more often, it's a matter of giving a patient an insight into what's going on and helping them find ways of coping. When Everett left us, I thought he would be able to deal with life okay. And I encouraged him to keep in touch with me."

"Did he?"

"Yes. Especially when his father died. That was very hard on him. He came back for a few more sessions with me. A lot of hand-holding, mostly. He needed someone, poor guy."

Markhal slowly spun her chair so she was facing Scott. He wondered how much baggage she was carrying because of Fine. In her list of fears, he imagined losing a patient would rank pretty high. Her pretty features were traced with sadness, as if confirming what he thought.

"When did he get into the paranormal research?" Scott asked.

"After his father died. It's not uncommon for people who have such an intimate loss to embrace spirituality, or religion or to start poking into the supernatural. It's a natural tendency to want to connect with someone we love who's passed away. Part of it is the denial of death. Part of it is the power of love. For some people, it's a passing thing. For others, it's the beginning of a true spiritual awakening.

"And for Everett?" Scott asked.

"For Everett, it led to a career."

"Maybe not a healthy one," said Scott.

"Maybe not. But perhaps doing paranormal investigations was a way for him to deal with his loss more openly. I can't say I thought it was the best thing for him to pursue, but he seemed to find it a good outlet for his curiosity and inventiveness. I was worried about it for him on an emotional level. But I think Everett was truly fascinated by the scientific challenge of finding and observing and documenting ghosts. I saw him a few times after he started doing that work, and he seemed to be coping pretty well. He seemed to have his feet on the ground."

"What about his paranormal work at Ledge Light? Did you know he wanted to go out there?"

"Well, I had told him to keep me abreast of his work. I said I was fascinated by it. I wasn't, really. I just wanted him to feel comfortable telling me what he was up to, so I could help if I felt he was having problems."

Scott remembered the note at the bottom of the page in Fine's notebook: *"Tell doctor."*

Markhal continued: "He came here a few days before he went to the lighthouse. He was excited. Maybe a little too excited. I remember what he said because it was vivid and he was so animated. He went on and on about seeing a sculpture hit by lighting, about a ghost at the lighthouse, a new invention he had and all sorts of stuff. I was worried about him. He was still grieving his father. He was vulnerable. I told him to wait, but he was determined to get out there."

"Not much you could do."

"No," said Markhal. She opened her top desk drawer and took out an amber pill bottle.

"But I did give him one of these," she said.

"What is it? A tranquilizer?"

"No. Not exactly. It's an experimental drug. Still in development. Its code name is TFD6, which stands for The Fear Drug, Formulation 6."

"The Fear Drug?" Scott asked.

"Yes. It's been in development trials by the military for some time now. And a few select places, like the Miskatonic Hospital, have also been in on the trials. Mostly it's been tested in Afghanistan. The Fear Drug, as its name implies, it's supposed to help with extreme fear. Like someone at war, in a combat zone. Or firefighters. Or police. When we are terrified, our adrenaline starts pumping, our cortisone levels spike — all sorts of physiological and psychological changes occur to help us deal with the situation."

"Fight or flight," said Scott.

"Yeah, the old survival mechanism. But like anything, all those chemical and mental changes have their side effects. Adrenaline gives us strength and stamina and maybe courage, but it can also skew our judgement and make us too jumpy. Too hair-triggered. The idea behind TFD is to help modulate the fear response to a level that is helpful, not overwhelming."

"Does it work?" asked Scott

Markhal shrugged. "Too early to tell. The problem with testing it in a war zone is that lots of the subjects get killed. We don't know if TFD helped them or not. There are always surprises when developing a new drug. Especially one dealing with the very difficult and elusive subject of human behavior."

"What about here at the hospital? What were the results"

"Fine was the only patient I gave a pill to. He was the only patient I've had that I knew was heading into a situation that might cause him extreme fear."

"Why did you think that?"

"Fine told me all about Ledge Light. When he got done, I concluded that his mental state was fragile enough that his imagination might turn on him and he might, essentially, scare himself to death. On the other hand, given what he'd told me, he might encounter a real ghost. That would terrify anyone.

"I had mixed feelings about Everett going out to Ledge Light. On the one hand, the best way to conquer our fears is to confront them. On the other, the best way to lose your mind is to be scared out of it."

Scott mulled over what Markhal had said. Then asked: "Did he take the pill?"

"I have no idea. I listened to the tape over and over. He mentions it, but I don't know if he took it. And, as you know, the tape ends before he experienced whatever it was in the basement that pushed him over the edge. If he took it, I guess it didn't work. Who knows?"

"He knew the pill was experimental?"

"Of course! I explained it to him. He knew what it was all about. I didn't promise him much. I just gave him one and told him to take it if it all got too much for him. It might help; it might not. It wasn't a silver bullet."

Scott eyed the pill bottle a moment. He thought about Fuzzy's suggestion he bring a silver bullet. TFD6 might not be one, but maybe it could be useful.

"Why don't you give me one?" he asked.

Markhal looked surprised. "Really?"

"Sure," said Scott. "I'm going to Ledge Light soon myself. When there is a full moon, just like the night Everett went out. I have no idea what lies in wait for me out there. I'm not as fragile as Fine was. But if I encounter the ghost of Ernie and get too spooked, maybe TFD will come in handy. I can tell you if it helped."

Markhal spun the bottle in her hand. The pills clattered inside, sounding like a rattlesnake. Scott saw a warning label. Markhal looked at it and then at him.

"You have to sign a waiver. Fine did. Anyone who takes an experimental drug has to acknowledge they know it's experimental, unproven, and may have side effects."

Scott hadn't thought about that. "Side effects? Do you know of any?"

"Not yet," said Markhal. "I expect a report to come in any time now." She looked at the pile of reports on her desk. "You know, my worst fear may be that I'll never get through these."

She looked at Scott. "Your call. You can have a pill. Whether you use it is entirely up to you."

Scott looked at the bottle. "What would you do?"

"I wouldn't go out to the lighthouse," she said.

Scott thought it over. He was going. No doubt about that. As for the pill, he figured there was no harm in at least having one, just in case. If he reached a point of absolute terror, he could take his chances with The Fear Drug and whatever side effects it might have. How bad could they be?"

"I'll take one," he said.

Markhal took off the bottle cap and took out a single pill. It was bright red. And big.

"I'm not very good at swallowing pills," said Scott. "Especially ones that big."

"Well, just take it with plenty of water and gulp." Markhal said. She went to a cupboard and took out a small plastic bag, dropped the pill in it and sealed it. She wrote "TFD6" on the bag. As she was about to hand it to Scott, she smiled and took it back and wrote some more.

"Here you go," she said. "I hope you don't have to use it. I'll go get the waiver for you to fill out." She gave him the bag and went into another room.

Scott looked at what she'd written: "*Take one at night if terrified by ghost.*" Well, at least she had a sense of humor.

Scott held the tiny bag in his hand and stared at the bright red pill. What would be the worst thing he could encounter out there? All he could think of was that sign on the high voltage cage.

"Danger."

20

"After what happened to Everett, you want to spend the night out there?" Chuck Freedman was incredulous. "Why?"

"Because the more pieces of the puzzle I put together, the more I can't decide if everything that happened was just Everett's imagination and fears running wild, or if he had some sort of genuine paranormal encounter out there. I think if I spend the night, I'll find out."

"So they're really going to let you stay the night?" Chuck asked.

"Yes," said Scott. "It was hard to get permission. I had to meet with the Ledge Light Foundation, convince them, sign a waiver. It wasn't easy."

"When are you going?"

"In a few days. Night of the full moon, just like Everett Line Fine."

Scott had returned to the office of the Groton Paranormal Group. He wasn't sure why. He had a few more questions about the world of the paranormal. And about Everett Fine. Maybe he was just looking for someone to talk him out of it. He had told Chuck about Everett's final break when he had jumped to his death from the hospital roof. Just like Ernie had done at the lighthouse. Apparently Chuck had not heard of Fine's fate. He was shocked. No doubt he felt some responsibility. Scott also told Chuck about the tape of Fine's night on Ledge Light and offered to share it.

Chuck had turned in his chair and was staring out the window.

Scott let it all sink in. He busied himself looking through his own notebook of research. Mary Angela Lenska came in from her office.

"Hi, Scott," she said. "What brings you back our way?"

"Scott is going out to Ledge Light," said Chuck. "He wants to experience what Everett Fine did."

"Really? Didn't he go mad?"

"Worse than that, Angie," Chuck said sadly. "He jumped off the roof of the mental hospital."

Angie looked stricken. "My God! That's terrible!" She sat down and shook her head. "Poor guy," she added. They sat in silence.

"Maybe we should come along with you," said Chuck at last. "We have expertise in this stuff, you know."

"I appreciate it, Chuck. Maybe another time. Right now, I want to put myself in Everett's position: alone at the lighthouse at night. See what happens."

"What happens if you see a ghost?" asked Angie in all seriousness. "What will you do?"

Scott hadn't really thought it through. "Probably shit in my pants," he said in all seriousness.

"Always a good investigative technique," muttered Chuck. After a moment he told Angie about the tape.

"Really!" she said. "I'd like to listen. Do you hear ghosts?"

"It's hard to tell what is going on at times," Scott said. "And everything is from Fine's perspective, so who knows what's real, what isn't."

"Can you hear what happened to him in the basement?" Chuck asked.

"No. The tape ends just as he's heading down there."

"Damn! We may never know," Chuck said, shaking his head.

"Chuck, I've been wondering about Everett. Do you know if he had any particular fears? Phobias?"

"Why do you ask?"

"I talked to his doctor at the mental hospital. She said if something had triggered a fear response in him that night, then he might have been more susceptible to his own imagination or …"

"A real ghost," Chuck finished.

"Yes."

"Scott, what more did he need? He was alone in a dark, creepy, deserted lighthouse a mile from shore. Wouldn't that be enough to spook him?"

"Maybe. Maybe not. You guys spend half your lives in dark, creepy, deserted places, don't you?"

"Yeah."

"So, maybe it was that. But maybe it started with something else."

Angie chimed in: "Scott, in your research, have you come across anything about the ombralogists?"

"No, I haven't."

"I'm not surprised. They are not very well known. You'd have to really be into this stuff to have come across them. The ombralogists were a small group of followers of an Italian named Francesco Lopergolo Tuti. He was around in the late eighteenth century. He wrote a book: *La Vita tra le Ombre*. 'Life in the Shadows.' He believed that shadows were a kind of life form. They are created by people and animals and objects, but Tuti believed they could and did lead their own lives. Separate from what created them. It's kind of hard to wrap your mind around. It might require drugs. But imagine that a shadow is like a photograph, and that once it is made, what made it can move on, but the record remains. We think of shadows as connected to what causes them, but what happens if they are just created and then have their own life?"

"Drugs might help," said Scott, having a hard time imagining what Angie was describing.

Angie laughed, then continued: "Francesco Tuti had some followers. The Italian word for shadow is 'ombra' so this little cult called themselves 'ombralogists.' Tuti went on to expand his theory. He came to believe that shadows were the home of spirits. He wrote a second book: *Spiriti nelle Ombre*, which translates to 'Spirits in the Shadows.' The books, Tuti, and the ombralogists were very obscure. It took me hours on the Internet to find a copy of the books. They make for interesting reading, so long as you can read Italian. Tuti makes a pretty good case for shadows being more than the absence of light. Read his books and you might start to believe that shadows possess paranormal life of some sort. You might come to not trust your own shadow."

"Shadows with their own lives. The mind boggles!" said Scott.

"My point is, Scott, that you shouldn't dismiss the darkness and shadows of Ledge Light. If you believe what Francesco Lopergolo Tuti wrote, as I do, shadows are full of malice and mischief. More than enough to drive Everett — or anyone for that matter — off the deep end."

"Duly noted," said Scott. "So it could have been something in the shadows. A real ghost. Or something else. Something that started to put him off balance. So I come back to my original question. Did Everett have any particular fears he might have mentioned?"

Chuck picked up a paperweight. Etched inside it was a question mark. Scott could see Chuck's focus change as he stared at it and roamed through his memories. After a minute Chuck spoke softly.

"I do remember that Everett told me once when we were in a dark basement somewhere that he was scared of rats. And with good reason. It was quite a story. If I remember right, as a kid he was pretending to be an archaeologist exploring a tomb. He climbed into a concrete storm drain and went in quite a ways. It was pitch dark. He heard scratching and turned on his flashlight. There were rats. Lots of rats. He was surrounded by dozens of beady red eyes, all looking at him. He ran out as fast as he could, but not before the rats swarmed around him. He never forgot it. Hell, who would?"

Scott had listened to the tape. He knew about Everett's encounter with the closet full of rats. He wondered, now, if there had been real rats or if Everett had just conjured them up in his fear. Scott had tried to hear the scratching Everett heard, but the tape had not been clear. He just couldn't tell. The problem with everything Scott had heard on the tape was that it was all subjective. It was Everett Fine's reporting of what he saw, or thought he saw. Heard, or thought he heard. Objective verification was hard to come by.

He looked at Chuck.

"On the tape, Everett heard scratching at a closet door in one of the rooms. He went to investigate. His fear of what was behind that door is palpable. You can hear it in his voice."

"We encounter a lot of closed doors in our line of work, Scott," said Angie. "And a lot of them are scary. You just don't know what you might find when you open them."

"Skeletons in closets," said Scott.

"Yeah. Something like that," said Chuck without humor.

"It is pretty obvious Fine was scared. He debated with himself quite a while whether or not he should open the door."

"Did he open it?"

"Yes, he did."

"And what was in the closet?"

"Rats. Hundreds of them."

"Jesus!" Chuck exclaimed.

"He actually saw rats?" Angie asked, incredulous.

Scott shrugged. "Who knows? Everett certainly thought so. It was the start of his coming unglued. Or maybe he was already unglued."

Chuck thought it over then said: "Interesting, isn't it, that he would encounter his worst fear out there."

"Yes, it is."

"Like the lighthouse knew," Chuck said.

"Or maybe it was Ernie," said Angie. "Softening him up."

"Maybe so," said Chuck. "Maybe so. To make him easier to possess. If a person is stressed, he's vulnerable. There are cracks in his armor, and the spirit finds them."

"You think Ernie took him over?" Scott asked.

"Possibly," said Chuck. "If you learned about Ka you know that the spirits of the dead look for a new home. That's the point of a Ka figure, isn't it? But in theory, if there is a living person handy, a spirit would prefer them. The term I use is 'corporeal inhabitation' — when a spirit possesses a living person."

"Someone who is fragile. Scared."

"Yes."

Angie explained: "We theorize about something called 'instigated memory hallucinations.' We think spirits can root around in someone's memory. Find scary things they have experienced, or seen, or maybe just a story they've heard. And then cause those fears to be manifested as very vivid hallucinations. Waking dreams. Very real when you experience them."

"The way dreams are," said Scott.

"Exactly," Angie replied. "When we dream, we don't question the reality of the experiences, no matter how weird. Dreams have their own logic, their own laws of nature. We accept them. They seem absolutely real to us."

Scott asked: "So the spirit of Ernie might have poked around in Everett Line Fine's memory and found what he was most scared of — rats — and made him believe there was a closet full of them."

"In theory," said Chuck.

"To soften him up. To cause a crack he could seep into to possess Fine."

"Quite possibly. That's one explanation," Chuck said.

"Is there another?" asked Scott.

"Yes. There could have been a closet full of rats. In either case, the terror was real."

Chuck let that sink in. He looked Scott in the eye and spoke firmly:

"You sure you don't want us to come with you? We could watch out for one another."

"Thanks, Chuck. But no. Everett was out there alone, and I want to be, too."

"Suit yourself. But listen, Scott: you're not dealing with a kid in a cheesy rubber monster costume out there. You may be getting in over your head. Especially if a ghost is really looking for a home. Be careful. Things at Ledge Light might not be what they seem to be."

21

The small skiff left the Project Oceanology docks, just east of Avery Point, at 5 p.m. It was a calm afternoon, and the captain, Russell, headed past the blue Envirolab II boat used for the tours. Russell rounded the stone jetty, heading south. As soon as they cleared the point, Ledge Light came into view.

Scott Edwards was excited. His time had finally come to spend the night at Ledge Light. It had not been easy to arrange. But he had been persistent.

"You're lucky to get to do this," said Russell, steering toward the light a mile out to sea. "Not many folks get to spend the night out there anymore."

"Have you?"

"Sure. Plenty of times. We used to take kids out on field trips, and I've been on work parties. But, with the rare exception, no overnights anymore."

"Why?"

Russell chuckled. "One bad experience. But now it's mostly liability issues. Lawyers and insurance agents. We fear them more than Ernie."

"Speaking of which," said Scott, "have you ever had any encounters with Ernie? Or ghosts?"

"Nope."

Russell kept his eyes on the light. It was so incongruous — it looked like a French chateau that had somehow found its away to the sea and was just drifting out there.

"Actually," Russell said, "I played Ernie in the orientation film they screen at the museum inside the light. We spent the night out there filming that."

"Really?" Scott said. "I saw that film. Quite good. Very evocative. I bought the DVD. I had no idea it was you."

Russell smiled.

"I didn't jump, though," he said. "I told the director I wouldn't go that far."

"Don't blame you."

Both men lapsed into silence as the boat bounced along to the lighthouse. It only took 10 minutes to reach Ledge Light. Scott observed again what he had experienced on his tour aboard the Mystic Whaler. Ledge Light appeared small until they got about 100 feet away, and then it seemed to suddenly grow larger. It was a trick of perspective: with nothing near it to provide scale, it was hard to judge its size. But now it loomed above them as they slowed and pulled alongside the base. Ledge Light was actually quite large: the monumental concrete base, the three-story brick building topped by the mansard roof punctured by a dozen dormers, and then a two-story light tower on top of that.

Russell flipped two white bumpers over the side and nudged the boat alongside the landing lip that circled the concrete base. The three-foot concrete deck was cracked and crumbling. The metal that sheathed it was rusting.

"We need to replace this," Russell said as he stopped the motor and gingerly held on to the metal. "We just need a few million to do it." Russell circled a rope around a cleat but kept the engine idling.

He turned to Scott and asked: "Got all you need?"

"Everything's in my pack."

Russell watched apprehensively as the high-speed ferry to Block Island approached from New London. He took out a single key attached by a chain to a small rubber shark bristling with teeth — a miniature of the great white in "Jaws."

"Here, take this," he said to Scott. "It unlocks everything on the lighthouse. All the locks are keyed the same. Don't go where you shouldn't! I have to get out of here before that ferry goes by," he said. "It kicks up a hell of a wake and it can smash the boat hard against the lighthouse. Nobody likes the Block ferry. You're on your own out here. The lights are funky, so don't be surprised if they flicker or just cut out. It's probably not Ernie. Or maybe it is. Who knows? Don't screw around with the light up top. Or the foghorn. The Coast Guard wouldn't appreciate it. You've been out on a tour, right?"

"Yes."

"Okay, so you know the layout of the place. Don't open any doors that say 'No Entry.' Heed the warning signs. Watch out for the foghorn. It can come on at any time. Be careful in the dark."

Russell shook Scott's hand. Scott grabbed his backpack. It was low tide and the lip was about four feet above the water, so it was a bit of a scramble to get up to it from the boat. Scott climbed onto the light as Russell pulled the rope off the cleat and put the engine in gear. He pulled away just as the ferry roared by. Thirty seconds later, as Russell had said, its wake hit the base of Ledge Light in a series of big, angry waves. He could see why Russell didn't want to have the small boat tied up to the light any longer than needed.

He yelled up at Scott: "Don't hurt yourself. Nobody will come to the rescue. You're out here for the night. I'll be back in the morning for you. Say 'hi' to Ernie. Good luck!" Then he turned the boat to the northeast and headed back to Avery Point.

Scott watched the small skiff head back to Avery Point. The sound of its motor was soon swallowed by the incessant sound of waves hitting the lighthouse. He watched until the boat disappeared around the point.

Scott was alone on Ledge Light.

22

S cott had a brief flash of trepidation. What had he gotten himself into? As he stood at the rail of the lighthouse and watched the sunset and darkness creep over the area like a blanket being pulled up, his isolation hit home. Ashore, talking about coming out here, planning his visit, the reality of being truly isolated was vague, theoretical. Now, he was here, and he was here alone.

He walked up the three granite steps and unlocked the front door. He pulled it open and, as he had seen Zook do, kept it open with a rope around the doorknob that hooked over a thick electrical conduit that snaked along the nearby bricks.

He stepped into the front hallway.

On his Mystic Whaler tour, on a sunny day, the place was full of people. The rooms were crowded with tourists talking about the exhibits, looking out the windows, posing for selfies with Ernie in the background, buying stuff at the gift shop. The place had burbled with the sounds of the orientation film, conversations, the talk of the tour guides, and the occasional cry of shock as someone walked into Ernie's room.

None of that now. Standing in the front hall, Scott found himself immersed in a profound silence. A frisson of expectancy hit him. He turned and looked out at the view of sky and water and land framed by the doorway. The distant sound of the waves wafted up from the base in a hissing, rhythmic cadence.

The blue door to his left was locked. "Danger: Battery Charging Area. No Smoking." He had the key to the lock, now, and was tempted to take a look. But he had been warned by Russell not to enter restricted areas or any door with a warning sign, so he wouldn't. Instead, he stepped into the room to his right — the gift shop.

He put his pack down on the table with the guest sign-in book. This had been Fine's "headquarters" and it would be his. He looked through the guest book, which covered four years, and browsed the comments people had made during the tours. There was a lot of praise for the hard work done by the Ledge Light Foundation in restoring the lighthouse and creating the museum.

"Always wanted to see inside! Now I have."

"Kudos to everyone who works on this beautiful building!"

"WOW! What a fabulous job you are doing. What a great treasure."

"Absolutely amazing! Very thought provoking."

"I loved the whole thing!! The movie made me cry!"

There were also numerous reactions to the figure of Ernie, the most colorful being:

"Loved the tour and Ernie mannequin. Scared the crap out of me!"

Scott flicked on the overhead light, which worked. He unpacked his supplies on the table. He had packed light. He was not armed with the tools of ghost hunting. No Phanoptiscope for him. He had a small notebook and pen, a couple of sandwiches, a thermos of coffee, some bottles of water, his cell phone, and Morgan. He wasn't sure why, but perhaps in Everett's memory, he thought his good luck mascot should come along. In his pocket he had a silver pill case containing the TFD-6 pill Dr. Markhal had given him "just in case his fears got the better of him."

Frowning, he searched the backpack. Where was his phone charger? The main part was empty so he searched the pockets. Nothing! He did not have his phone charger!

"Damn!" He couldn't believe he had forgotten it! Fool! He turned the phone on and checked the battery level. 73 percent. Well, that should last him the night if he didn't tax it too much.

He wandered next door to the briefing room. He admired the mural of the lighthouse on the wall, then sat on the padded bench beneath it. Though he didn't plan on sleeping much, he stretched out to see how comfortable it was in case he wanted to nap. He closed his eyes. It was comfortable enough. It would do.

He remembered he had promised to text Anne when he was at the light. So he did.

Scott: Hi, Sweetie. Here at Ledge Lighthouse. Safe and sound. Sun just set. Beautiful out here. Wish you were here to enjoy it with me. I sure do miss you. Well, you'll be with me in spirit tonight. Love you!

He decided not to tell her about the charger. She would think he was an idiot. Which he was. He waited a few minutes, but there was no reply. She was probably out to dinner or at some conference function.

Scott decided to tour the building, this time with nobody else to elbow out of the way. The light was waning. It wouldn't be long before the bright rooms were filled with shadows. His footsteps sounded loudly as he roamed about. The sense of isolation was palpable. On the Mystic Whaler tour, he knew he was only on the light for an hour or so, and with plenty of people. The boat had bobbed outside, visible through the windows, a comforting presence. Now, there was no boat. No deadline for departure. No companions. He was out here for hours, for the whole night. He shook away the vague uneasiness.

As he wandered around, he thought about Everett's tape and what he'd seen through the Phanoptiscope, the layered apparitions of generations of keepers. It was an odd feeling to think of them here, now, working, playing cards, listening to the radio, walking about, doing chores, partying with college girls — all invisible to him. Without the Phanoptiscope, or a mind going mad, perhaps, he would not see them as Fine had.

Maybe that was a good thing.

Scott had avoided Ernie's room on his solitary tour of the light, but eventually his path took him back to the furnished keeper's room on the third floor. "Ernie's Room" a sign on the closed door read. As he grabbed the brass door handle, Irma Streeter's words came back to him: *"You can't help but wonder what you'd do if you opened a door and there he was."*

Scott let go of the doorknob. He stared at the door.

"I'm being silly," he said to himself. "I've seen the mannequin and that's all it is. Creepy to be sure, but just a fake figure."

He grabbed the doorknob again.

"Sure, just a mannequin," his little inner voice said. "But what happens if you open the door and he IS standing there? What are you gonna do? Where are you gonna run?"

"Shit." Scott took a deep breath.

Stop this nonsense. The night is young. Don't talk yourself into being afraid. Just open the damned door.

"You can't help but wonder what you'd do if you opened a door and there he was."

Scott hesitated again, then turned the knob and opened the door.

No Ernie. Just the barrier to his left, an exhibit about ghosts on the wall to his right, and a small dormer window dead ahead. Another small sign on the wall read: "Caution. Ghost Area. Beware!" Ha, ha.

He stepped into the room.

He had seen the creepy mannequin, so there was no surprise when he stood at the barrier and saw it again. Still, he recoiled a bit. With the sunset, just a bit of dusky light hit Ernie's face and the letter of betrayal in his hand. He looked so angry! Ernie was so lifelike it would not surprise Scott if he turned his head and looked at him. Or took a step forward. He was glad there was a wood barrier across the room.

Then Scott laughed at himself. It was just this kind of thinking that would get him in trouble! The figure he saw was just some pipes and stuffing, a mask and some mannequin hands, a wig and glass eyes. It was just a representation of a human.

Now it was Fuzzy's words that came back to him.

"Ka could be the spirit returning to the body, but if there was no body, a statue or a representation of a human could work."

In the gathering gloom of dusk, the mannequin of Ernie faded into the shadows, giving him an even more menacing look. Scott didn't like it. He didn't like the thought of being out here all night, alone with this spooky figure. He backed out of the room, out of the "Ghost Area." He closed the door.

Ding! Ding!

Anne: Just got your text. How is it going out there?
Scott: Okay. Wandering around. It's getting dark.
Anne: Any ghosts?
Scott: Not yet.
Anne: Are you scared?
Scott: Not yet. How is it going with you?
Anne: Good. Keeping very busy. Learning a lot. Nice people.
Scott: Any time to relax?
Anne: Not too much. Just a little at the end of seminars. They keep us busy. Talks. Meals. Breakout sessions. The trade show. A field trip. But it's good to keep my mind off the other thing.

"The other thing." Yes, he knew what she meant. She was away at her conference, and he was on the lighthouse after spending days on the trail of Everett Line Fine. For both of them, they were escaping the grinding worrisome reality and fears of "the other thing." He sighed. He looked at his phone: 55 percent. He texted back.

Scott: Good. Keep busy. Don't worry. About anything, including me.
Anne: I'll try. You have a rescue plan?
Scott: Of course.

He lied. His only rescue plan was to swim a mile to shore.

Anne: That's good.
Scott: And if all else fails, my love, you can rescue me!
Anne: You got it! You get in a jam, just conjure me up!
Scott: I will.
Anne: So you have a good ghost story going?
Scott: Not sure. It's all pretty shadowy. Maybe tonight will tell the real tale.
Anne: Be safe out there. Don't do anything foolish, okay?
Scott: I won't. Promise.
Anne: Good. Well, off to my night's fun. We're learning about team building.
Scott: You with a team. Me alone.
Anne: You have me. In your heart.
Scott: Always and forever!
Anne: Gotta run.
Scott: Me too. The ghosts await me.
Anne: Say hi to them. Keep in touch.
Scott: Will do. Love you.
Anne: Love you more.

Scott looked at their text bubbles. His eyes fixed on one phase: "The other thing." He had almost forgotten about it. Now that she had reminded him, he wondered if he could cast it off, let it drift away from his thoughts like something thrown into the sea. He hoped so. Scott stared at his phone. At their conversation preserved in a string of bubbles on the glowing screen. They were together on that screen, but in reality they were in very different worlds!

It was nearly dark now. Scott walked into the long room on the third floor, where Fine had seen the men with his Phanoptiscope. Having seen Richard Moore's Twice Seen Scenes, Scott could easily imagine what it looked like to Fine. That evocative overlapping of people from different eras, their odd unawareness of someone standing so close in space, yet so far away in time.

Scott walked slowly around the room looking at the exhibits on the walls. One explained the workings of the light. Another chronicled the harrowing saga of the men in the hurricane of 1938. Yet another told the story of Ernie.

As Scott was reading about the keeper and his ghost, the ceiling lights flickered and went off.

Perfect.

Scott laughed. He already knew from talking with Zook during his Mystic Whaler tour that the lights in this room were constantly going off. The Ledge Light Foundation had hired a number of electricians to examine the lights, but fix them as they might, the lights remained finicky.

Proof of the ghost of Ernie!

Well, not very persuasive proof. He'd need to do better. In part, that's what Scott's investigation of Fine's night had become. He had caught the investigator's obsession with getting irrefutable and unambiguous proof of a ghost. A photograph used to be considered that proof. But the power of digital software to convincingly manipulate images — and by extension the reality they documented — had made photographic evidence less trusted.

David had assured him that he hadn't fooled with frame 13. So Scott could rule that out. But the ambiguity of what the photo really showed was haunting in its own right. Those who saw a face in the photo — the face of a keeper, the face of Ernie, perhaps — had their proof of a ghostly apparition. Those who saw just streaks and reflections had proof only of others' imaginations and their ability to find a face in a meaningless jumble of shadows and light.

When proof becomes ambiguous, it's no longer proof. It's just interpretation. It loses its persuasiveness.

It was impossible to read the exhibits without light, so Scott left the long room. He stood in the third floor hall and listened. He closed his eyes. Beyond the stillness and silence of the building, Scott heard things. The waves hitting the base, their slap wafting through the open front door. The distant cry of a bird. A gentle electric hum. The faintest whistle of wind through a cracked window. His own heartbeat.

Scott found himself alert. A bit tense. He knew too much about this place not to be wary. For over a century, men's lives had played out in these rooms. Adrift from everyday life ashore, isolated and at the mercy of the seas, the men who served on Ledge Light were still travelers. Their journey went nowhere through space as their home was bound to the ledge beneath it. But their voyage took them through days of routine and through hours alone with their own thoughts and feelings, fears, and dreams.

Countless men had spent countless hours polishing brass and painting walls and fixing things. And countless men had spent countless hours playing cards and Monopoly, building model ships and cooking meals. They'd measured their days by the coming and going of ferries. They'd seen the buildings and industries along the shore change over time. They'd watched white schooners become black submarines. They'd felt the savage assault of storms and the dreamy stillness of a foggy morning.

How many of the keepers had been burdened by loneliness and stifling boredom? By the grinding anxiety of isolation? By conflicts with their partners? By their own inner demons with plenty of time to wreak havoc on their minds?

Two men who had been on this light had committed suicide. One off the light itself and one off the roof of the mental hospital a night on the lighthouse had sent him to.

Scott began to think about Ka and thought forms, about panicked voices on tape, about rooms full of unseen men.

"I'm thinking too much," he said to himself again. "I don't want to talk myself into something. I have a long night ahead."

"Alone," a tiny voice in his head added.

Again that slight feeling of trepidation swept over him. Scott pushed it away.

He went down to the second floor. Though it had banisters, he didn't shy away from them or the shadows that lay below them like a deep dark sea. In defiance of fear, he held on to the railing as he went down the stairs and arrived at the second floor. As he rounded the corner and headed down the hallway toward the theater, he thought he heard something. He stopped. Listened.

There, again. He closed his eyes to concentrate.

Yes, he definitely heard it. A scratching sound. Behind him. Scott turned around and walked back down the hall. He stopped before the room at the end. Its door was closed. He heard the scratching faintly through the door.

"Just like on the tape," Scott thought to himself. Would he open the door and find a room full of rats? If so, it would certainly add credence to Everett's description of what was happening to him. But what would Scott do about a room full of rats? If he opened the door and they were there, they'd swarm all over the building. Not a good idea, as Fine had remarked. Yet how would he know what was behind the door if he didn't open it?

Scott pondered the problem. He realized there was a sensible solution. He would open it just a crack and peek in. If he saw so much as a single rat's whisker, he'd slam the door. He wouldn't give them a chance to escape. Scott grabbed the knob and pressed his ear to the door. He didn't hear the scratching now. He slid his head along the door until his eye was near the edge of it.

He gripped the door handle and took a deep breath and opened the door a crack.

He looked down.

Though it was almost dark out, the small room's three windows let in a dim glow.

Enough for him to see the room was empty.

No rats.

Scott exhaled and opened the door wider. The room was indeed empty. It was a cozy little room, with two walls finished in wood, the other two painted a dark blue. Scott walked in and saw the closet in the corner.

He heard scratching behind it.

This was the closet Everett had found the rats in. Scott stared at the wood door. He had opened it on his daytime visit and found nothing but some junk inside. Certainly no rats. Though he had found some scratch marks. He remembered asking Zook where the pipe inside went. Zook had told him to the cistern in the basement. Scott had to push away images of a tank full of rats down there, of rats climbing up the pipe, pouring out, massing inside the closet.

Did he see a thin pink tail flick by under the door?

Scott licked his lips. His throat was dry. He wanted to think this through. Again he worried that if he opened that door and rats swarmed out, they would spread all over the lighthouse. He'd be dealing with them everywhere all night. He could contain them by closing the door to this room. But then he would be trapped in a very small room full of rats.

Not a good thought.

Shit! He was thinking as Everett had thought, and he was beginning to feel the fear Everett had felt standing in front of this door at night. Alone in the lighthouse. Hearing things.

He wished the lighthouse didn't have so many doors. Closed doors are like closed boxes. You have no idea what might be inside. It was a damned box that had launched this whole journey! Again Scott shook his head trying to dispel his fearful thoughts.

"This is silly," he said to himself. "I'm letting my imagination run wild, and I haven't been here more than an hour or so. Be fearless." He had tried to make this his motto of late. Be fearless. Don't overthink things. Be brave and act. He was learning it from Anne.

He decided to leave the door to the room open. If rats came tumbling out of the closet, let the damned things swarm. Before he could talk himself out of it, he turned the brass doorknob and opened the closet door.

Did he see something move in there? Did he hear scratching?

Quickly, he turned on his phone's flashlight and shone it around the closet.

Nothing.

It was the same as when he'd looked in before. Just some harmless junk. The shag carpet. The loose-fitting pipe. But no rats. If they had been in there, they had heard him and fled. Scott examined the pipe. He started to imagine ... then stopped. He exhaled and gave a nervous laugh. Okay. He had opened two menacing doors and found nothing bad behind them. He wouldn't think about maybe seeing something in the closet before he turned his light on. No, the closet was empty. That was that.

Scott left the room. Directly across from it was another closed door with a sign on it that read "No Entry." He'd heed Russell's words and not go there. "Fine with me," he mumbled aloud. "If it says not to enter, I won't. Maybe the Ledge Light Foundation or the Coast Guard knows where the monsters are and sticks them in rooms marked 'No Entry.'" He chuckled at that. But, who knew? Maybe it was true.

He turned back toward the theater. It was nine o'clock. He hadn't really planned what he would do all night at the lighthouse. He had a vague notion to follow Everett's timetable and path through the building. Scott went back down to the first floor. It was dark now. He looked out the front door and was struck by how it framed the night sky and sea outside. It was a funny illusion. The doorframe looked like a picture frame, and the scene was a nice painterly seascape. But unlike a painting, this scene moved. Scott was drawn to it, and when he stepped through the doorway he had the strangest sensation of walking into another world. The confined spaces inside the lighthouse gave way to a place with no boundaries. Above, the sky feathered off to infinity, and all around the sea spread out and the distant land gave no sense of any limitations. A full moon tugged the tide higher and cast its mesmerizing shimmering silver beam across the water.

Scott undid the line keeping the door open and was going to close it. But he turned and was seduced by the view. Scott walked to the rail at the top of the stairway on the north side and looked at the lights on shore. They cast streaks on the water. He could see Mythic Mystery, a black smudge in the moonlit landscape. It was remarkably clear. He felt like he was looking at forever.

After a few minutes, Scott walked back toward the southwest corner.

The foghorn came on.

It was ahead of him about 20 feet. The sudden, unexpected blast of the horn on this clear night hit him like an explosion. His hands shot to his ears and he stumbled backwards and around the corner. The sound of the horn diminished. Scott lowered his hands.

And froze.

Someone was standing at the railing, a dark silhouette against the night sky.

23

Dr. Markhal hunched over the report on her desk. A single lamp lit the paper, her face, and a small area around her. Otherwise, her office was dark. She closed the report on "Convergence of Intelligence and Emotion in Dealing with Grief" and took off her glasses. She rubbed her eyes. The stack of reports she had read was getting taller, but the stack of unread reports was still higher. Would they never end?

She sat back in her chair and looked out the window. Above the dark pointed branches of a fir tree, the full moon was bright. Beautiful. Maybe when she was done, she would take a stroll around the grounds. It may have been her work place, but Markhal had come to enjoy the spookiness of a moonlit walk through the shadows of the trees and the silhouettes of the gothic building. The slight shiver of fear as she roamed about made the walk vivid and somehow invigorating. She might never conquer her fear of the jar at the Mütter, but she could find strength in her solo nighttime forays through the darkness.

Markhal poured herself some tea. Did she have it in her to read another report? She debated. Then made up her mind. One more. Then a little walk to clear her mind, home to a hot bath, and the blessed oblivion of sleep.

She grabbed the next report on the pile and opened to the title page.

FINAL REPORT on TFD-6
(The Fear Drug, Formulation 6)

Chemical Formulation
Animal Study Results

Afghanistan Field Study Results
Institutional Test Results
Data Analysis
Expert Interpretation
Summary of Efficacy
Side Effects
Potential
Conclusion & Recommendations

Presented By
Drs. B. Munson and B. Buckley
Review Committee Co-Chairpersons
Institute of Psychoactive Pharmaceuticals

Blackstone, MI.
June 3, 2014

The report had been sitting on her desk all summer.

With the approval of the researchers and the informed consent of Everett Fine, she had given him a TFD-2 pill years ago. She never knew if he took it or not when he went to Ledge Lighthouse. And now she had given Scott Edwards the newer TFD-6 formulation because he was going to the lighthouse, too. It seemed that place was a hotbed of fear. It might help him. She tried to remember when he was going out. The glow of the moonlight on her desk reminded her. He had wanted to go out the next full moon, just like Everett Fine had.

"He's out there tonight!"

The report took on immediate relevance. She started to read. It was a thick report, dense with charts and graphs, statistics, analyses, and narratives. They were stultifyingly dense and dry, and almost impenetrably wordy. Reading the report was like walking in wet sand.

Slow and tedious.

24

Scott stood at the base of the steps, stunned, unable to move. The foghorn blasted around the corner. He couldn't believe someone else was on the lighthouse. He was about to speak when a few clouds drifted, and the moon shone brighter, and Scott could see the man better. He was thin as a rail, with long fingers and claw-like nails, big pointy ears, a bald head, and sharp teeth — something out of a nightmare.

Forget talking! Scott turned and ran up the stairs and into the lighthouse.

He didn't remember slamming the door closed, but when he recovered himself a bit, it was shut tight. He threw the inside bolt. He backed away from the door and stared at it a moment, imagining what was on the other side. Then he went through the gift shop into the briefing room and sat down on the bench below the mural of the lighthouse. He tried to calm his breath. The foghorn wailed, its deep mournful cry reverberating through the empty rooms of Ledge Light.

He couldn't believe someone else was on the lighthouse! But it was possible. Nothing to keep someone from coming out, tying up, and climbing the stairs to the main deck. Maybe someone had done just that.

The horn sounded every twelve seconds. Scott tried to replay what had just happened in his mind. He tried to remember the Mystic Whaler tour and what was at that corner of the deck when he had wandered around outside. Like rewinding a tape, he replayed the memory of sailing up to the light, docking, climbing the stairs, listening to the briefing outside. The images flashed back. Wayne talking to the crowd of people. The flags flapping in the breeze. He had been in the corner.

Wasn't there a hoist? A curved metal pole and a pulley? Yes! Right near the corner where he had just seen the man. And they were probably what he saw in the dark and took for a ghoul. No, not just a ghoul — it was the picture of that vampire on the movie poster at the Groton Paranormal Group office.

Scott believed he knew what had happened. The foghorn had scared him, and the hoist had confused him. His imagination had turned a pitted shadowy round pulley into a face. Scott was surprised at how easily he had started to imagine things once darkness had fallen on Ledge Light. There was something about the place. Or at least about being alone on it at night. It was like being under the influence of a strange drug. Or being in a dream. He was beginning to understand how Everett might have slipped down the slippery slope of sanity. He'd have to be careful.

Scott believed his analysis of the frightening occurrence. All the same, he felt no need to open the door, go outside, and double check. He felt in his pocket and took out the silver pill case. He opened the lid. Nestled inside was a red pill. The TFD-6 pill Dr. Markhal had given him. If things got worse, if he felt himself overwhelmed by fear, for whatever reason, he would take it. He certainly wasn't there yet. He was on edge, a bit spooked, but still in control of himself.

He snapped the lid closed and put the box away.

25

The lights went out.

All of them.

Scott was plunged into a world of darkness. He went around the lighthouse, using the flashlight on his iPhone to light the way. He tried the light switches, but none worked. Russell had warned him the lights were undependable. High voltage electricity flowed into the building from a cable linking it to shore. In the transformer in the cage in the basement, it was stepped down to lower voltage and split into the major circuits servicing the lighthouse. The light and horn were independent, powered from the batteries connected to the solar panels. Strangely, even when the lights were out, the high voltage transformer was aglow and working. Since no one lived at Ledge Light any longer, it was only during the tours or when volunteers were out doing restoration work that anyone cared about the electricity.

Ghost hunters were on their own.

On the west side of the lighthouse, moonlight came in the windows to add light to a few rooms. Other than that, it was very dark, even with his little phone light. Scott sat in the gift shop, at the table with the guest book, and looked at Morgan, barely visible in the gloom.

"Earn your keep, little guy. If something out here needs a Ka figure for the night, why don't you volunteer? Do it for Everett."

Morgan just stood there on the table, a small, carved wood figure of a sailor.

Scott had a quick dinner of a sandwich and some water. It was almost 10 p.m., and his phone's power was down to 34 percent. The flashlight used a lot of juice. He cursed himself again for forgetting the charger. He'd have to watch it.

Ding! Ding!

Anne: Hi, honey. Thought I'd check in with my ghost boy to see how he is doing.

Scott: Fine. Had something to eat. The lights are out here.

Anne: Really? Is it spooky?

Scott: Actually, yes. I'm in a world of shadows now.

Anne: Be careful.

Scott: I'm being careful, believe me. How's it going with you?

Anne: So-so. Nothing happening tonight so I'm up in my room alone. I'm worried. In my own darkness.

Scott: The test.

Anne: Yes. You know how important it is. How hard I've battled the past few years. What I've been through. WE'VE been through.

Scott: I do. You've been very brave. You never gave up.

Anne: I came close. After the last round of treatments. I almost called it quits. You remember.

Scott: I do. But you didn't give up. You hung in there. Got better. No more shadows.

Anne: They think.

Scott: They were pretty sure, as I recall.

Anne: Yeah, but they still wanted this test.

Scott: It's been a while since the last one. And it was okay.

Anne: But they still wanted this test. Dr. Falk said they were "keeping an eye on things." Like what? I never really understand him.

Scott: You'll be fine.

Anne: Easier to say than know or believe. The results were due yesterday. Don't know why the delay. It's killing me.

Scott: Dr. Falk promised to call.

Anne: He hasn't yet. I just checked the messages at home.

Scott: Don't fret. Distract yourself with something.

Anne: Yeah. Maybe. I just need a hug.

Scott: We'll be together in a few nights. The test will be good, you wait and see. You'll get your hug and we'll go out and celebrate. Deal?

Anne: Sure.
Scott: Okay. I love you. If you hear anything, let me know.
Anne: Of course. Okay. Gotta go. Say hi to any ghosts you meet.
Scott: Will do. I love you.
Anne: Love you more! XX000XX

Scott stared at the text bubbles. He knew how to read Anne's texts. She was afraid. With good reason. Her sickness had been a tough journey. She had glimpsed her own mortality. So had he. And he had had to contemplate the possibility of life without her. All their other worries had seemed trivial.

Scott remembered that day when Dr. Falk had told them of a little shadow on a routine scan. Falk had walked into the small, cold exam room and closed the door. That was when Scott first felt the fear in his gut. The next half hour was a foggy memory. Just impressions as the doctor explained the situation. Only a few words stayed in memory. "Caught it early … treatments … with luck … a pretty good chance … take your time deciding … some new procedures … you have youth on your side … of course, nothing is certain …"

The shadow on the scan took on a life of its own. It became the focus of their fears. It was what kept them up at night staring at the ceiling, what turned her incandescent smile into a frown when she thought he wasn't looking. It was what made them forgetful and preoccupied and irascible. It was what made them cry when they were alone. Like a black hole, the shadow had a gravity of fear that sucked all the happiness from them. It had been a rough few years.

And now they awaited a crucial test that would show if all the treatments and procedures had succeeded. Had she rid herself of the shadow? Or had it come back to haunt her?

Scott sighed and sat back. He rubbed his eyes and sighed again. Outside, the foghorn wailed.

"I'll make a sound that's so alone that no one can miss it, and whoever hears it will know the sadness of eternity and the briefness of life."

26

The foghorn repeated its cry every 12 seconds, as regular as a heartbeat. Which it was, in a way. Scott decided to see if he could find a flashlight. He remembered seeing one on the shelf in Ernie's room. Whether it worked or not, he had no idea. But it was worth a look. If not, there was sure to be one someplace — maybe in the basement or in the closet in the theater.

Scott walked out of the gift shop into the hallway. Moonlight came in the window of the utility room and kitchen area and shone as two elongated rectangles on the wall of the hallway. It was enough to see by, and the light cast a glow throughout space. Scott turned and walked to the front door. It was still closed. As he turned to the bottom of the stairs, he thought he saw something out of the corner of his eye. Movement. He stopped and looked back. Nothing. He started up the stairway. The banisters cast striped shadows on the wall of the stairwell, like the bars of a prison cell.

He looked down through the banisters at the wall. Again he thought he saw a shadow moving across the light cast by the moonbeam. But a shadow of what?

He stopped halfway to the second floor and watched. He waited 10, 20 seconds. And then the unmistakable silhouette of a man slowly moved across the patch of light into the darkness on the other side. Scott backed away from the banister and pressed his back to the railing that ran along the wall. Dr. Markhal's fear had become his. Keeping his back to the wall and peering through the banister, he went up the stairs to the second floor.

Scott realized he had been holding his breath, and at the next sounding of the foghorn, he exhaled. He could feel his heart beat. To his right was the history room, right above the foghorn. To his left, the theater, its doorway blocked by heavy black velvet curtains. And down the hall, the room where Everett had seen the rats and across from it the room with the "No Entry" sign. On this floor, too, the moonlight came in the history room windows on the west side and shone through the doorway onto the hallway wall. Enlargements of the lighthouse's original blueprints hung on that wall. Those drawings from 1909 defined the physical parameters of the building, but did little to capture its essence or its history. That would come only after Ledge Lighthouse had been constructed and lived in, abandoned and restored.

His steps energized by nerves, Scott walked down the hallway, past the big center column, and around to the base of the stairs to the third floor. This time, he did not dally on the stairs or wait for a shadow to pass across the moonlight on the wall. He ascended the stairs quickly.

A gallery of exhibits was on his right, the long room of exhibits to his left. And at the end of the hallway was Ernie's room. His destination. Creepy mannequin or not, he wanted the flashlight on the shelf in that room.

His heart beating rapidly, his breathing a bit ragged, Scott made his way down the dark corridor and without giving himself a chance to think or lose his nerve, he opened the door to Ernie's room. He waited a heartbeat or two to make sure nothing was going to surprise him.

Nothing did.

Scott walked in and turned to face the barrier and beyond it the mannequin of the keeper who legend says took his own life at Ledge Light.

Ernie was gone.

27

Scott froze.

The mannequin of Ernie was not there.

"Damn!" Scott hissed. Then he simply stared. The shock of the missing mannequin seemed to paralyze him. He couldn't even blink. He had the sensation of a delicate set of gears in his mind slowly turning, loosening, causing some other part of his mind to spin and wobble.

It took him a moment to understand what he was seeing. Or not seeing. Ernie was not there. That awareness was followed by a sudden rush of adrenaline he could feel in his gut, like an electric current being switched on. He took a step backward and bumped into the wall where an exhibit about Ernie hung along with the sign "Caution. Ghost Area. Beware!"

It happened fast. To his left, at the far end of the hall, he saw a figure silhouetted in front of the window. Scott could not tell for sure, but it looked like the apparition was looking at him. Maybe there really had been someone outside who had somehow managed to get inside? It was there no more than a few seconds before it moved forward and started to descend the stairs to the second floor.

Then, thought returned. The talks with Chuck about the world of the paranormal and with Fuzzy about the Egyptian Ka and Fine's tape and Markhal's insights into mental states and Streeter's lore of Ledge Light all came together. Scott realized the ghost of Ernie had found in the mannequin of Ernie the perfect Ka figure. The perfect vessel to inhabit to walk again inside this lighthouse.

Forget the flashlight!

Scott turned from Ernie's room and walked down the hallway to the top of the stairs. The banisters glowed with reflected moonlight. Their shadows striped the wall. And at the bottom of the stairs he saw Ernie turn and walk down the hall into the shadows.

Scott took two steps down the stairs and stopped.

Was he chasing Ernie, or was Ernie leading him? And if so, where? Was Ernie trying to trap him and possess him? Was he desperate to taste the sweet elixir of life again?

Like a prisoner, Scott looked through the banisters and saw the shadow of Ernie as he walked past the blueprints. What to do? Follow or hide? Hide where?

The foghorn stopped. Suddenly, Ledge Light sank into a sea of silence. It was unsettling. Scott leaned back against the wall and tried to calm himself. His heart beat so fast and loudly he was sure even a ghost could hear it. He wished the foghorn would start up and mask the drumbeat in his chest. But it remained silent.

"Get a grip," he said to himself. "This is what happened to Fine. He saw a few shadows and got a little scared. And then his imagination kicked in and he got a little more scared and then maybe he started to see things that weren't there, even with the damned Phanoptiscope and goggles, and then he was in a free-fall to madness."

Scott thought he heard a door creak.

He started down the stairs again, because not knowing what was going on and where Ernie was going seemed more terrifying than knowing.

He reached the bottom of the stairs. The rat room, as he had come to think of it, was to his right, its door still closed. Again he heard a faint scratching beyond that door. Well, screw it! He wasn't going in there again. He stood in front of the door and turned around and looked at the door across the narrow hall, the one marked "No Entry." It was open a crack.

As Scott stood transfixed with his back against the door to the rat room, the door to the "No Entry" room began to swing open. Slowly. Very, very slowly. It creaked loudly. When it was finally fully open, there sat an enormous glass jar. It rose about 7 feet from the floor. The bright moonlight shown through the jar so that the fluid inside glowed. The side of the jar facing the door was black. Scott couldn't see what was in it.

A young boy with a round face and bright red hair stepped from the shadows next to the glowing jar. He looked at Scott and smiled. "You gonna go take a look, or are you chicken?"

The huge jar began to turn.

Scott's knees buckled. He staggered down the hall and was about to go down the stairs when he spotted something small and dark in a patch of moonlight at the top of the stairs.

It was Morgan, the little carved sailor.

Scott turned to the only place left to go. The theater. Thick black velvet curtains hung in its doorway. Without a thought as to what might lay beyond, he parted them and stepped inside.

It was like going blind. Not a bit of light shone in the theater. Blackout curtains over the windows kept out the moonlight and the shore lights. He could see nothing. Complete and absolute darkness. Scott remembered from his daytime visit that the room was filled with chairs, and a narrow aisle ran along the left wall.

If Ernie was in here, Scott would never know it.

In a panic, he took out his iPhone and turned it on, touched it with his finger and got to the home screen. He was shaking so much he dropped the phone.

He cursed, knelt, and picked it up.

He turned on the flashlight and shone it wildly around the room. It was as he had remembered it. Curtains, an AC unit, chairs, and the TV.

No lurking possessed mannequin.

He stumbled to the front of the room. There was a closet to the left of the TV.

"You can't help but wonder what you'd do if you opened a door and there he was."

"Well, to hell with him!" He decided to act, for his thinking was slow and getting more confused as this funhouse of a lighthouse worked on him. "Be fearless," he told himself, though it was getting hard to be so.

He grabbed the doorknob and opened the door.

He held his iPhone out in front of him like a sword. Maybe it was. Maybe ghosts don't like light. The closet was small, only a few feet deep, and lined with shelves. Scott scanned the light quickly across them. There was the audio-visual gear to run the show, some tools, notebooks, tape, boxes, and a flashlight. A flashlight! Thank God!

Scott took the flashlight and turned it on. Nothing. Dead as dead could be.

"Shit!"

He pawed around inside some boxes, hoping to find batteries, but there were none. In disgust, he threw the flashlight on the floor of the closet. He looked at his iPhone. 16 percent. He was using up a lot of battery power. He shut the phone off and felt his way along the wall to the doorway. He needed to get back to the halls and the rooms where at least a little moonlight trickled in.

Scott found the heavy velvet curtains.

He parted them.

And found himself face to face with Ernie.

28

D r. Markhal had been reading the report on TFD-6 for almost an hour. More than once, her eyes had closed and her head had drooped. The report was numbing, and while she had a keen interest in it, getting through the text was like hacking through a thick jungle. Finally, she gave up and jumped to the conclusion:

"Institutional testing has been too limited to yield statistically significant data. Field tests of TFD-6 in Afghanistan have shown some positive results, though the fog of war makes it difficult to assess efficacy as well as contraindications. Furthermore, the combat environment makes it difficult to determine with certainty if deaths were caused by TFD-6 or other factors. However, given the high incidence of mortality in laboratory simian subjects upon ingestion of the drug, or as a delayed reaction, as well as potential long-term deleterious psychological effects observed in human subjects, it is the recommendation of this review committee that further lab, field, clinical, or institutional testing of TFD be terminated immediately. While a pharmaceutical of great promise, in its current formulation it is flawed and potentially lethal."

Markhal looked at the words again: "Flawed and lethal."
Scott Edwards!
She had to warn him not to take it. She hoped it wasn't too late. Panicky, she shuffled through the papers on her desk trying to find the slip of paper with his phone number on it. Papers flew to the floor as she scrambled to find it. Finally, she

saw the paper with her doodle of a lighthouse and a ghost and, next to them, Scott's number.

She picked up her phone and, with trembling fingers, punched in his number.

29

S cott screamed. He was inches away from the dead keeper's wild angry face. Scott looked into the wide eyes. He saw a curled lip, a shock of grey hair beneath a keeper's cap with a gold emblem of a lighthouse. He could feel the chill of the creature, like a wind from the grave. He saw the ghost for just an instant, like a scene illuminated by a flash of lightning or a camera strobe. Sometimes, the eye sees before the mind comprehends.

Scott recoiled as if shot and fell back over the chairs in the theater. He ended up in a tangle of plastic arms and legs, panicking, wanting to get away, get away, get away from Ernie and the shadows and the apparitions. Wanting to get away from this damned lighthouse.

He disentangled himself from the chairs. He again found himself alone in a pitch-black room. Or was he? Who knew what phantoms lurked in the shadows. Watching. Waiting.

The curtains had closed when he'd backed away from the ghost. Scott didn't know if Ernie was still there or whether he had come into the room. Scott did not know what to do. He waited in the darkness, senses alert. He was scared, not thinking clearly. The adrenaline was pumping. And, as Dr. Markhal had explained, sometimes it gets in the way. Was it time to take the pill? Let it calm him down, push away the fear and restore rational thought?

As he was trying to decide, Scott heard a door open upstairs. It was distant, but he heard it. The creak and clang of a very heavy door. He hoped it was Ernie. He hoped that Ernie had not come in after him. That he had moved on to somewhere else. Scott hoped that if he parted those curtains again,

Ernie would not be there. He sure as hell couldn't stay in this pitch-black room until dawn. He'd go mad. He laughed at that thought. How did he know he hadn't gone mad already? Hadn't Dr. Markhal called madness a kind of waking dream? If it was, how would he know? When we dream, we don't know we're dreaming. Does a mad man know he's mad? Probably not.

Well, mad or not, he was getting out of this room, Ernie be damned!

Scott stepped forward, took hold of the edges of the velvet curtains, took a deep breath, and opened them.

Ernie was not there.

Scott exhaled and quickly stepped into the hallway. Glancing down, he saw that Morgan was no longer standing at the top of the stairs.

"Damn!" he said again. Things were happening, and happening quickly. Scott had the feeling of being pulled along, acting less of his own will and more at the whim of unseen forces. Again he heard a clang upstairs. He jumped. His nerves were frayed. He heard it again. Way up, in the light tower. The hatches of the tower levels were metal. And so was the massive door out to the catwalk.

Scott wanted to get away from the second floor. It offered only a pitch-black room, the horror of the Mütter Museum, and possibly a room full of rats. When he thought about the lantern room with the lighthouse's light, it seemed appealing. Up there, that bright light spun and shone. White. Black. Red. Light was better than darkness, as hope was better than fear. Maybe he could find both up there.

From the light tower, he would be able to see for miles — all the way to the horizon. There would be the moon and the stars. Fresh air and calming sea. He'd see boats and the lights on land and not feel so alone. The claustrophobia of the inside of the light would give way to the embrace of infinity.

But what about Ernie?

Scott didn't know what he would do if he encountered Ernie again up there. And he probably would. But the thought of the light overshadowed his fear of the ghost.

He went up the stairway to the third floor and down the hall to Ernie's room. Maybe Ernie had gone back to his room.

The door to the room was closed. Scott left it that way and climbed the curving ladder from the third floor to the lantern room. The metal hatch was open. The hatch was about a third of the circular metal floor and just wide enough to get through. He paused at the top of the ladder. The hatch opened into a dark space above, the lower level of the light tower. It flickered with the light of the spinning lens. The light, reflected back from the curved window above, came down through another hatch that was the floor of the actual lantern room.

What if Ernie was waiting for him? Scott stood on the ladder and, like the little boy on the tour, looked down at the stairway dropping away below. As he looked, a shadow moved across the wall toward his end of the hall.

Scott shot up the ladder and through the hatch and into the lantern room.

Ernie was not lying in wait.

There was barely room to move in the small space. Two round portholes in the brick walls let in a bit of moonlight, and Scott saw the metal spiral ladder continue up into the light room. On the wall he saw, or thought he saw, the word "DIE" stenciled on the white paint.

As if he wasn't frightened enough! His hand went into his pocket and he felt for the little silver pillbox. He took it out and snapped the lid open. Nestled inside was the red TFD-6 pill. Was it time to take it? Had his fear reached the point where it was clouding his reason? He looked at the stencil on the wall again.

"DIE." It made no sense. Or it made perfect sense if this was all a dream. Scott had no way of knowing. Whatever was happening — whatever was about to happen — he had to ride it out. Play his part in the shadow play of this night on Ledge Light. He stood in the cramped space. He didn't know what was above him. He didn't know what was below. As he started up the ladder to the light, Everett's panicky words from the tape came back to him:

"What if Ernie is up there and as I come through he grabs my hair and pulls my head back and cuts my throat with that razor? I'm defenseless."

Scott wished he'd never listened to that damned tape. Never heard of Everett Line Fine. Never found that box of mysteries. But he had. He turned the red pill over in his shaking hand. He closed his eyes. He shook his head. "Not yet. I can still cope." He put the pill away and grabbed the sides of the metal ladder. He started up, sticking his head into the small metal light room where the light spun, sending its beam of hope and safety 19 miles to sea.

Ernie was not there. He didn't grab his hair and slit his throat. Scott clambered up into the small chamber, metal to waist level, then a surrounding circle of windows. The heavy metal-and-windowed door to the catwalk was open. Scott inched his way around the light. For a few seconds he was bathed in bright white light, then lost in the dark as the black-out panel spun into place, then illuminated by a demonic red. From the sea or shore, the pattern read as three blinking white lights and one red. But here, inches from the slowly spinning lantern, it was a blinding assault of light and color.

Without even thinking, Scott stepped out onto the narrow catwalk that circled the lantern room.

It was like before, when he had stepped out the front door. He stepped from a world of confinement to one of infinite expanse. The fresh air was sweet, the stars twinkled, the lights of Electric Boat and Pfizer lit up the Groton shoreline. New London Harbor Light flashed its white light every three seconds. Buoys and boats cast streaks across the dark waters. The moon blazed bright like a cyclops eye in the night sky. Its beam was a shimmering path across the sea.

Scott relaxed a bit as he took in the beautiful scene around him. The foghorn was still on, a little fainter from up here, but audible. Then he tensed again. Where was Ernie?

He walked around the catwalk. He looked through the scratched glass panes of the lantern room. Every scrape and gouge caught the brilliant light and refracted it. The thick windows nearest him reflected the windows on the opposite side of the room, and they in turn reflected the light and its reflections. It was a kaleidoscope of lights and reflections, exactly as Scott had seen it in frame 13 of Everett's roll of photographs. And just as in frame 13, as Scott peered closely through the window, he thought he saw a face across the lantern room, out on the catwalk, peering through the glass back at him.

Ernie.

Or was it? Was it a face or just some shadows and light that looked like a face? Was it his *own* face, reflected and distorted?

Scott didn't move. If it was Ernie, they were out on the catwalk together. Man and ghost. Flesh and unearthly Ka inhabiting and animating a mannequin. Or maybe it wasn't the mannequin anymore. Maybe the ghost of Ernie had abandoned it and had become a ghostly apparition as it stalked him. As it sought to possess, at least for a while, a being of living flesh and blood. Whether the mannequin was a simulacrum of the ghost, or the ghost had become a simulacrum of the mannequin, Scott couldn't know. It didn't matter.

The light turned. White. Black. Red. Scott squinted and tried to look past it through the far side of the tower window at Ernie.

The face was gone. Where was it? Where was Ernie now?

Scott turned and looked down at the roof below that surrounded the lantern room. It was no more than 20 feet square. A silhouetted figure stood at the edge of the roof. His long shadow, cast by the moonlight, led to the base of the tower.

The figure lifted an arm and motioned back at Scott, waving him forward. "Come to me," he seemed to be saying. Scott stood riveted, alternately bathed in white light, then in shadow, then in red. The relentless spin of the light and the rhythmic sounding of the horn were hypnotic. Scott let himself be carried by them. He saw nothing but that figure at the edge of the roof, beckoning him forward. Time seemed to stop.

Without thinking, without intent, unable to resist, Scott knelt on the catwalk, climbed under the railing, and dropped down onto the roof. He stood and faced the ghost.

"Come to me."

Scott took a step forward. He was obeying an irresistible compulsion. He moved slowly, aware of each step he took, unable to stop himself from taking another.

"Come to me."

He took another step toward Ernie. And then another.

Scott again felt the chill of the creature, which stood at the edge of the roof, almost 50 feet above the water. Ernie stood as he had stood almost a hundred years ago, broken and despairing and ready to jump.

He raised his hand and beckoned Scott forward.

"Come to me. Come to me. Come to the edge."

Scott took another step. He felt like he was a film of himself. Both present and detached at the same time.

Ernie gestured again, a shadow waving him toward the darkness. Scott was almost there now.

How easy it would be. Step to the edge. Look out at that beautiful glowing moonbeam streaking across the water like a path. Yes, a path through the darkness, a path beyond the doubt and the worry and the fear. So much fear. That black spot on the scan. The looming test results. The possibility of losing Anne. How nice it would be to escape it all.

Ernie turned and looked down. He turned back to Scott and gestured again.

"Come with me into the darkness, my friend. We will go there together. You will see. It is not so bad. Just a few steps. That's it, come closer. Join me. I will show you the way."

Scott was almost at the edge now. Just a few feet from Ernie, who, with his back to the moon, was all shadow. It was cold. Scott took a step to the very edge. There was no barrier.

The top edge of a building is a strange thing. Scott knew. He once lived in an apartment on the 18th floor. It had a balcony. Sometimes he would stand at the railing and look down. It was scary. Dizzying. It wouldn't take much to bend over too far and fall over the rail and plummet to his death. A terrible thought. Yet he would sometimes see that very image play out in his mind, and fight a vague urge to act on it. The thought of oblivion was both frightening and inexplicably appealing. He had heard the same from other people who had stood someplace high and exposed. He wondered what Dr. Markhal would say about it.

Scott swayed at the edge of the lighthouse roof. The slightest breeze would push him over. The light spun.

White. Black. Red.

Ernie reached a shadowy arm toward him.

At that instant, out of the night sky, a bird swooped by, very close to Scott. He saw it for only a second, lit by the red light. Its shape was unmistakable. It was a falcon. It flew so close, Scott felt the draft from it. As it passed it screeched loudly.

Scott woke up. Woke up from whatever dream state or ghost trance or desire for oblivion had overtaken him.

As Ernie reached for him, Scott turned away and fell back onto the roof. Suddenly, he was terrified to realize how close to the edge he had been. He started to scramble back toward the lantern room. He was surprised at how steep the roof seemed. He hadn't noticed on his trip out to the edge. Now he felt like he was climbing uphill. Scott struggled against gravity. He felt the roof slant more. Fighting his terror, and fighting the roof that pitched ever steeper, Scott flailed and crawled, slid back down and dove forward. The dried bird droppings and the copper roof surface gave him little to hold on to. The roof pitched more and more, and he slid back, back toward Ernie, toward the edge, toward the drop into the darkness and the cold black sea below.

Scott lunged forward. Upward. Slid back. Lunged again. He focused on the railing of the catwalk. Five feet away.

Lunge. Slide. Six feet away.

Lunge. Four feet away.

He felt an icy wind. Ernie coming up behind him.

Lunge. Lunge. Two feet from the catwalk.

Wild with fear, Scott pushed with his feet and reached with his arms and lunged forward and up. His hand slapped against the iron railing of the catwalk. He tried to grab. Missed.

As he fell away, he flailed his arm, and his hand hit one of the railing supports, scraping along the rust. He grabbed it and held on. He pulled himself up and wrapped his other arm around the support. He took a few deep breaths and then pulled himself back onto the catwalk, like a man overboard climbing back onto a ship.

Scott sat on the catwalk. He gulped air as if he had been drowning. He had been. He had been immersed in a suffocating nightmare from which he had barely surfaced. He struggled to get his breath back, to get his wits back, to let his heart slow down. The light spun above him sending its beam out into the darkness.

White. Black. Red.

When he had regained his composure, Scott stood. His palm was cut, dripping blood. The moon was bright, hanging in the night sky like a ghost of the lighthouse beam. A bird flew across it and back into the night. Scott looked down at the roof. It was flat.

There was no sign of Ernie.

30

S cott was sitting on the bench in the briefing room on the first floor. He had beat a hasty retreat back inside the lantern room and down the tower ladders and stairs to the first floor. After his experience out on the roof, the small, claustrophobic rooms of Ledge Light were comforting. He sat with his back to the mural of Ledge Light. A small sign below it told the story of the painting and quoted a poem one of the keepers had written:

> *Rock of slow torture. Ernie's domain.*
> *Hell on earth — may New London Ledge's light*
> *shine on forever because I'm through.*
> *I will watch it from afar while drinking a brew.*

Scott understood now. Ledge Light *was* a rock of slow torture. And it *was* Ernie's domain. And now he was in that domain, and Ernie was intent on possessing him. Probably as he had Everett Line Fine.

There were still hours of darkness. Ernie's ghost was somewhere. Behind a door. Waiting in the shadows. Somewhere. And he would come after Scott again. It had been a close thing on the roof. If that falcon hadn't come by, Scott knew he had been just a step away from going over the edge.

Scott wondered: did Ernie want him dead? Maybe. But what use would he be to Ernie dead? Didn't the ghost want a living person to possess? Maybe he just wanted him terrified and weak. To that end, Scott wondered if he had really been out on the roof. Maybe Ernie had just pulled a scene from Fine's tape and instigated a memory hallucination. Maybe the ghost had been doing that all night?

If so, it was working. Scott was certainly terrified. He had thought it would be easy to be out here alone. After all, shadows were just shadows, right? Now Scott wasn't so sure. And Everett Fine's tape did not seem so crazy, either. Not after what he'd been through.

The briefing room was dark. Just a faint trace of moonlight came in through the windows. The foghorn had stopped. Scott sat in the darkness and the silence and tried to make sense of what was happening. As he did so, he noticed a faint glow on the opposite side of the room. Had it been there all along? He wasn't sure. As Scott stared into the darkness and his eyes adjusted to it, he saw that the glow was the white smock of a man sitting in a chair in the corner. The man seemed familiar, but Scott could not place him.

The man raised his head and looked directly at Scott. Then, very slowly, he raised his right hand. He was holding something. As he raised it to shoulder level, it caught a bit of light and glinted.

It was a straightedge razor.

Scott stood up and walked out of the briefing room. Quickly.

He was in the main hallway on the first floor.

He took out his phone and pressed the home button. After a soft bell, he spoke: "Siri, how do I get rid of a ghost?" A few seconds later, Siri's voice replied: "Okay, here's what I've found." It was a bunch of Internet pages about paranormal groups, the movie Ghostbusters, exorcists, and the cartoon Casper, the Friendly Ghost. Scott frowned. Siri hadn't been much help. He was on his own. He put the phone away.

Scott thought he heard something. Cocking his head, he closed his eyes and listened. Yes, he heard it: music and talking, coming from upstairs. He walked to the bottom of the stairs. The music was louder. Its tinny sound meant it was coming from an old radio. It was Glenn Miller's *Moonlight Serenade*.

Scott took a few steps up the stairway. He heard voices. Young men talking. They seemed to be in the room to the right at the top of the stairs — the museum's "History Room." Scott had no doubt that if he went up there, even without a Phanoptiscope and goggles, he'd see young Coast Guardsmen sitting around a radio sometime in the1940s. And perhaps other men from other eras. Like the mix of people in Moore's photos, the men would inhabit the same space but at different times. Ghosts of the future. Ghosts of the past. Together, but, like oil and water, never really mixing.

A new piece of music played. Cab Calloway singing *Minnie the Moocher*. Scott retreated down the stairs. He really didn't need to go up there. He toyed with going out the front door, but he was afraid he might run into the ghoulish figure out there. Maybe he wasn't there at all, and there was nothing more menacing than an old worn pulley hanging from a rusty old davit.

On the other hand … well, that was his problem, right now. If he was hallucinating, what he saw sure seemed real. And if the men were real, he didn't want to tangle with them. He wasn't sure there was any real difference. What had Dr. Markhal said? "If you believe something strongly enough, it might as well be true." Whether imaginary or real, Scott had to deal with the truth. His truth. Here. Now.

Alone on this isolated lighthouse, Scott had few options. Though he had calmed a bit, he felt the creep of panic again. Ledge Light was alive with spirits of the dead. He was trapped out here with them. There was no place to run, no place to hide. It was dark. Shadows were everywhere. And things lurked in the shadows.

Ding! Ding!

Anne: Hi, Sweetie. Hope all is okay out there. I checked the messages at home. Nothing from Dr. Falk. But there was one from a Dr. Marcol or Mark Hall or something like that. She said it was urgent.
Scott: What did she want?
Anne: She said that you shou

Scott waited. The text app disappeared. The screen turned dark. A little graphic of an empty battery came up. Below it was a plug and a lightning bolt. Then a warning message flashed in red on the screen:

Your phone has 0% battery charge
Plug it in <u>immediately</u>!

Then the screen went black.

31

"Shit!" Scott had lost his only communication with the outside world. And his only light, too.

It was 3 a.m. The dead of night. Scott had been throughout the building except for one place. The basement.

In spite of his fear, he knew he had to go down there. It was in the basement that Everett lost the battle for his mind and his soul. Nobody knew what had happened down there. His tape stopped just as he descended into the darkness.

Scott walked back to the end of the hallway, past the briefing room with the man in the white smock and the straightedge razor. He walked into the room that was part storage and work area and part kitchen. It had a small refrigerator, microwave, cupboard, coolers, and a charcoal grill. He supposed that Ledge Light Foundation work crews used the stuff. The room had a heavy metal door at the back, along the northwest wall. The door led to the stairway to the basement. Scott opened it, and again read the warning sign: "Watch Your Step." Somehow, it seemed more meaningful after the night he'd had. Yes, he would have to be careful down there.

He stood at the top of the stairway. Moonlight from a window high on the wall lit the stairway with a faint blue light and spilled into the basement at the bottom. It was at the top of these stairs that they had found Fine the morning after.

Scott heard the hum of the high voltage transformer in the caged-off alcove.

The blood red stairs went down and then turned right, out of view. Scott knew he had to go down to the basement. There was no turning back. He had come this far. He took a step down into the darkness. He heard something and stopped. There it was again. It sounded like someone yelling. Muffled. Distant.

Scott descended a few more steps. He heard it again. It was coming from the cistern! He took another step and stood before the small square hatch labelled "Fresh Water." Another door. What was behind this one?

Taking a deep breath, Scott opened the hatch and swung it open. He peered into a black void.

"Hey, thank God! I thought nobody would ever hear me!" yelled a frantic voice from inside. It echoed like a cave.

"Who are you?" Scott yelled back.

"It's Rick! You know, the guy in the photo upstairs. The guy crouching on top of the divider between the cistern tanks. It wasn't such a good idea. I fell in."

A bit of moonlight trickled in the open hatch. Scott's eyes had accommodated to the darkness. He saw again what he had seen on his daylight visit on the *Mystic Whaler*: the tops of two deep tanks, a bunch of pipes, and some structural supports. He couldn't see a person.

"Where are you?" he asked.

"I'm down in the back tank, man. I think I might have a broken ankle or leg. Hard to move. The water seems to be rising, and I think there are some rats scurrying around down here. You gotta get me out!"

Crawling inside the cistern was about the last thing Scott wanted to do. He leaned in and over, trying to see if he could spot the man.

"You have to get me out of here! I'll drown if the water keeps rising. Imagine that: drowning inside a lighthouse! Come and help me!"

The panic in Rick's voice was palpable. Scott could only imagine his terror at being in that tomb-like space, hollowed out deep in the base of the lighthouse. Even with the moonlight, the place was dark. With the hatch closed, it would be pitch black.

"What are you waiting for? Help me! Get me out of here!"

The foghorn came on like an imitation of the desperate man's cries. It reverberated through the building.

Scott leaned in a bit further. His feet no longer touched the stairs. He was balanced on the lip of the cistern. If he went much further, he'd tumble in himself. They'd both be trapped. It was then he heard the heavy steel door at the top of the basement stairs swing closed and latch with a loud thunk.

Scott heard footsteps on the stairs.

It was Ernie. Ernie was coming down and would push him into the cistern and lock the hatch. Scott would be in there with the water and the rats and Rick. If there was a Rick.

Scott pulled himself out and dropped back down onto the stairs. Looking up the stairs to his right, he saw a man silhouetted against the barred window high up on the wall.

Rick yelled: "Hey what are you doing? You can't leave me! You have to …"

Scott slammed the hatch shut, cutting off Rick's pleas. In the gloom, he noticed a faint red handprint on the wall next to it. Was it his own, made by his cut palm? Or had it been there? At the moment, he didn't care. He had Ernie to worry about.

Scott backed down a step. The figure above descended a step, too. He backed down another step. Ernie did too. He was being stalked by a ghost.

He heard the humming of the high voltage cage behind him. Only a little moonlight shone down the stairway into the basement. A few feet in, it was a dark cavern.

Scott stepped backwards and down again, never taking his eyes off Ernie. Ernie followed. He could feel the cold of the ghost in the confined space of the stairway. Scott ducked under the pipes that cut across the last few stairs and stepped back and down, back and down.

Ernie stepped forward and down. Forward and down.

Scott reached the basement. He backed through the arched brick doorway, flicking the light switch as he did. Just in case the power was back on. Nothing. He looked up the stairs and saw the menacing silhouetted figure take another step down.

Scott was scared. Very scared. He was cornered in the deep dark damp basement of Ledge Light. He was feeling panicky. He didn't want to be trapped in the dark with Ernie. He didn't want to be near that humming cage of high voltage. He didn't want to be out at Ledge Lighthouse at all.

Things were happening quickly. Too quickly. He was off balance. He didn't know what was real anymore. He was dealing with a ghost. An angry ghost. And other things. Shadows. Phantoms. God knows what. Scott knew he would have to keep his sanity to survive. Everett had not been able to do so, and it had cost him dearly. It was time to take the TFD-6 pill. If the pill could help, even a little, it was worth trying. To hell with any side effects.

Scott took out the little pillbox. He opened it and took out the red pill, all the while keeping his eyes on the stairway.

He popped the pill in his mouth.

32

The big red TFD-6 pill stuck to Scott's tongue. He tried to generate some spit, but his mouth was cotton dry. If he tried to get it down his throat, he might choke on it. He could never swallow a pill this big without water. And his water was upstairs.

Scott shook his head, reached in, and took the pill off his tongue. He put it back in the silver box. The Fear Drug, Formulation 6, would not be getting a field test this night. He'd have to deal with his fear and Ernie without any help.

His hand shook as he put the pillbox in his pocket. As he backed into the main area of the basement, Scott realized his legs were shaking too. A streak of moonlight cut across the damp brick floor. The transformer apparatus in the high voltage cage crackled and sizzled. It sparked like flashbulbs going off, momentarily illuminating the basement in blue light.

Scott went past the center column towards the workroom. When he got to the doorway, he saw the table saw. Power or not, he had seen enough horror movies to know to stay away from saws when there is a monster after you.

He quickly turned to take the few steps across the main basement space to the utility room when he saw Ernie at the bottom of the stairs. Too late. To get to the utility room he'd have to walk right by Ernie. Scott didn't want to do that. He didn't know if a ghost could physically attack him, but now was not the time to find out.

"Shit!" He was running out of options. He glanced to his right and saw, high up on the wall, the storm hatch that led to the outside. There were ladders piled beneath it. If he could get to the hatch and open it, he could escape the basement — and Ernie. It was his only hope.

Scott ran to the wall and scrambled up a big rolling ladder to the hatch. By the flashes from the transformer, he found the bolt to the hatch and tried to throw it. It didn't move. He pushed harder.

Then he felt the cold. That icy cold that told him Ernie was near. Looking down the ladder, Scott saw the dark figure of the ghost keeper climbing up.

Frantically, Scott pulled at the bolt. Rust flaked off, but it didn't turn. The cold of Ernie started to flow about him, an icy fog.

Scott didn't look down again. He didn't wait to feel cold fingers grab his ankle. He jumped sideways, onto another ladder leaning against the wall. In the dark he couldn't see the rungs. He missed. He started to fall, then managed to grab on. The shadowy figure of Ernie retreated down the ladder.

Scott half scrambled, half fell down the ladder. He landed hard on the brick floor and fell. As he rolled onto his knees, Scott thought about bolting up the stairs, but Ernie was already back down and too close to them. Scott got to his feet. Ernie stood there, a menacing figure in the archway to the stairs. He was barely visible in the shadows, but he was there, blocking Scott's only way out.

Scott backed away from the ghost until he bumped up against the blue mesh of the high voltage door.

"Danger. Keep Out. High Voltage."

Scott could smell the electricity just a few feet away.

Electricity.

Hadn't he talked about electricity with Chuck on his first visit to the Groton Paranormal Group? As Ernie stood blocking the stairs and Scott stood a few feet away, back to the cage, he tried to remember what Chuck had said. Bits and pieces came back to him.

"Can't kill something already dead ... electricity ... attract a spirit's energy ... capture it ... store it."

Scott realized his only chance was to get into the high voltage electrical cage. He had to get into that alcove with its thick black cables and sparking transformer apparatus in spite of his fear of electricity.

His worst fear.

Ernie took a shuffling step toward him.

By the sparking blue light behind the mesh door, Scott pulled out the key and fumbled to get it into the big brass lock. His hands were shaking too much.

"Come on! Come on!" Scott said aloud. He heard the ghost take a shuffling step toward him. The air turned icy. Ernie was only a few feet away.

"COME ON! COME ON!" Scott yelled at the lock. At himself. The cold air worsened the clumsiness of his already trembling hands.

He managed to get the key in. He turned it. The lock opened, and Scott pulled at the hasp. It was about six inches long and wedged tightly against the edge of the door. Scott twisted the hasp and pulled hard, but it didn't want to come out — as if it was fighting him. He heard Ernie take another step. He yanked at the hasp and finally got the right angle and it slid free.

The blue metal mesh door swung open, and Scott stepped into the dark alcove. It was like walking into a crypt in a catacomb. It was almost pitch black inside. The alcove was about 7 feet long and 4 feet wide. The intense electrical power from the underwater cable made the transformer glow. The glow and the sparks flashing from rusted and frayed contact points were the only light.

The door creaked behind him, and a shadow fell across the darkness.

Scott was inside the electrical cage now. A ghost blocked the only way out. He had to act fast before it got into the alcove with him. He moved closer to the electric transformer. He acted out of pure terror and desperation.

In the brief flashes of illumination from the sparking wires, Scott could see the thick underwater cable coming through the bricks high on the back wall of the alcove. It split to four smaller high voltage cables that sagged toward the floor and then snaked back up the transformer apparatus, a big black box. It stepped down the power to a usable level. A panel behind it had three thick wires — probably feeds to the lighthouse's main circuits.

Scott hesitated. All that high voltage! Frayed wires! The infernal hum of power, like a slumbering beast! Did he dare wake it?

Ernie took a step toward the alcove. The shiny brass buttons of his coat glinted in the light of the sparking electricity.

Scott abandoned rational thought. He reached up to a knurled metal coupling that secured one of the four high voltage cables to the transformer. He turned it, but it didn't budge. He tried another. It also was too hard to turn. He might need a wrench. Too late. The third was also stuck. A final cable remained. The humming of the transformer was very loud. He could feel the heat of the high voltage just inches away, a stark contrast to the chill he felt behind him.

With a strength born of fear, Scott put both hands around the coupling and twisted. It turned slightly. Frantically, he turned the coupling around the three-inch wide cable. It was agonizingly slow. Finally, it came loose. The cable was free. Scott pulled it from the transformer. It was like holding the deadliest of snakes in his hands. The thick cable's bite would kill him as certainly as any venom.

Holding the thick cable, Scott turned toward the door.

And stopped.

He could not move.

Suddenly, he was not in an alcove in the basement of Ledge Light. He was back in his yard on a stormy day many years ago. The rain pelted down. The wind howled. A trash can banged against the house. Scott was holding a downed electric line. In a few seconds, he would feel the excruciating fire of electricity surging through his hands and up his arms.

The memory of that terrible accident that had almost killed him paralyzed Scott with fear.

The sound of another shuffling step snapped him out of his hallucination. Scott looked into the shadows and saw Ernie about to step into the mouth of the alcove.

In the dim moonlight and the flashes of the transformer, Scott saw the ghost's face. It was a mask of rage mixed with eyes that spoke of a deep and desperate need. Ernie longed to possess Scott. He wanted to feel life once again. Ernie's wide eyes burned into him like the electricity had all those years ago.

Scott's mind was running fast. His fears, his adrenaline, the instinct of flight or fight all tumbled across his thoughts, as bright and brief as the sparks behind him. And through them, an image surfaced.

Anne.

He saw her face, a vision in this dark nightmare.

With her image came memories. Memories of her courage. Her will. Her fierce resolve as she had battled *her* worst fear. Anne hadn't flinched at the critical moments. She had fought. Maybe she had won. Maybe she would survive.

Together, he and Anne had faced the darkness. And it was their love that had shown the way through it. A love Scott knew would unite them forever, in this life or beyond it. At that moment, Scott realized that while Ernie's wife had given him a reason to die, his had given him a reason to live.

The ghost of Ernie took a step toward Scott.

"Damn you, Ernie!" Scott yelled. "Damn you to hell!"

Scott lunged forward. With one hand he reached out, grabbed the mesh door and pulled it closed. Ernie continued forward and pressed against it. His face, his hat, his coat, all started to evanesce through the mesh, his spectral form barely slowed.

Scott jammed the live high voltage cable against the door. It took the charge: 13,800 volts of electricity flowed into the metal.

There they stood, Scott and Ernie, human and spirit, on either side of a metal door that sparked and sizzled with electricity. Ernie stopped as the power surged through him. It would not kill him, for he was already dead. But it could attract and possess his energy field.

Scott held the hot deadly cable in his hands, trembling, determined. If he touched the door he would be killed instantly. He'd join Ernie in the world beyond life. Their faces were only inches apart. Scott gazed into the angry hurt eyes of the spirit. And the spirit gazed into the terrified defiant eyes of the man. Scott felt the gravity of evil pulling him toward the door. He fought it. He felt the icy cold of the ghost. The frigid air enveloped him and he started to shiver, despite the heat from the electricity. He struggled to keep the cable against the metal door.

A hand came through the mesh. Then an arm. The ghost was trying to grab him, pull him to the door. Scott ducked out of the way, still holding the cable to the metal.

For long seconds, man and ghost stood at that door in the dark basement of Ledge Lighthouse. It was a battle between life and death.

Then Ernie opened his mouth. What came out was not a voice, not a scream. It was a simulacrum of the cry of the foghorn, deafeningly loud in the confined brick basement. Ernie bellowed once and then again. Scott wanted to put his hands over his ears. He wanted to block out that loud wail of the betrayed keeper. But he did not. He held the sizzling high voltage cable against the door to keep Ernie at bay.

As Ernie cried his unearthly wail again and again, Scott heard in it the sadness of eternity and the briefness of life.

Then, Scott screamed too, letting out all the rage and frustration and terror of this nightmarish night and of the past few years. He screamed out his fear of the electricity he held in his hands. He unburdened his soul from its darkest demons.

Ernie's ghost gave a horrific roar, a sound from beyond the

beyond. The being, the ghost, the Ka — whatever it was — disintegrated into a sparkling cloud that clung to the mesh door like glowing drops of rain. Smoke wafted off the metal.

The spirit's energy began to flow along the mesh toward the middle of the door, pulled to the center of the powerful electric field where the cable touched the metal. The glowing mass gathered there for a few seconds, a bright ball of energy. Strange sounds came from it, cries no longer, just pitiful whimpering. Then with a blinding flash and a deafening crackle like thunder, the glowing ball was sucked into the end of the cable and down to the transformer at the other end.

The ghost of Ernie was gone.

Scott waited a few seconds, and then let the cable drop.

The mesh door glowed a molten red. Scott panted, his face beaded with sweat, his hands cramped from his death grip on the cable. The basement was silent, except for the hum of the high voltage transformer. Was it a little louder? Perhaps. Scott could barely hear it over the pounding of his heart.

He had vanquished the ghost of Ernie.

He had bottled up the genie. At least for now.

Scott leaned back against the wall of the alcove, then slid to the floor, carefully avoiding the live wire.

In the dark basement of Ledge Light, in a tiny alcove, trapped and terrified, Scott had conquered his worst fear.

He had survived.

33

Scott sat on the floor of the alcove. A man in a dark cage. He watched as the mesh door lost its heat and its glow slowly dimmed.

In no rush to move, he let thoughts drift across his mind. He thought about Everett and what he might have encountered in this basement. He thought about his own night on Ledge Light. He thought about Anne, and her illness. He thought about shadows and fear, about imagination and paranormal apparitions.

After a few minutes, he stood. With care but without fear, he attached the cable to the transformer.

He closed and locked the mesh door, shaking his head at its warning sign.

DANGER
DO NOT ENTER
HIGH VOLTAGE

He'd have to be careful whom he told about his foray into that forbidden zone. He'd gone where he shouldn't have. What choice did he have? We confront our fears when and where they decide we must.

Scott was exhausted. Spent. He climbed the steep steps from the basement, passing the red handprint on the wall next to the hatch to the cistern. He pulled open the heavy metal door at the top of the stairs, stumbled through the kitchen area and across the hall to the briefing room. He sat on the padded bench. He put his head back against the mural of Ledge Light and closed his eyes. He let his waking dream carry him to sleep.

Scott was awakened by the foghorn announcing a misty dawn.

He was startled out of his sleep. He was disoriented. It took him a few minutes to grasp where he was. To remember what had happened. He stood and walked into the gift shop. Morgan was on the table, where he was supposed to be. But last night, the little figure had been upstairs. Scott wondered if he had taken him there, then later returned him here. Markhal had said such a thing was entirely possible. She had called it a "memory blackout." Then again, before the spirit of Ernie had inhabited the mannequin and come after him, perhaps it had found Morgan a suitable Ka figure. That was possible, too.

Scott poured a cup of coffee from his thermos. It was luke-warm but tasted wonderful. He looked at Morgan. If the little figure knew what had really happened, it would remain his secret. Gazing out the window, Scott saw the sun was up, a glowing ball in the heavy mist. The dawn was glowing orange with the sun, its streaks floating on the glassy calm water as the moonbeam had done at night.

It would be a while before Russell came for him, so Scott decided to look around Ledge Light. Daylight brought with it calm and a sense of order. Things that were mysterious or frightening by night became benign and rational by day.

The briefing room was empty. No man sat there brandishing a menacing razor. As Scott walked up to the second floor, there was no menacing darkness to avoid, no prison-like shadows of the banisters on the wall.

On the second floor, he looked in the history room. No men were gathered around an old radio listening to Glenn Miller. Scott walked down to the other end of the hall. The door to the "No Entry" room was closed. Wasn't it open last night? Hadn't he seen a huge glass jar and a red-haired boy? Warily, he pushed the door open. The room it revealed looked like it had once been a bathroom. Tile floors, lots of pipes. But no jar. No boy. Though looking at the tile floor, Scott saw a wide circle in the dust and grime. The imprint of the jar? Or just a vestige of some long gone tank?

He closed the door.

Across the hall was the rat room. He opened its door slowly. Daylight streamed in from the east-facing window. Seeing nothing, he went in and over to the closet. So many doors to open. So many chances to be surprised.

He recalled the terror on the tape when Everett had come in here and found a room full of rats. Scott recalled his own fear standing here in the dark, hearing something, maybe seeing something, debating what to do.

"Be fearless."

He hesitated a second more then opened the wooden closet door.

No rats. Just space heaters, some bulbs, a shag rug, paint chips, and a jar on the shelf. A pipe from the cistern ran from the floor up and through the ceiling with plenty of space around it. He again noted the scratches and gouges on the edges of the wooden door.

A harmless closet. At least so long as the rats weren't in it.

He left the room and went up to the third floor. He looked in the two rooms at the top of the stairs and, seeing nothing, went down the hall to "Ernie's Room."

The door was closed. Scott wondered if he should go in. So far, everything seemed fine. No demons, no jars of horror, no misplaced shadows, no rats. Maybe he should leave well enough alone. Why tempt fate?

But he knew he had to open the door to Ernie's room. He knew he had to go in and see if the mannequin was there. He was certain it had been a Ka figure last night. Or at least, for some of the night.

What was it now? Where was it?

He opened the door, ready to run if he again came face to face with the ghost. But Ernie did not greet him on the other side of the door.

No, the spooky statue of Ernie stood in the room as it always does, with its expression of betrayal and anger, clutching the letter that pushed him into madness.

Scott stared at the intense face that seemed to stare back at him. Did those glass eyes see? Did the figure remember their encounter on the roof, their battle in the basement? Was there a spirit inside the cloth and rubber, just waiting for a living person to tempt him with the sweet elixir of life?

Scott looked at the mannequin. He frowned. Something was different. He couldn't figure out what. Nothing dramatic. Nothing obvious. But something, something subtle. He let his gaze roam over Ernie's hat and face, his hands, the letter, his coat.

What was it?

His attention returned to the coat. It was a dark pea coat with six brass buttons, each adorned with an anchor and rope. Traditional garb for men of the sea.

One button was missing.

Scott searched his memory. When he had come out here on the Mystic Whaler tour he had seen this mannequin. He closed his eyes and thought back to that sunny day. Back to standing here looking at Ernie, then being surprised by Zook, who had been crouched in the shadows, turning on a light.

How many buttons had it had? Five or six? He tried to remember.

But memory is not like a photograph. It's not fixed. The vivid reality of what we experience is softened into vague impressions.

Scott could not remember how many buttons were on Ernie's coat. Six buttons … five buttons … the film in his mind replayed it both ways. Which was truth, which was fiction, he did not know.

Shaking his head, Scott gave Ernie a final look, saluted him, and left the keeper's room.

He climbed the metal spiral ladder into the light tower. The stencil on the wall was still enigmatic: "018" or "DIE"? For him and for Everett, in the middle of their nights of fear, it had read, "DIE." Now, by the light of day, it seemed to read "018." Its interpretation was a function of one's mental state.

Scott went to the light room. The light spun as it always did. The door to the catwalk was closed, but not locked. He remembered going out on the roof — almost going off the edge of the roof. In his mad scramble back, he must have slammed the door. He threw the bolt to lock it.

He descended from the tower to the second floor and then to the first. On the first floor he headed to the room that led to basement. He stopped at the top of the stairs. Did he really want to go down there again? Ever?

Steeling himself, he descended the stairs. He stopped at the cistern hatch. He opened it. Ducked his head in and listened. He heard no pleas for help. He closed the hatch. It was then he noticed a faint red handprint on the wall. He looked at his palm. It was cut. He couldn't be sure, though, if the print was his or had been there all along.

Scott continued down the stairs to the basement. Enough sunlight came in the window at the top of the stairs to cast some light into darkness. He stood by the center column and looked around. Nothing seemed out of place. The sound of the foghorn drifted down from above. How different it seemed from a few hours ago, when he had been trapped here in the shadows, chased by the icy apparition of Ernie. He relived what he could remember of their confrontation. It was a jumble of images — images from the shadows of the basement that surfaced from the shadows of his memory.

He walked over to the high voltage cage and peered in, as the ghost of Ernie had done. He heard the hum. A few sparks threw blue bursts of light into the dark alcove. By the light of one spark, Scott saw something glint on the grimy floor. He bent down for a closer look.

He saw it more clearly, and knew exactly what it was.

It was a single brass button. Polished and decorated with an anchor and rope. Just like the five buttons on Ernie's coat. It was nothing more than a simple brass button. It could have been here for years. Or perhaps it had been ripped off Ernie's coat last night. Perhaps it was proof that the ghost of Ernie was as real as a ghost can be. Scott did not know which. He could only imagine.

He stared at the button a long time. Then he stood up. He looked around the basement one last time. He never wanted to come down here again.

Scott headed up the stairs and down the front hall. He muscled open the door and stepped outside. The sun was out, but so was the fog, diffusing the light in a luminous glow. The calm golden water feathered into the sky. There was no horizon line. It was dream like. And beautiful. He walked over to the davit and pulley. Had they been what he had seen at night and thought to be a ghoul? Probably. But he couldn't be sure.

Nothing was certain. It was all as vague as the foggy morning, which softened and dissolved hard lines and shapes into mere suggestions. Scott turned and went back inside to wait for Russell to come and pick him up.

Scott realized he hadn't checked the theater. He went to the second floor. He crossed the hall and parted the velvet curtains. A few chairs were overturned. He remembered recoiling when he had come face to face with Ernie and falling over them. He remembered opening the closet looking for a flashlight.

At some point the power had come back on. The TV in the theater was on. Text scrolled up. "Your guide will start the orientation film, which tells the true story of Ledge Lighthouse."

The true story of Ledge Lighthouse. What *was* the true story of this lighthouse? Ledge Light was an isolated place of shadows, a place where a man's fears could mingle with spirits from a realm unknown. It was a place where memories lived on like echoes, echoes that never faded away. The lighthouse was where dreams became real, and reality became a dream.

Was the truth of Ledge Light sunny rooms full of tourists, laughing and talking about the exhibits? Buying "I saw Ernie" T-shirts at the gift shop? Or was it the truth of dark nights, of isolated men alone with their worst fears, filling the shadows with demons of their own design? The true story of Ledge Light? Who could possibly know? At best, one could only fashion an interpretation.

Scott heard a motor. Looking out the window, he saw Russell's small skiff appear in the distance, just a dark shape in the fog. He went down to the first floor. As he passed the gift shop, he glanced in and saw the guest book. He went in and opened it to the last page of the season. He thought a moment then penned an entry:

"Scott Edwards spent the night here with Ernie on October 3, 2014.
There is life in the shadows."

34

Scott stood outside at the railing of Ledge Lighthouse. He had gathered his supplies and locked the front door. He sat on a bench by the front door where a single black feather was caught between two planks. He plucked it out of the crevice and kept it as a souvenir.

As he waited, he put his hand in his pocket and felt the pill case. Scott took it out and opened it. Nestled inside was the TFD-6 pill. He took it out, looked at it a moment, then flicked it over the rail into the water. He'd call Dr. Markhal and tell her he had been able to deal with his fear without it. Not quite true. He would have taken the pill if he could have, but he was too scared to swallow it. A perfect irony.

When Russell drew near, Scott put the chain across the top of the stairway and went down to meet the skiff.

He caught a line Russell threw and tied the boat to a cleat. He handed down his backpack, jumped into the boat, then scrambled to the bow to untie the line. Only when he had pulled it in and helped stow the bumpers did they speak.

"So you survived," Russell said.

"I did."

"You doing okay?" asked Russell.

"Yeah, okay," said Scott. "A little worse for the wear."

"Spooky out there at night, isn't it?"

"Yes, it is. Beyond imagining."

Russell took the skiff on a slow circle around Ledge Lighthouse. It changed as they went around it. Facing the sun, even through the thick morning fog, the building glowed bright red as the bricks caught the light. As they swung around the back, the light lost its color, and the structure just became a looming dark shape. It looked ominous, its black silhouette reflected in the calm waters and disturbed by the boat wake. To Scott it seemed an apt expression of the minds of men disturbed by the dark menace of the light.

Scott looked up at the window of Ernie's room. He could well imagine the mannequin up there, frozen in its pose of shock and anger.

Russell completed the circle, then pointed the skiff north toward Avery Point. Scott watched as the lighthouse grew smaller and slowly faded away like a dream. Only the disembodied voice of the foghorn remained, echoing across the water.

The lighthouse that was a home to ghosts had become a ghost itself.

35

Scott walked down the hallway to the offices of the Groton Paranormal Group. He stood before the glass door.

Groton Paranormal Group
Shedding Light on the Dark Side

How different was his appreciation of those words now. When he first come here, he had been skeptical, perhaps mildly scornful of them. Not any more.

Scott's night on Ledge Light had changed his mind about the paranormal world. He believed in it now. He had been chased by a ghost and tormented by all sorts of apparitions. He had shared the shadows with spirits, and come face to face with his own darkest fears. He had spent a night in the dark side.

He entered the office and was greeted like an old friend by Chuck and Angie. They wanted to hear everything.

So he told them. He told them all about his journey through Everett Line Fine's story. His visit to the Miskatonic Mental Hospital, Fuzzy and her Egyptian deities, the Twice Seen Scenes exhibit, the Mythic Mystery sculpture, Everett's tape, Dr. Markhal's story, the Custom House, frame 13, and his own ghost-filled night on the lighthouse. When he was done, Angie and Chuck stared at him a moment.

"That's some story!" said Chuck.

"Man, I may do my doctoral work about you!" said Angie.

"So you used electricity to capture the ghost of Ernie," said Chuck.

"Yes. I remembered something you'd said," said Scott. He was quiet a moment and then added. "But it was more, Chuck.

It was my love for Anne that gave me the strength to overcome my fear and use the electricity."

Chuck nodded, then turned his chair to look out the window. Scott knew he was thinking. After a moment, Chuck turned back.

"Scott, everything you've told us is fascinating. Dramatic. It would make a great ghost story or page-turner of a thriller. But as for telling us what really happened to Everett, or as paranormal investigation … I don't know."

Scott was taken aback. "What do you mean?"

"What Chuck means," said Angie, "is that everything you've told us could be explained in paranormal terms or in psychological terms."

"You sound like Dr. Markhal," said Scott.

"Angie is right, Scott," said Chuck. "Everything you've told us makes sense if there were real ghosts out there. And everything you've told us makes sense if you were very stressed and your imagination was running wild. People get spooked alone in the dark."

Scott shook his head.

"What I saw — at least most of it — was real. I'm sure of it."

Chucked pressed: "What's your proof of a ghost, Scott? A blurry, ambiguous photograph and a brass button? Not much."

"No, not much, but maybe enough."

Chuck was tapping a pencil against the desk slowly, considering. Angie was lost in thought, too, idly turning a ring on her finger.

Scott asked: "Tell me: how does a button go from a coat on a mannequin on the third floor to behind a locked door in the basement if the mannequin wasn't inhabited by Ernie's ghost and chasing me around the lighthouse?"

Chuck said: "Well, let's see if we can figure out a way that that could have happened. Other than your ghost theory, that is. Describe Ernie's room to us."

Scott described the keeper's room.

"Does anyone go behind that barrier?" asked Angie.

"No. It keeps people away from Ernie. And the guides …"

Scott stopped. Thought a moment. "No. Wait. Somebody *did* go back there on my tour. One of the guides. A guy named Zook. He went in the corner and turned on a lamp."

"Is Zook a big guy?"

"Yes."

"And is it cramped back there where the mannequin of Ernie is?"

"Very. There's a table, a bed with a chest at the end, another table with photos and a lamp, another with a ship's model, and a chair."

"So not much open space."

"No. Zook had to squeeze around everything to get to the light."

"I see," said Chuck. He put his hands over his eyes.

"He's visualizing," said Angie.

Scott looked around the room, and his gaze settled on the poster from the film *Nosferatu*. He remembered that creepy guy. Hadn't he seen him for real outside Ledge Light at night? Or had he just been something out of a nightmare, like Angie had said?

Chuck dropped his hands from his eyes. "Scott, let me try this scenario out on you. Maybe when Zook goes back one time, he bumps into Ernie. He reaches out to catch the mannequin, snags the button, and it pulls off. He picks it up. He intends to give it to somebody to sew back onto the coat. He puts it on the barrier while he climbs over. As he climbs over, someone distracts him. He wanders off and forgets about the button. Later on that tour, or maybe on the next, a kid comes along and sees that shiny button and takes it. At some point, the kid is in the basement and starts playing with the button, the way kids do. He drops it and it rolls under the cage door. So the button has mysteriously gone from Ernie's coat to the basement cage."

"Sounds a bit far-fetched, Chuck," said Scott.

"No more so than a ghost inhabiting a mannequin and walking around."

"So you don't believe in ghosts?" Scott asked.

"It's not that. It's that I believe in proof. My scientific training makes me want evidence. My scenario is a possible explanation. Maybe not probable, but certainly possible. From your perspective, there was a button on Ernie's coat that somehow ended up in the basement cage. Must be a ghost. And maybe it was. But maybe, if my scenario is true, it wasn't the work of a ghost.

"We have to consider the possibility that your experience may be missing some steps — the tour guide bumping the mannequin, the kid finding a shiny button. Without them, what happened is a mystery. But add them in, and it's not a very mysterious chain of events. I suppose we could imagine any number of scenarios that would get that button from A to B. One of them would be your ghost hypothesis. But is that proof?"

"Believe it or not, Scott," Angie added, "we start from a position of skepticism. You give us unambiguous evidence, irrefutable proof of a ghost, and we'll believe you. But if there is reasonable doubt, we won't."

"I know what I saw. I know what I heard. I know what I felt. It was real!" Scott said defiantly.

Chuck shook his head. He was sympathetic, but unwavering. "Subjective experience," he said, "doesn't count for much. Take some shadows, add fear and confusion, and things get muddled. What you saw and felt may lead to proof — or reinforce it — but they can't stand alone."

Scott shook his head. "Not so easy to prove a ghost."

"No, it's not," said Chuck.

"And the photo?" Scott asked.

"Who knows what the photo shows," said Angie.

"I see a face," said Scott.

"Maybe. Once you pointed it out, I saw it too," said Chuck. "But whose face? Ernie's? Could be. Or maybe it's a self-portrait of Everett."

There was silence. Scott was disappointed that Chuck and Angie weren't ready to drop everything and write up his story as a paper for the *Journal of Paranormal Research* or wherever it was that their kind published their papers. But he also understood their point of view, and why they clung to it to add credibility to what they did.

"Well, you skeptics," said Scott at last. "I may not have the proof you want, but I know what happened to me at Ledge Light."

"Welcome to the world of the paranormal, Scott," Angie said. "Certainty — of anything — is hard to come by. Mental states and ghosts are both as amorphous as a fog. You can sense them, see them, believe in them. But it's damned hard to put your arms around them."

"Who said I wanted to put my arms around *them*?" Scott said shaking his head. "Seems it was *they* who wanted to put their arms around *me*!"

Chuck asked: "So, are you going to write your book?"

"I think so," said Scott.

"Fiction or nonfiction?" Angie asked.

Scott thought a moment. He thought about Ka figures and ghosts, mummified falcons and instigated memory hallucinations. He thought about the ombralogists and Everett's tape, about the Phanoptiscope and the Mythic Mystery. He remembered the coldness of Ernie nearby, and the sparking transformer in the high voltage alcove.

He looked at Angie: "Welcome to the world of writing, Miss Lenska. Certainty is sometimes hard to come by. Fiction or nonfiction? I'm not sure I'll ever really know."

"Well, whatever story you tell," said Angie," I can't wait to read it. I hope you'll put me in it somewhere."

"I probably will," Scott said. He looked around the office a minute and then commented: "You know, it's kind of strange. Everyone I've talked to has some experience with, or opinion about, or story connected to ghosts."

Angie laughed. "That's because you're researching ghosts. So naturally, everyone you talk to filters what they say through that particular prism. If you were writing about chickens, everybody would have chicken stories."

"I suppose," said Scott, unconvinced.

"Ghosts say a lot about our perceptions and memories," Chuck said. "Like I said when we first talked, the paranormal lies somewhere in that murky area between the real and the imaginary."

"I think my book will, too," said Scott. "Oh, I almost forgot. I thought you might want some of Everett's stuff. Maybe it will do you some good." He opened a shoebox and took out some of Everett's gear. "I think the Phanoptiscope and goggles worked, from what I could tell by Everett's tape. And here's the tape. Give it a listen. Maybe you'll stumble on some proof. As for Morgan, I'm not so sure he's good luck."

Angie picked up the Phanoptiscope and fiddled with its buttons and knobs. Chuck picked up the little carved figure of Morgan and turned it over in his hands a few times then put it on a shelf above his computer.

"So, Scott," Angie asked. "Any final thoughts about Ledge Lighthouse?"

Scott thought a moment and replied, seriously: "Yes. Don't go out there at night."

36

The brisk October afternoon was clear and beautiful. Not a single cloud darkened the sky. It was late in the day. The shadow of the Mythic Mystery stretched across the grass like a sundial.

Scott sat at the base of the obelisk, looking out across the water at Ledge Lighthouse. A flock of geese flew by, a dark arrow against the sky. They followed the shoreline of Avery Point, then veered west toward New London. Scott had once heard that birds were the spirits of those we have lost, returning to us in another form, graceful and free of earthly bonds.

Scott felt free himself. Earlier that day, a great dark weight had been lifted from him. For maybe the twentieth time, he looked at the text he'd received from Anne that morning.

Anne: Dr. Falk finally called. My test results came in. All good!!!! No shadows! No signs of any problems at all! I did it, Sweetie! I have a future. WE have a future! Thank you for everything! I love you! I love you! I love you!

He had wept when he'd first read it.
Their ordeal was over.
They were both survivors now.

He couldn't wait to see her. He couldn't wait to hear her laugh, to share meals, to just sit and talk, to listen to Hot Jazz and dream of the past, or take walks and plan their future. Scott wanted to hold Anne and never let her go.

For years he had thought his greatest fear was electricity. But it wasn't. It was losing Anne. She had inhabited his heart like a Ka spirit. He had willingly let her possess him. They had become as one. Maybe Chuck had a term for it, or maybe it was more in Dr. Markhal's realm. No matter. He and Anne had a deep enduring love. It was that love that had given Scott the strength to overcome his worst fear. To vanquish Ernie as they faced each other on either side of that metal door — on either side of life.

Ernie with his letter and Scott with his texts had both found the truth of their lives while in the shadows of Ledge Light.

Scott had come to believe that the lighthouse was merely a stage upon which our darkest fears play out their dramas. A place we inhabit with demons of our own design. He remembered a line from the orientation film that expressed the life of the lighthouse: "From men in storms to the storms in men." Keepers had faced hurricanes at Ledge Light. And they had faced the storms that sometimes raged within themselves. Those who survived learned to savor the sweet elixir of life.

He had not really solved the mystery of what had happened to Everett Fine that night in the basement of Ledge Light. From his own experience, he thought he knew. But he couldn't be sure. Like the letters of Mythic Mystery, the story was jumbled. And like frame 13, the evidence was open to interpretation.

Fiction or nonfiction? He'd write the story and let people decide for themselves.

Scott marveled at how the chance purchase of a locked box had led him on this journey. A journey through men's lives, through ancient beliefs and local legends, a journey into his own heart and soul.

It was time to pick Anne up at the train station. Scott Edwards left the Mythic Mystery obelisk, crossed the grass, and walked along the memorial brick path. His mind was filled with his own memories.

In the dusk, the light on Ledge Lighthouse came on. And even though the night was clear and dry, so did the foghorn. Perhaps it was Ernie, calling out in anguish. Or warning of the dangers that lurked in the shadow of the light.

EPILOGUE

The season is over. The tourists are gone. Ledge Light is locked up.

As winter weaves its cold around and through the lighthouse, the mannequin of Ernie stands alone in its third floor room. He is posed in his moment of betrayal and anger, his wife's letter in his hand, a ferocious look of hurt and vengeance on his face. He is just rubber and glass, wood and cloth — and an odd number of brass buttons.

But perhaps he is more.

Perhaps all the fears of all the men who have served on Ledge Light, and all those who have investigated and visited it, have gathered in the shadows. At night, those fears seek out the mannequin as their home. The Ka of Ernie joins them. The hum of energy flowing into the deep dark basement breaks free of its cage and drifts upward, too. The mannequin, now something from another realm, slowly raises its head and looks out the window at a black obelisk on the distant shore, a mythic mystery silhouetted in the moonlight.

The figure begins to move.
Once again, Ernie roams Ledge Light.
A lost soul.
A ghost.
Once a keeper of the light, now master of the darkness.

Author's Notes

You can visit Ledge Light on tours during the summer. You may even see some of the mysteries in this book on your visit. You will most certainly see Ernie. Go to www.LedgeLighthouse.org to find out about tours and more. And join us on Facebook at: www.facebook.com/NewLondonLedgeLighthouse

My cousin Chuck Freedman really did play a monster in *Horror of Party Beach*. It is a world-class bad movie. Our family takes great pride in knowing that *Horror* often makes top-ten lists of worst movies ever made.

I corresponded with artist Penny Kaplan about the letters on the Mythic Mystery obelisk. The mystery of their meaning is safe with me.

Photographer Richard Moore does create Twice Seen Scenes. You can find some here: www.richardmoorephotography.com or www.facebook.com/twiceseenphoto

There is a Mütter Museum full of medical abnormalities and horrors in Philadelphia. Go at your own peril.

This author has spent the night on Ledge Light and lived to tell the tale. I had no need for TFD-6.

You really can get a good haircut for $15 at Danielle's Barber Shop on Thames Street in Groton. And the apple cinnamon cobbler dessert at Par 4 is to die for.

If you would like to see a film I made of the area of Avery Point, including Mythic Mystery, go to YouTube and search for "X100 Gipstein."

Mary Angela really does think "The Walking Dead" is a reality show.

Thanks To

My wonderful wife Marcia for her encouragement as I wrote and for sharing the adventures of life, including preserving Ledge Lighthouse.

My mom, Fuzzy, for letting my brother and me stay up late to watch "Chiller Theater," where we became versed in the stories of the Wolfman, the Mummy, Frankenstein, and all the other classic horror movies.

My brother, Rick, for our shared loved of horror stories and films — though *not* for reaching through the banister of our stairway at home when we were kids and grabbing my ankle, thus instilling in me a lifelong wariness of shadowy stairways.

My dear friend of over thirty-five years, Nan Shnitzler, for proofing yet another of my stories.

Jim Streeter, for historical background material and for getting Marcia and me involved with Ledge Light in the first place.

And finally, thanks to all the volunteers who have helped restore Ledge Lighthouse, who lead the tours, and who have imbued the brick and mortar — and perhaps the shadows — with their spirit.

Also by Todd A. Gipstein

"LEGACY of the LIGHT "

Legacy of the Light is an historical thriller. It is the story of two generations of lighthouse keepers at Race Rock Lighthouse off the shore of New London, Connecticut. The action takes place in 1907 and a generation later, much of it the day of the great hurricane of 1938. Storms, ships at sea, and the isolated lighthouse are the stages of this drama. *Legacy* is a story of how the past influences the present, of fathers and sons, failure, guilt, love, and redemption. As the story unfolds, men and women visit the lighthouse and mysterious objects wash up on the rocks that surround it. Storms bear down on this man-made island in the middle of the sea, and those trapped at Race Rock – the keeper, his fiancée, and a mysterious stranger – must fight the forces of nature and the demons within that threaten to destroy them. All the while, they are trying to keep the light lit for ships at sea and to unravel a puzzle that could dramatically change their lives. *Legacy of the Light* takes readers into a face-paced adventure and love story full of twists and turns.

WHAT READERS ARE SAYING ABOUT
"*LEGACY of the LIGHT*"

"This is an absolutely riveting, mesmerizing and spellbinding novel. Its description of the 1938 Hurricane is so lifelike that I felt like I was right there. Once I started *Legacy*, I couldn't put the book down."

— *A reader in New London, CT.*

"I started reading this book on a flight from Boston. I continued reading once I got home, and kept reading all night. I could not put it down. What a thrilling ride! Todd Gipstein's many years working as a photographer comes through in his ability to paint a picture with his words. He renders a scene so well that you can feel the wind on your face, hear the crash of the waves, taste the salt in the air, and feel the electricity on the back of your neck. This is best kind of historical fiction: well researched, beautifully crafted, and a joy to read."

— *A reader in Atlanta*

"Gipstein's prose is crisp and direct and his characters well-formed. He has clearly done his research, and the period details of life in an early-20th-century lighthouse are fascinating, adding considerable depth to the narrative. A well-wrought tale of family, duty, honor and redemption." — *Kirkus Reviews*

"Todd Gipstein has produced a first-rate fact-based thriller that had me up all night. Thanks to Gipstein's deft fast-paced writing, crisp dialogue and well-defined characters, this tale about the lonely life of a lighthouse keeper ... is packed with drama and excitement as well as a sprinkling of humor. Legacy of the Light would make a great movie and I hope the folks in Hollywood will take note and grab the film rights. It would be a smash hit in the hands of a good director and cast."

— *A reviewer in Wisconsin*

"What a fascinating, thrilling, extraordinarily well written novel you produced in Legacy of the Light. I was very happy that I have retired because I couldn't put the damn book down once I got into it. It was like being there every moment of their lives with your central characters. Thank you for a great book."
— *A reader in New London, CT.*

"I loved it! I could hardly put the book down and the day I finished it I spent all afternoon and early evening reading it until I finished. What a great movie this would make. It was a real thriller for me right to the end. I always felt like I was in the scene you were describing. You certainly captured my attention with your unforgettable characters, and tension-building scenes. Congratulations. This is a great read. Thank you for writing the book."
— *A reader in Mystic, Ct.*

"Outstanding book! ...The characters, the setting, the tension of each storm...it's all written in a way that makes you FEEL it... I love when a book makes you care about the characters and care about their lives ... Overall, an awesome book that I absolutely recommend. I'm bummed to be done with it, but very happy with the way things turned out."
— *Amazon review*

"Incredible read! It is a fast-paced novel written with stunning geographical details and enjoyable characters. A great read that will have you looking for more novels written by this talented author. One of my top five books of 2011."
— *Anonymous Nook Reader*

"Behind this riveting storyline filled with mystery, agony, hope and the power of love, is a profound intelligence that brings this novel to a different level. It is not just a thriller that keeps you turning the page, but a journey filled with poignant pauses where some little detail suddenly holds great meaning. Give yourself time to read this in a few sessions because there will come a point where it will be very hard to put it down."
— *A reader in New Hampshire*

"At one point I was so taken in by Nathanial's feelings for the sea and the light that I was wishing I could be his friend. That is how compelling and real the characters were. Thank you Todd, for such a wonderful story hope you will write more."

— Amazon review

"There is great human involvement with love, drive, devotion, concern, despair, fear, and many other emotions that give the story life. The mystery provides a treasure hunt and a battle royal between good and evil. Not to be missed for both the learning and the entertainment."

— A reader in New York

"He paints a vivid picture of the critical and demanding, yet lonely job of a lighthouse keeper and uses powerful imagery, great photos and a vivid cast of characters to bring this realistic, compelling story to 'light' … A love story, a mystery, and good vs. evil, "Legacy of Light" is an engaging, entertaining read you won't want to put down."

— Amazon review

MAGICIAN'S CHOICE

A NOVEL BY
TODD A. GIPSTEIN

Foreword by Gay Blackstone

"MAGICIAN'S CHOICE"

This historical fiction novel follows the story of Guy, a young man coming of age in the 1930s and 1940s. As a birthday present for his thirteenth birthday, Guy's mother takes him to see the great Harry Blackstone Sr.'s 1001 Wonders Magic Show. Guy helps on stage, meets Blackstone, gets a magic set, and decides he wants to become a magician himself. Seeking his destiny, Guy encounters some of the great figures in magic of the era including Blackstone, Lou Tannen and Dai Vernon. He joins a carnival where he has many adventures with an oddball assortment of colorful characters. Eventually, he finds his way back to New York, begins a career there, and discovers that there are more illusions in life than just on the magician's stage. Guy's journey features the Garde Theater and other locations in New London, Connecticut; small towns of the South; the deserts of Africa in WWII; and the theaters, magic stores and night clubs of New York. Along the way, there are guest appearances by Albert Einstein and Ella Fitzgerald. "Magician's Choice" is an exploration of youth and age, fame and betrayal, vengeance and compassion, love and forgiveness. As it transports readers inside the world of performers, the story explores themes of free will and fate. "Magician's Choice" is a tale full of surprises, secrets, and wonder. A story where things and people are not always what they seem to be. With a foreword by Harry Blackstone Sr.'s daughter-in-law Gay Blackstone.

WHAT READERS ARE SAYING ABOUT
"MAGICIAN'S CHOICE"

"I loved this book! The characters really come alive and suck you into the story. This is a perfect example of 'write about what you know'. Todd has been practicing magic as long as Guy and the whole story just glows because of it. I didn't want the story to end."

— A reader in Boston

"One of the most readable and enjoyable books I have read in years. Couldn't put it down. Moved along at an excellent pace, yet full of details. Great pathos. Laughed and cried more than once. Beautifully written. A fitting bookend to 'Legacy of the Light'. Todd has done it again. Bravo!!! Encore!!!"

— A reader in Connecticut

"I was captured from the first page and did not want the story to end... I thoroughly enjoyed this coming of age story and the rise to stardom of the main character. What a great story! It will put some magic and inspiration back into your life."

— Amazon review

"Great Story! This author has a talent for giving the reader a wonderful experience from the first page to the last page...Gipstein weaved a yarn that has many different facets, and expertly pulled it all together with a great ending. I highly recommend this book to all who have an interest in the art of magic, and also to everyone who just likes a great story! Looking forward to more of his books."

— A reader in Florida

"The story is intertwined with famous and not so famous magicians and celebrities from the past. This only serves to make the story a more interesting read... you get the feeling these conversations are real, and then in turn, Guy is real. Guy's journey through the world of magic is a varied and interesting one. His time with the carnival and his reaction to the 'freaks' is eye opening and heartwarming. Guy's need for revenge and the ultimate outcome presents much food for thought. Things aren't always what they seem! My new favorite book!"

— *Amazon review*

"Todd takes you through the wonderful world of magic and the magicians that bring us the wonder we all seek in life. It is a great story that once you start reading you will find it hard to put down. I loved it!"

— *A reader in Connecticut*

"I read the book last night. It was wonderful ... I loved the way you presented the hope and disappointment of a magician's obsession with new tricks and props ... I loved the little twist at the end and the threads of compassion that run throughout and give the story it's real heart."

— *Managing Editor of Reel Magic Magazine*

A delightful story of a young man growing up in the 1930s ... Gipstein skillfully unfolds Guy Borden's life ... Doors close as others open, and we, the readers, wonder what fate has in store for his future ... In the final chapters of the book, Gipstein nicely brings the story full circle, neatly tying together the subplots of Guy Borden's life. His best writing, in a well-written book, is in this section, in which the character of Guy deepens as he learns several enduring lessons about life while at the same time coming to maturity as a magician."

— *Review in MUM - The Society of American Magicians Magazine*

"Todd Gipstein has written a fictional account of a young man's rise to magic that is surprisingly both nostalgic in its setting and yet current in capturing the mood of many magicians … Gipstein does a great job keeping the plot lively and maintains a good pace… I genuinely liked his use of 'magician's choice' as a theme and he gives the term a philosophical twist I hadn't considered before that ties the book together well. It's a fun read … and an easy book to recommend."

— *Review in The Linking Ring Magazine*
of the International Brotherhood of Magicians

"All magicians have a box or drawer where they discard tricks — a graveyard of shattered dreams … I am willing to bet that nobody who buys a copy of *Magician's Choice* will consign it to their drawer of disappointment."

— *Review in Genii, the Conjurors' Magazine*

Todd Gipstein has been a writer, photographer and producer for 40 years. Since 1987 he has worked with the National Geographic Society as a photographer, producer and lecturer. Todd grew up in New London, Connecticut, where the story of "In the Shadow of the Light" takes place. He is a graduate of Harvard College, where he studied writing and filmmaking. Todd has traveled the world photographing for documentaries and lecturing. He has written hundreds of scripts for multimedia shows. Todd and his wife Marcia, a former pharmacist, live in Groton, Connecticut, a short walk from the Mythic Mystery sculpture and the von Schlippe gallery featured in this book. Marcia is Todd's muse and photo editor as well as a yoga teacher. Todd is president of the all-volunteer Ledge Light Foundation, which is dedicated to restoring New London Ledge Lighthouse. Together, Todd and Marcia have spearheaded the restoration of Ledge Light, creation of a museum inside it, and often serve as tour guides. When not working on the lighthouse, they travel the world to photograph and lecture for National Geographic, screen films at festivals, attend magic conventions, and study yoga. To learn more about their many and varied adventures, go to www.Gipstein.com or visit the Facebook page "Gipstein Books." This is Todd's third novel. He is currently working on several books, including "Elephant Island," a thriller about Ernest Shackleton's journey to Antarctica in 1914 and modern day meteorite hunters.

The Ledge Light Foundation has been the steward of the lighthouse since the Coast Guard automated it and left in 1987. The non-profit, all-volunteer Foundation's mission is to restore the building, create a museum inside it, facilitate public tours, and create educational programs focused on the light's history. Ledge Light is still an active aid to navigation. In 2014, the National Park Service awarded the deed to the light to the New London Maritime Society, who also owns Race Rock and the New London Harbor Light. The Ledge Light Foundation will continue to manage the building and the musuem. To learn about tour schedules, volunteer opportunities, membership information, events, products and more, please go to: www.LedgeLighthouse.org and follow us on Facebook: www.Facebook.com/New LondonLedgeLighthouse.
A portion of the sales of this book will be donated to help ongoing work on New London Ledge Lighthouse.

CPSIA information can be obtained
at www.ICGtesting.com
Printed in the USA
FFOW04n2016150915
16864FF